THE SANTAROGA BARRIER

SANTAROGA

Dasein pictured the Santaroga Valley as a swarming place behind a façade like a pyramid: solid, faceless, enduring. In there, behind the façade, Santaroga did something to its people . . .

He sensed a one-pointedness here such that every Santarogan became an extension of every other Santarogan. They were like rays spreading out from a pinhole in a black curtain.

What lay behind the black curtain?

FRANK HERBERT

THE SANTAROGA BARRIER

Published by
BERKLEY PUBLISHING CORPORATION
Distributed by
G. P. PUTNAM'S SONS: New York

1

The sun went down as the five-year-old Ford camper-pickup truck ground over the pass and started down the long grade into Santaroga Valley. A crescent-shaped turn-off had been leveled beside the first highway curve. Gilbert Dasein pulled his truck onto the gravel, stopped at a white barrier fence and looked down into the valley whose secrets he had come to expose.

Two men already had died on this project, Dasein reminded himself. Accidents. *Natural* accidents. What was down there in that bowl of shadows inhabited by random lights? Was there an accident waiting for him?

Dasein's back ached after the long drive up from Berkeley. He shut off the motor, stretched. A burning odor of hot oil permeated the cab. The union of truckbed and camper emitted creakings and poppings.

The valley stretching out below him looked somehow different from what Dasein had expected. The sky around it was a ring of luminous blue full of sunset glow that spilled over into an upper belt of trees and rocks.

There was a sense of quiet about the place, of an island sheltered from storms.

What did I expect the place to be? Dasein wondered.

He decided all the maps he'd studied, all the reports on Santaroga he'd read, had led him to believe he knew the valley. But maps were not the land. Reports weren't people.

Dasein glanced at his wristwatch: almost seven. He felt reluctant to continue.

Far off to the left across the valley, strips of green light glowed among trees. That was the area labeled "green-

5

houses" on the map. A castellated block of milky white on an outcropping down to his right he identified as the Jaspers Cheese Cooperative. The yellow gleam of windows and moving lights around it spoke of busy activity.

Dasein grew aware of insect sounds in the darkness around him, the swoop-humming of air through nighthawks' wings and, away in the distance, the mournful baying of hounds. The voice of the pack appeared to come from beyond the Co-op.

He swallowed, thinking that the yellow windows suddenly were like baleful eyes peering into the valley's darker depths.

Dasein shook his head, smiled. That was no way to think. Unprofessional. All the ominous nonsense muttered about Santaroga had to be put aside. A scientific investigation could not operate in that atmosphere. He turned on the cab's dome light, took his briefcase from the seat beside him. Gold lettering on the brown leather identified it: "Gilbert Dasein—Department of Psychology—University of California—Berkeley."

In a battered folder from the case he began writing: "Arrived Santaroga Valley approximately 6:45 p.m. Setting is that of a prosperous farm community . . ."

Presently, he put case and folder aside.

Prosperous farm community, he thought. How could he know it was prosperous? No—prosperity wasn't what he saw. That was something he knew from the reports.

The real valley in front of him now conveyed a sense of waiting, of quietness punctuated by occasional tinklings of cowbells. He imagined husbands and wives down there after a day of work. What did they discuss now in their waiting darkness?

What did Jenny Sorge discuss with her husband —provided she had a husband? It seemed impossible she'd still be single—lovely, nubile Jenny. It was more than a year since they'd last seen each other at the University.

Dasein sighed. No escaping thoughts of Jenny—not here in Santaroga. Jenny contained part of Santaroga's mystery. She was an element of the Santaroga Barrier and a prime

6

subject for his present investigation.

Again, Dasein sighed. He wasn't fooling himself. He knew why he'd accepted this project. It wasn't the munificent sum those chain stores were paying the university for this study, nor the generous salary provided for himself.

He had come because this was where Jenny lived.

Dasein told himself he'd smile and act normal, *perfectly normal*, when he met her. He was here on business, a psychologist detached from his usual teaching duties to make a market study in Santaroga Valley.

What was a perfectly normal way to act with Jenny, though? How did one achieve normalcy when encountering the paranormal?

Jenny was a Santarogan—and the normalcy of this valley defied normal explanations.

His mind went to the reports, "the known facts." All the folders of data, the collections of official pryings, the second-hand secrets which were the stock in a trade of the bureaucracy—all this really added up to a single "known fact" about Santaroga: There was something extraordinary at work here, something far more disturbing than any so-called market study had ever tackled before.

Meyer Davidson, the soft looking, pink fleshed little man who'd presented himself as the agent of the investment corporation, the holding company behind the chain stores paying for this project, had put it in an angry nutshell at the first orientation meeting: "The whole thing about Santaroga boils down to this—Why were we forced to close our branches there? Why won't even *one* Santarogan trade with an outsider? That's what we want to know. What's this Santaroga Barrier which keeps us from doing business there?"

Davidson wasn't as soft as he looked.

Dasein started the truck, turned on his headlights, resumed his course down the winding grade.

All the data was a single datum.

Outsiders found no houses for rent or sale in this valley.

Santaroga officials said they had no juvenile delinquency figures for the state's statistics.

Servicemen from Santaroga always returned when they

were discharged. In fact, no Santarogan had ever been known to move out of the valley.

Why? Was it a two-way barrier?

And the curious anomalies: The data had included a medical journal article by Jenny's uncle, Dr. Lawrence Piaget, reputedly the valley's leading physician. The article: "The Poison Oak Syndrome in Santaroga." Its substance: Santarogans had a remarkable susceptibility to allergens when forced to live away from their valley for extended periods. This was the chief reason for service rejection of Santaroga's youths.

Data equaled datum.

Santaroga reported no cases of mental illness or mental deficiency to the State Department of Mental Hygiene. No Santarogan could be found in a state mental hospital. (The psychiatrist who headed Dasein's university department, Dr. Chami Selador, found this fact "alarming.")

Cigarette sales in Santaroga could be accounted for by transient purchasers.

Santarogans manifested an iron resistance to national advertising. (An un-American symptom, according to Meyer Davidson.)

No cheese, wines or beers made outside the valley could be marketed to Santarogans.

All the valley's businesses, including the bank, were locally owned. They flatly rejected outside investment money.

Santaroga had successfully resisted every "pork barrel" government project the politicians had offered. Their State Senator was from Porterville, ten miles behind Dasein and well outside the valley. Among the political figures Dasein had interviewed to lay the groundwork for his study, the State Senator was one of the few who didn't think Santarogans were "a pack of kooks, maybe religious nuts of some kind."

"Look, Dr. Dasein," he'd said, "all this mystery crap about Santaroga is just that—crap."

The Senator was a skinny, intense man with a shock of gray hair and red-veined eyes. Barstow was his name; one of the old California families.

8

Barstow's opinion: "Santaroga's a last outpost of American individualism. They're Yankees, Down Easters living in California. Nothing mysterious about 'em at all. They don't ask special favors and they don't fan my ears with stupid questions. I wish all my constituents were as straightforward and honest."

One man's opinion, Dasein thought.

An isolated opinion.

Dasein was down into the valley proper now. The two-lane road leveled into a passage through gigantic trees. This was the Avenue of the Giants winding between rows of *sequoia gigantea.*

There were homes set back in the trees. The datum-data said some of these homes had been here since the gold rush. The scroll work of carpenter gothic lined their eaves. Many were three stories high, yellow lights in their windows.

Dasein grew aware of an absence, a negative fact about the houses he saw: No television flicker, no cathode living rooms, no walls washed to skimmed-milk gray by the omnipresent tube.

The road forked ahead of him. An arrow pointed left to "City Center" and two arrows directed him to the right to "The Santaroga House" and "Jaspers Cheese Co-op."

Dasein turned right.

His road wound upward beneath an arch: "Santaroga, The Town That Cheese Built." Presently, it emerged from the redwoods into an oak flat. The Co-op loomed gray white, bustling with lights and activity behind a chain fence on his right. Across the road to his left stood Dasein's first goal here, a long three-storey inn built in the rambling 1900 style with a porch its full length. Lines of multipaned windows (most dark) looked down onto a gravel parking area. The sign at the entrance read: "Santaroga House — Gold Rush Museum — Hours 9 a.m. to 5 p.m."

Most of the cars nosed to a stone border parallel to the porch were well-kept older models. A few shiny new machines were parked in a second row as though standing aloof.

Dasein parked beside a 1939 Chevrolet whose paint

9

gleamed with a rich waxy gloss. Red-brown upholstery visible through the windows appeared to be hand-tailored leather.

Rich man's toy, Dasein thought.

He took his suitcase from the camper, turned to the inn. There was a smell of new mown lawn in the air and the sound of running water. It reminded Dasein of his childhood, his aunt's garden with the brook along the back. A strong sense of nostalgia gripped him.

Abruptly, a discordant note intruded. From the upper floors of the inn came the raucous sound of a man and woman arguing, the man's voice brusk, the woman's with a strident fishwife quality.

"I'm not staying in this godforsaken hole one more night," the woman screamed. "They don't want our money! They don't want us! You do what you want; I'm leaving!"

"Belle, stop it! You've . . ."

A window slammed. The argument dimmed to a muted screeching-mumbling.

Dasein took a deep breath. The argument restored his perspective. Here were two more people with their noses against the Santaroga Barrier.

Dasein strode along the gravel, up four steps to the porch and through swinging doors with windows frosted by scroll etching. He found himself in a high-ceilinged lobby, crystal chandeliers overhead. Dark wood paneling, heavily grained like ancient charts enclosed the space. A curved counter stretched across the corner to his right, an open door behind it from which came the sound of a switchboard. To the right of this counter was a wide opening through which he glimpsed a dining room—white tablecloths, crystal, silver. A western stagecoach was parked at his left behind brass posts supporting a maroon velvet rope with a "Do Not Touch" sign.

Dasein stopped to study the coach. It smelled of dust and mildew. A framed card on the boot gave its history: "Used on the San Francisco-Santaroga route from 1868 to 1871." Below this card was a slightly larger frame enclosing a yellowed sheet of paper with a brass legend beside it: "A note from Black Bart, the Po-8 Highwayman." In sprawling script on the yellow paper it read:

> *"So here I've stood while wind and rain*
> *Have set the trees a-sobbin'*
> *And risked my life for that damned stage*
> *That wasn't worth the robbin'."*

Dasein chuckled, shifted his briefcase to his left arm, crossed to the counter and rang the call bell.

A bald, wrinkled stick of a man in a black suit appeared in the open doorway, stared at Dasein like a hawk ready to pounce. "Yes?"

"I'd like a room," Dasein said.

"What's your business?"

Dasein stiffened at the abrupt challenge. "I'm tired," he said. "I want a night's sleep."

"Passing through, I hope," the man grumbled. He shuffled to the counter, pushed a black registry ledger toward Dasein.

Dasein took a pen from its holder beside the ledger, signed.

The clerk produced a brass key on a brass tag, said: "You get two fifty-one next to that dang' couple from L.A. Don't blame me if they keep y' awake arguing." He slapped the key onto the counter. "That'll be ten dollars . . . in advance."

"I'm hungry," Dasein said, producing his wallet and paying. "Is the dining room open?" He accepted a receipt.

"Closes at nine," the clerk said.

"Is there a bellboy?"

"You look strong enough to carry your own bag." He pointed beyond Dasein. "Room's up them stairs, second floor."

Dasein turned. There was an open area behind the stagecoach. Scattered through it were leather chairs, high wings and heavy arms, a few occupied by elderly men sitting, reading. Light came from heavy brass floor lamps

11

with fringed shades. A carpeted stairway led upward beyond the chairs.

It was a scene Dasein was to think of many times later as his first clue to the real nature of Santaroga. The effect was that of holding time securely in a bygone age.

Vaguely troubled, Dasein said: "I'll check my room later. May I leave my bag here while I eat?"

"Leave it on the counter. No one'll bother it."

Dasein put the case on the counter, caught the clerk studying him with a fixed stare.

"Something wrong?" Dasein asked.

"Nope."

The clerk reached for the briefcase under Dasein's arm, but Dasein stepped back, removed it from the questing fingers, met an angry stare.

"Hmmmph!" the clerk snorted. There was no mistaking his frustration. He'd wanted a look inside the briefcase.

Inanely, Dasein said: "I . . . uh, want to look over some papers while I'm eating." And he thought: *Why do I need to explain?*

Feeling angry with himself, he turned, strode through the passage into the dining room. He found himself in a large square room, a single massive chandelier in the center, brass carriage lamps spaced around walls of dark wood paneling. The chairs at the round tables were heavy with substantial arms. A long teak bar stretched along the wall at his left, a wood-framed mirror behind it. Light glittered hypnotically from the central chandelier and glasses stacked beneath the mirror.

The room swallowed sounds. Dasein felt he had walked into a sudden hush with people turning to look at him. Actually, his entrance went almost unnoticed.

A white-coated bartender on duty for a scattering of customers at the bar glanced at him, went back to talking to a swarthy man hunched over a mug of beer.

Family groups occupied about a dozen of the tables. There was a card game at a table near the bar. Two tables held lone women busy with their forks.

There was a division of people in this room, Dasein felt. It was a matter of nervous tension contrasted with a

12

calmness as substantial as the room itself. He decided he could pick out the transients—they appeared tired, more rumpled; their children were closer to rebellion.

As he moved farther into the room, Dasein glimpsed himself in the bar mirror—fatigue lines on his slender face, the curly black hair mussed by the wind, brown eyes glazed with attention, still driving the car. A smudge of road dirt drew a dark line beside the cleft in his chin. Dasein rubbed at the smudge, thought: *Here's another transient.*

"You wish a table, sir?"

A Negro waiter had appeared at his elbow—white jacket, hawk nose, sharp Moorish features, a touch of gray at the temples. There was a look of command about him all out of agreement with the menial costume. Dasein thought immediately of Othello. The eyes were brown and wise.

"Yes, please: for one," Dasein said.

"This way, sir."

Dasein was guided to a table against the near wall. One of the carriage lamps bathed it in a warm yellow glow. As the heavy chair enveloped him, Dasein's attention went to the table near the bar—the card game . . . four men. He recognized one of the men from a picture Jenny had carried: Piaget, the doctor uncle, author of the medical journal article on allergens. Piaget was a large, gray-haired man, bland round face, a curious suggestion of the Oriental about him that was heightened by the fan of cards held close to his chest.

"You wish a menu, sir?"

"Yes. Just a moment . . . the men playing cards with Dr. Piaget over there."

"Sir?"

"Who are they?"

"You know Dr. Larry, sir?"

"I know his niece, Jenny Sorge. She carried a photo of Dr. Piaget."

The waiter glanced at the briefcase Dasein had placed in the center of the table. "Dasein," he said. A wide smile put a flash of white in the dark face. "You're Jenny's friend from the school."

The waiter's words carried so many implications that

13

Dasein found himself staring, open-mouthed.

"Jenny's spoken of you, sir," the waiter said.

"Oh."

"The men playing cards with Dr. Larry—you want to know who they are." He turned toward the players. "Well, sir, that's Captain Al Marden of the Highway Patrol across from Dr. Larry. On the right there, that's George Nis. He manages the Jaspers Cheese Co-op. The fellow on the left is Mr. Sam Scheler. Mr. Sam runs our independent service station. I'll get you that menu, sir."

The waiter headed toward the bar.

Dasein's attention remained on the card players, wondering why they held his interest so firmly. Marden, sitting with his back partly turned toward Dasein, was in mufti, a dark blue suit. His hair was a startling mop of red. He turned his head to the right and Dasein glimpsed a narrow face, tight-lipped mouth with a cynical downtwist.

Scheler of the independent service station (Dasein wondered about this designation suddenly) was dark skinned, an angular Indian face with flat nose, heavy lips. Nis, across from him, was balding, sandy-haired, blue eyes with heavy lids, a wide mouth and deeply cleft chin.

"Your menu, sir."

The waiter placed a large red-covered folder in front of Dasein.

"Dr. Piaget and his friends appear to be enjoying their game," Dasein said.

"That game's an institution, sir. Every week about this hour, regular as sunset—dinner here and that game."

"What do they play?"

"It varies, sir. Sometimes it's bridge, sometimes pinochle. They play whist on occasion and even poker."

"What did you mean—*independent* service station?" Dasein asked. He looked up at the dark Moorish face.

"Well, sir, we here in the valley don't mess around with those companies fixin' their prices. Mr. Sam, he buys from whoever gives him the best offer. We pay about four cents less a gallon here."

Dasein made a mental note to investigate this aspect of the Santaroga Barrier. It was in character, not buying from

14

the big companies, but where did they get their oil products?

"The roast beef is very good, sir," the waiter said, pointing to the menu.

"You recommend it, eh?"

"I do that, sir. Grain fattened right here in the valley. We have fresh corn on the cob, potatoes Jaspers—that's with cheese sauce, very good, and we have hot-house strawberries for dessert."

"Salad?" Dasein asked.

"Our salad greens aren't very good this week, sir. I'll bring you the soup. It's borscht with sour cream. And you'd like beer with that. I'll see if I can't get you some of our local product."

"With you around I don't need a menu," Dasein said. He returned the red-covered folder. "Bring it on before I start eating the tablecloth."

"Yes, sir!"

Dasein watched the retreating black—white coated, wide, confident. Othello, indeed.

The waiter returned presently with a steaming bowl of soup, a white island of sour cream floating in it, and a darkly amber mug of beer.

"I note you're the only Negro waiter here," Dasein said. "Isn't that kind of type casting?"

"You asking if I'm their *show* Negro, sir?" The waiter's voice was suddenly wary.

"I was wondering if Santaroga had any integration problems."

"Must be thirty, forty colored families in the valley, sir. We don't rightly emphasize the distinction of skin color here." The voice was hard, curt.

"I didn't mean to offend you," Dasein said.

"You didn't offend me." A smile touched the corners of his mouth, was gone. "I must admit a Negro waiter is a kind of institutional accent. Place like this . . ." He glanced around the solid, paneled room. " . . . must've had plenty of Negro waiters here in its day. Kind of like local color having me on the job." Again, that flashing smile. "It's a good job, and my kids are doing even better. Two of 'em

15

work in the Co-op; other's going to be a lawyer."

"You have three children?"

"Two boys and a girl. If you'll excuse me, sir; I have other tables."

"Yes, of course."

Dasein lifted the mug of beer as the waiter left.

He held the beer a moment beneath his nose. There was a tangy odor about it with a suggestion of cellars and mushrooms. Dasein remembered suddenly that Jenny had praised the local Santaroga beer. He sipped it—soft on the tongue, smooth, clean aftertaste of malt. It was everything Jenny had said.

Jenny, he thought. *Jenny . . . Jenny . . .*

Why had she never invited him to Santaroga on her regular weekend trips home? She'd never missed a weekend, he recalled. Their dates had always been in mid-week. He remembered what she'd told him about herself: orphaned, raised by the uncle, Piaget, and a maiden aunt . . . Sarah.

Dasein took another drink of the beer, sampled the soup. They did go well together. The sour cream had a flavor reminiscent of the beer, a strange new tang.

There'd never been any mistaking Jenny's affection for him, Dasein thought. They'd had a *thing,* chemical, exciting. But no *direct* invitation to meet her family, see the valley. A hesitant probing, yes—what would he think of setting up practice in Santaroga? Sometime, he must talk to Uncle Larry about some interesting cases.

What cases? Dasein wondered, remembering. The Santaroga information folders Dr. Selador had supplied were definite: "No reported cases of mental illness."

Jenny . . . Jenny . . .

Dasein's mind went back to the night he'd proposed. No hesitant probing on Jenny's part then— Could he live in Santaroga?

He could remember his own incredulous demand: "Why do we have to live in Santaroga?"

"Because I can't live anywhere else." That was what she'd said. "Because I can't live anywhere else."

Love me, love my valley.

16

No amount of pleading could wring an explanation from her. She'd made that plain. In the end, he'd reacted with anger boiling out of injured manhood. Did she think he couldn't support her any place but in Santaroga?

"Come and see Santaroga," she'd begged.

"Not unless you'll consider living outside."

Impasse.

Remembering the fight, Dasein felt his cheeks go warm. It'd been finals week. She'd refused to answer his telephone calls for two days . . . and he'd refused to call after that. He'd retreated into a hurt shell.

And Jenny had gone back to her precious valley. When he'd written, swallowed his pride, offered to come and see her—no answer. Her valley had swallowed her.

This valley.

Dasein sighed, looked around the dining room, remembering Jenny's intensity when she spoke about Santaroga. This paneled dining room, the Santarogans he could see, didn't fit the picture in his mind.

Why didn't she answer my letters? he asked himself. *Most likely she's married. That must be it.*

Dasein saw his waiter come around the end of the bar with a tray. The bartender signaled, called: "Win." The waiter stopped, rested the tray on the bar. Their heads moved close together beside the tray. Dasein received the impression they were arguing. Presently, the waiter said something with a chopping motion of the head, grabbed up the tray, brought it to Dasein's table.

"Doggone busybody," he said as he put the tray down across from Dasein, began distributing the dishes from it. "Try to tell me I can't give you Jaspers! Good friend of Jenny's and I can't give him Jaspers."

The waiter's anger cooled; he shook his head, smiled, put a plate mounded with food before Dasein.

"Too doggone many busybodies in this world, y' ask me."

"The bartender," Dasein said. "I heard him call you 'Win.'"

"Winston Burdeaux, sir, at your service." He moved around the table closer to Dasein. "Wouldn't give me any
17

Jaspers beer for you this time, sir." He took a frosted bottle from the tray, put it near the mug of beer he'd served earlier. "This isn't as good as what I brought before. The food's real Jaspers, though. Doggone busybody couldn't stop me from doing that."

"Jaspers," Dasein said. "I thought it was just the cheese."

Burdeaux pursed his lips, looked thoughtful. "Oh, no, sir. Jaspers, that's in all the products from the Co-op. Didn't Jenny ever tell you?" He frowned. "Haven't you ever been up here in the valley with her, sir?"

"No." Dasein shook his head from side to side.

"You *are* Dr. Dasein—Gilbert Dasein?"

"Yes."

"You're the fellow Jenny's sweet on, then." He grinned, said: "Eat up, sir. It's *good* food."

Before Dasein could collect his thoughts, Burdeaux turned, hurried away.

"You're the fellow Jenny's sweet on," Dasein thought. Present tense . . . not past tense. He felt his heart hammering, cursed himself for an idiot. It was just Burdeaux's way of talking. That was all it could be.

Confused, he bent to his food.

The roast beef in his first bite lived up to Burdeaux's prediction—tender, juicy. The cheese sauce on the potatoes had a flowing tang reminiscent of the beer and the sour cream.

The fellow Jenny's sweet on.

Burdeaux's words gripped Dasein's mind as he ate, filled him with turmoil.

Dasein looked up from his food, seeking Burdeaux. The waiter was nowhere in sight. *Jaspers.* It was this rich tang, this new flavor. His attention went to the bottle of beer, the non-Jaspers beer. *Not as good?* He sampled it directly from the bottle, found it left a bitter metallic aftertaste. A sip of the first beer from the mug—smooth, soothing. Dasein felt it cleared his head as it cleared his tongue of the other flavor.

He put down the mug, looked across the room, caught

18

the bartender staring at him, scowling. The man looked away.

They were small things—two beers, an argument between a waiter and a bartender, a watchful bartender—nothing but clock ticks in a lifetime, but Dasein sensed danger in them. He reminded himself that two investigators had met fatal accidents in the Santaroga Valley—*death by misadventure* . . . a car going too fast around a corner, off the road into a ravine . . . a fall from a rocky ledge into a river—drowned. *Natural* accidents, so certified by state investigation.

Thoughtful, Dasein returned to his food.

Presently, Burdeaux brought the strawberries, hovered as Dasein sampled them.

"Good, sir?"

"Very good. Better than that bottle of beer."

"My fault, sir. Perhaps another time." He coughed discreetly. "Does Jenny know you're here?"

Dasein put down his spoon, looked into his dish of strawberries as though trying to find his reflection there. His mind suddenly produced a memory picture of Jenny in a red dress, vital, laughing, bubbling with energy. "No . . . not yet," he said.

"You know Jenny's still a single girl, sir?"

Dasein glanced across to the card game. How leathery tan the players' skin looked. *Jenny not married?* Dr. Piaget looked up from the card game, said something to the man on his left. They laughed.

"Has . . . is she in the telephone directory, Mr. Burdeaux?" Dasein asked.

"She lives with Dr. Piaget, sir. And why don't you call me Win?"

Dasein looked up at Burdeaux's sharp Moorish face, wondering suddenly about the man. There was just a hint of southern accent in his voice. The probing friendliness, the volunteered information about Jenny—it was all faintly southern, intimate, kindly . . . but there were undertones of something else: a questing awareness, harsh and direct. The psychologist in Dasein was fully alert now.

19

"Have you lived very long here in the valley, Win?" Dasein asked.

" 'Bout twelve years, sir."

"How'd you come to settle here?"

Burdeaux shook his head. A rueful half-smile touched his lips. "Oh, you wouldn't like to hear about that, sir."

"But I would." Dasein stared up at Burdeaux, waiting. Somewhere there was a wedge that would open this valley's mysteries to him. *Jenny not married?* Perhaps Burdeaux was that wedge. There was an open shyness about his own manner, Dasein knew, that invited confidences. He relied upon this now.

"Well, if you really want to know, sir," Burdeaux said. "I was in the N'Orleans jailhouse for cuttin' up." (Dasein noted a sudden richening of the southern accent.) "We was doin' our numbers, usin' dirty language that'd make your neck hair walk. I suddenly heard myself doin' that, sir. It made me review my thinkin' and I saw it was kid stuff. Juvenile." Burdeaux mouthed the word, proud of it. "Juvenile, sir. Well, when I got out of that jailhouse, the high sheriff tellin' me never to come back, I went me home to my woman and I tol' Annie, I tol' her we was leavin'. That's when we left to come here, sir."

"Just like that, you left?"

"We hit the road on our feet, sir. It wasn't easy an' there was some places made us wish we'd never left. When we come here, though, we knew it was worth it."

"You just wandered until you came here?"

"It was like God was leadin' us, sir. This place, well, sir, it's hard to explain. But . . . well, they insist I go to school to better myself. That's one thing. I can speak good standard English when I want . . . when I think about it." (The accent began to fade.)

Dasein smiled encouragingly. "These must be very nice people here in the valley."

"I'm going to tell you something, sir," Burdeaux said. "Maybe you can understand if I tell you about something happened to me here. It's a thing would've hurt me pretty bad one time, but here . . . We were at a Jaspers party, sir. It was right after Willa, my girl, announced her engage-

20

ment to Cal Nis. And George, Cal's daddy, came over and put his arm across my shoulder. 'Well there, Win, you old nigger bastard,' he said, 'we better have us a good drink and a talk together because our kids are going to make us related.' That was it, Mr. Dasein. He didn't mean a thing calling me nigger. It was just like . . . like the way we call a pale blonde fellow here Whitey. It was like saying my skin's black for identification the way you might come into a room and ask for Al Marden and I'd say: 'He's that red-headed fellow over there playing cards.' As he was saying it I knew that's all he meant. It just came over me. It was being accepted for what I am. It was the friendliest thing George could do and that's why he did it."

Dasein scowled trying to follow the train of Burdeaux's meaning. Friendly to call him nigger?

"I don't think you understand it," Burdeaux said. "Maybe you'd have to be black to understand. But . . . well, perhaps this'll make you see it. A few minutes later, George said to me: 'Hey, Win, I wonder what kind of grandchildren we're going to have—light, dark or in between?' It was just a kind of wonderment to him, that he might have black grandchildren. He didn't care, really. He was curious. He found it interesting. You know, when I told Annie about that afterward, I cried. I was so happy I cried."

It was a long colloquy. Dasein could see realization of this fact come over Burdeaux. The man shook his head, muttered: "I talk too much. Guess I'd better . . ."

He broke off at a sudden eruption of shouting at the bar near the card players. A red-faced fat man had stepped back from the bar and was flailing it with a briefcase as he shouted at the bartender.

"You sons of bitches!" he screamed. "You think you're too goddamn' good to buy from me! My line isn't good enough for you! You can make better . . ."

The bartender grabbed the briefcase.

"Leggo of that, you son of a bitch!" the fat man yelled. "You all think you're so goddamn' good like you're some foreign country! An *outsider* am I? Let me tell you, you pack of foreigners! This is America! This is a free . . ."

21

The red-headed highway patrol captain, Al Marden, had risen at the first sign of trouble. Now, he put a large hand on the screamer's shoulder, shook the man once.

The screaming stopped. The angry man whirled, raised the briefcase to hit Marden. In one long, drawn-out second, the man focused on Marden's glaring eyes, the commanding face, hesitated.

"I'm Captain Marden of the Highway Patrol," Marden said. "And I'm telling you we won't have any more of this." His voice was calm, stern . . . and, Dasein thought, faintly amused.

The angry man lowered the briefcase, swallowed.

"You can go out and get in your car and leave Santaroga," Marden said. "Now. And don't come back. We'll be watching for you, and we'll run you in if we ever catch you in the valley again."

Anger drained from the fat man. His shoulders slumped. He swallowed, looked around at the room of staring eyes. "I'm glad to go," he muttered. "Nothing'd make me happier. It'll be a cold day in hell when I ever come back to your dirty little valley. You stink. All of you stink." He jerked his shoulder from Marden's grasp, stalked out through the passage to the lobby.

Marden returned to the card game shaking his head.

Slowly, the room returned to its previous sounds of eating and conversation. Dasein could feel a difference, though. The salesman's outburst had separated Santarogans and transients. An invisible wall had gone up. The transient families at their tables were hurrying their children, anxious to leave.

Dasein felt the same urgency. There was a pack feeling about the room now—hunters and hunted. He smelled his own perspiration. His palms were sweaty. He noted that Burdeaux had gone.

This is stupid! he thought. *Jenny not married?*

He reminded himself that he was a psychologist, an observer. But the observer had to observe himself.

Why am I reacting this way? he wondered. *Jenny not married?*

22

Two of the transient families already were leaving, herding their young ahead of them, voices brittle, talking about going "on to the next town."

Why can't they stay here? he asked himself. *The rates are reasonable.*

He pictured the area in his mind: Porterville was twenty-five miles away, ten miles outside the valley on the road he had taken. The other direction led over a winding, twisting mountain road some forty miles before connecting with Highway 395. The closest communities were to the south along 395, at least seventy miles. This was an area of National Forests, lakes, fire roads, moonscape ridges of lava rock—all of it sparsely inhabited except for the Santaroga Valley. Why would people want to travel through such an area at night rather than stay at this inn?

Dasein finished his meal, left the rest of the beer. He had to talk this place over with his department head, Dr. Chami Selador, before making another move. Burdeaux had left the check on a discreet brown tray—three dollars and eighty-six cents. Dasein put a five dollar bill on the tray, glanced once more around the room. The surface appeared so damn' normal! The card players were intent on their game. The bartender was hunched over, chatting with two customers. A child at a table off to the right was complaining that she didn't want to drink her milk.

It wasn't normal, though, and Dasein's senses screamed this fact at him. The brittle surface of this room was prepared to shatter once more and Dasein didn't think he would like what might be revealed. He wiped his lips on his napkin, took his briefcase and headed for the lobby.

His suitcase stood atop the desk beside the register. There was a buzzing and murmurous sound of a switchboard being operated in the room through the doors at the rear corner. He took the suitcase, fingered the brass room key in his pocket—two fifty-one. If there was no phone in the room, he decided he'd come down and place his call to Chami from a booth.

Feeling somewhat foolish and letdown after his reaction to the scene in the dining room, Dasein headed for the

23

stairs. A few eyes peered at him over the tops of newspapers from the lobby chairs. The eyes looked alert, inquisitive.

The stairs led to a shadowy mezzanine—desks, patches of white paper. A fire door directly ahead bore the sign: "To Second Floor. Keep this door closed."

The next flight curved left, dim overhead light, wide panels of dark wood. It led through another fire door into a hall with an emergency exit sign off to the left. An illuminated board opposite the door indicated room two fifty-one down the hall to the right. Widely spaced overhead lights, the heavy pile of a maroon carpet underfoot, wide heavy doors with brass handles and holes for old-fashioned passkeys gave the place an aura of the Nineteenth Century. Dasein half expected to see a maid in ruffled cap, apron with a bow at the back, long skirt and black stockings, sensible shoes—or a portly banker type with tight vest and high collar, an expanse of gold chain at the waist. He felt out of place, out of style here.

The brass key worked smoothly in the door of two fifty-one; it let him into a room of high ceilings, one window looking down onto the parking area. Dasein turned on the light. The switch controlled a tasseled floor lamp beside a curve-fronted teak dresser. The amber light revealed a partly opened doorway into a tiled bathroom (the sound of water dripping there), a thick-legged desk-table with a single straight chair pushed against it. The bed was narrow and high with a heavily carved headboard.

Dasein pushed down on the surface of the bed. It felt soft. He dropped his suitcase onto the bed, stared at it. An edge of white fabric protruded from one end. He opened the suitcase, studied the contents. Dasein knew himself for a prissy, meticulous packer. The case now betrayed a subtle disarray. Someone had opened it and searched it. Well, it hadn't been locked. He checked the contents—nothing missing.

Why are they curious about me? he wondered.

He looked around for a telephone, found it, a standard French handset, on a shelf beside the desk. As he moved, he caught sight of himself in the mirror above the
24

dresser—eyes wide, mouth in a straight line. Grim. He shook his head, smiled. The smile felt out of place.

Dasein sat down in the straight chair, put the phone to his ear. There was a smell of disinfectant soap in the room—and something like garlic. After a moment, he jiggled the hook.

Presently, a woman's voice came on: "This is the desk."

"I'd like to place a call to Berkeley," Dasein said. He gave the number. There was a moment's silence, then: "Your room number, sir?"

"Two fifty-one."

"One moment, please."

He heard the sound of dialing, ringing. Another operator came on the line. Dasein listened with only half his attention as the call was placed. The smell of garlic was quite strong. He stared at the high old bed, his open suitcase. The bed appeared inviting, telling him how tired he was. His chest ached. He took a deep breath.

"Dr. Selador here."

Selador's India-*cum*-Oxford accent sounded familiar and close. Dasein bent to the telephone, identified himself, his mind caught suddenly by that feeling of intimate nearness linked to the knowledge of the actual distance, the humming wires reaching down almost half the length of the state.

"Gilbert, old fellow, you made it all right, I see." Selador's voice was full of cheer.

"I'm at the Santaroga House, Doctor."

"I hear it's quite comfortable."

"Looks that way." Through his buzzing tiredness, Dasein felt a sense of foolishness. Why had he made this call? Selador's sharp mind would probe for underlying meanings, motives.

"I presume you didn't call just to tell me you've arrived," Selador said.

"No . . . I . . . " Dasein realized he couldn't express his own vague uneasiness, that it wouldn't make sense, this feeling of estrangement, the separation of Santarogans and Outsiders, the pricklings of warning fear. "I'd like you to look into the oil company dealings with this area," Dasein

25

said. "See if you can find out how they do business in the valley. There's apparently an independent service station here. I want to know who supplies the gas, oil, parts—that sort of thing."

"Good point, Gilbert. I'll put one of our . . ." There was a sudden crackling, bapping sound on the line. It stopped and there was dead silence.

"Dr. Selador?"

Silence.

Damn! Dasein thought. He jiggled the hook. "Operator. Operator!"

A masculine voice came on the line. Dasein recognized the desk clerk's twang. "Who's that creating all that commotion?" the clerk demanded.

"I was cut off on my call to Berkeley," Dasein said. "Could you . . . "

"Line's out," the clerk snapped.

"Could I come down to the lobby and place the call from a pay phone?" Dasein asked. As he asked it, the thought of walking that long distance down to the lobby repelled Dasein. The feeling of tiredness was a weight on his chest.

"There's no line out of the valley right now," the clerk said. "Call can't be placed."

Dasein passed a hand across his forehead. His skin felt clammy and he wondered if he'd picked up a germ. The room around him seemed to expand and contract. His mouth was dry and he had to swallow twice before asking: "When do they expect to have the line restored?"

"How the hell do I know?" the clerk demanded.

Dasein took the receiver away from his ear, stared at it. This was a very peculiar desk clerk . . . and a very peculiar room the way it wavered and slithered with its stench of garlic and its . . .

He grew aware of a faint hissing.

Dasein's gaze was drawn on a string of growing astonishment to an old-fashioned gaslight jet that jutted from the wall beside the hall door.

Stink of garlic? Gas!

26

A yapping, barking voice yammered on the telephone. Dasein looked down at the instrument in his hand. How far away it seemed. Through the window beyond the phone he could see the Inn sign: *Gold Rush Museum*. Window equaled air. Dasein found muscles that obeyed, lurched across the desk, fell, smashing the telephone through the window.

The yapping voice grew fainter.

Dasein felt his body stretched across the desk. His head lay near the shattered window. He could see the telephone cord stretching out the window. There was cool air blowing on a distant forehead, a painful chill in his lungs.

They tried to kill me, he thought. It was a wondering thought, full of amazement. His mind focused on the two investigators who'd already died on this project—accidents. Simple, easily explained accidents . . . just like this one!

The air—how cold it felt on his exposed skin. His lungs burned with it. There was a hammering pulse at his temple where it pressed against the desk surface. The pulse went on and on and on . . .

A pounding on wood joined the pulse. For a space, they beat in an insane syncopation.

"You in there! Open up!" How commanding, that voice. *Open up,* Dasein thought. That meant getting to one's feet, crossing the room, turning a door handle . . .

I'm helpless, he thought. *They could still kill me.*

He heard metal rasp against metal. The air blew stronger across his face. Someone said: "Gas!"

Hands grabbed Dasein's shoulders. He was hauled back, half carried, half dragged out of the room. The face of Marden, the red-haired patrol captain, swung across his vision. He saw the clerk: pale, staring face, bald forehead glistening under yellow light. There was a brown ceiling directly in front of Dasein. He felt a rug, hard and rasping, beneath his back.

A twanging voice said: "Who's going to pay for that window?" Someone else said: "I'll get Dr. Piaget."

Dasein's attention centered on Marden's mouth, a

27

blurred object seen through layers of distortion. There appeared to be anger lines at the corners of the mouth. It turned toward the hovering pale face of the desk clerk, said: "To hell with your window, Johnson! I've told you enough times to get those gas jets out of this place. How many rooms still have them?"

"Don't you take that tone with me, Al Marden. I've known you since . . . "

"I'm not interested in how long you've known me, Johnson. How many rooms still have those gas jets?"

The clerk's voice came with an angry tone of hurt: "Only this'n an' four upstairs. Nobody in the other rooms."

"Get 'em out by tomorrow night," Marden said.

Hurrying footsteps interrupted the argument. Dr. Piaget's round face blotted out Dasein's view of the ceiling. The face wore a look of concern. Fingers reached down, spread Dasein's eyelids. Piaget said: "Let's get him on a bed."

"Is he going to be all right?" the clerk asked.

"It's about time you asked," Marden said.

"We got him in time," Piaget said. "Is that room across the hall empty?"

"He can have 260," the clerk said. "I'll open it."

"You realize this is Jenny's fellow from the school you almost killed?" Marden asked, his voice receding as he moved away beside the clerk.

"Jenny's fellow?" There was the sound of a key in a lock. "But I thought . . . "

"Never mind what you thought!"

Piaget's face moved close to Dasein. "Can you hear me, young fellow?" he asked.

Dasein drew in a painful breath, croaked, "Yes."

"You'll have quite a head, but you'll recover."

Piaget's face went away. Hands picked Dasein up. The ceiling moved. There was another room around him: like the first one—tall ceiling, even the sound of dripping water. He felt a bed beneath his back, hands beginning to undress him. Sudden nausea gripped him. Dasein pushed the hands away.

Someone helped him to the bathroom where he was sick.

28

He felt better afterward—weak, but with a clearer head, a better sense of control over his muscles. He saw it was Piaget who'd helped him.

"Feel like getting back to bed now?" Piaget asked.

"Yes."

"I'll give you a good shot of iron to counteract the gas effect on your blood," Piaget said. "You'll be all right."

"How'd that gas jet get turned on?" Dasein asked. His voice came out a hoarse whisper.

"Johnson got mixed up fooling with the valves in the kitchen," Piaget said. "Wouldn't have been any harm done if some idiot hadn't opened the jet in your room."

"I coulda sworn I had 'em all turned off." That was the clerk's voice from somewhere beyond the bathroom door.

"They better be capped by tomorrow night," Marden said.

They sounded so reasonable, Dasein thought. Marden appeared genuinely angry. The look on Piaget's face could be nothing other than concern.

Could it have been a real accident? Dasein wondered.

He reminded himself then two men had died by accident in this valley while engaged in the investigation.

"All right," Piaget said. "Al, you and Pim and the others can clear out now. I'll get him to bed."

"Okay, Larry. Clear out, all of you." That was Marden.

"I'll get his bags from the other room." That was a voice Dasein didn't recognize.

Presently, with Piaget's help, Dasein found himself in pajamas and in the bed. He felt clearheaded, wide awake and lonely even with Piaget still in the room.

Among strangers, Dasein thought.

"Here, take this," Piaget said. He pressed two pills into Dasein's mouth, forced a glass of water on him. Dasein gulped, felt the pills rasp down his throat in a wash of water.

"What was that?" Dasein asked as he pushed the glass away.

"The iron and a sedative."

"I don't want to sleep. The gas . . . "

"You didn't get enough gas to make that much dif-

29

ference. Now, you rest easy." Piaget patted his shoulder. "Bed rest and fresh air are the best therapy you can get. Someone'll look in on you from time to time tonight. I'll check back on you in the morning."

"Someone," Dasein said. "A nurse?"

"Yes," Piaget said, his voice brusk. "A nurse. You'll be as safe here as in a hospital."

Dasein looked at the night beyond the room's window. *Why the feeling of danger now, then?* he wondered. *Is it reaction?* He could feel the sedative blurring his senses, soothing him. The sense of danger persisted.

"Jenny will be happy to know you're here," Piaget said. He left the room, turning off the light, closing the door softly.

Dasein felt he had been smothered in darkness. He fought down panic, restored himself to a semblance of calm.

Jenny . . . Jenny . . .

Marden's odd conversation with the clerk, Johnson, returned to him. " . . . *Jenny's fellow from the school . . .* "

What had Johnson thought? What was the thing Marden had cut short?

Dasein fought the sedative. The drip-drip of water in the bathroom invaded his awareness. The room was an alien cell.

Was it just an accident?

He remembered the fragmented confusion of the instant when he'd focused on that hissing gas jet. Now, when the danger was past, he felt terror.

It couldn't have been an accident!

But why would Johnson want to kill him?

The disconnected telephone call haunted Dasein. Was the line really down? What would Selador do? Selador knew the dangers here.

Dasein felt the sedative pulling him down into sleep. He tried to focus on the investigation. It was such a fascinating project. He could hear Selador explaining the facets that made the Santaroga Project such a glittering gem—

"Taken singly, no item in this collection of facts could be considered alarming or worthy of extended attention.

30

You might find it interesting that no person from Clover-dale, California, could be found in a mental hospital. It might be of passing interest to learn that the people of Hope, Missouri, consumed very little tobacco. Would you be alarmed to discover that all the business of Enumclaw, Washington, were locally owned? Certainly not: But when you bring all of these and the other facts together into a single community, something disturbing emerges. There is a difference *at work here."*

The drip of water in the bathroom was a compelling distraction. *Dangerous difference,* Dasein thought. *Who'll look in on me?* he wondered.

It occurred to him to ask himself then who had sounded the alarm. The breaking window had alerted someone. The most likely person would be Johnson, the room clerk. Why would he bring help to the person he was trying to kill? The paranoia in his own thoughts began to impress itself on Dasein.

It was an accident, Dasein thought. *It was an accident in a place of dangerous difference.*

Dasein's morning began with a sensation of hunger. He awoke to cramping pains. Events of the night flooded into his memory. His head felt as though it had been kicked from the inside.

Gently, he pushed himself upright. There was a window directly ahead of him with the green branch of an oak tree across it. As though his muscles were controlled by some hidden force, Dasein found himself looking up at the door to see if there was a gas jet. Nothing met his questing gaze but a patch on the wallpaper to mark the place where a jet had been.

Holding his head as level as possible, Dasein eased himself out of bed and into the bathroom. A cold shower restored some of his sense of reality.

He kept telling himself: *It was an accident.*

A bluejay was sitting on the oak branch screeching when Dasein emerged from the bathroom. The sound sent little clappers of pain through Dasein's head. He dressed hurriedly, hunger urging him. The bluejay was joined by a

31

companion. They screeched and darted at each other through the oak tree, their topknots twitching. Dasein gritted his teeth, faced the mirror to tie his tie. As he was finishing the knot, he saw reflected in the mirror the slow inward movement of the hall door. A corner of a wheeled tray appeared. Dishes clattered. The door swung wider.

Jenny appeared in the doorway pushing the tray. Dasein stared at her in the mirror, his hands frozen at the tie. She wore a red dress, her long black hair caught in a matching bandeaux. Her skin displayed a healthy tan. Blue eyes stared back at him in the mirror. Her oval face was set in a look of watchful waiting. Her mouth was as full as he remembered it, hesitating on the edge of a smile, a dimple flickering at her left cheek.

"Finish your tie," she said. "I've brought you some breakfast." Her voice had a well-remembered, throaty, soothing tone.

Dasein turned, moved toward her as though pulled by strings. Jenny abandoned the cart, met him half way. She came into his arms, lifting her lips to be kissed. Dasein, feeling the warmth of her kiss and the familiar pressure of her against him, experienced a sensation of coming home.

Jenny pulled away, studied his face. "Oh, Gil," she said, "I've missed you so much. Why didn't you even write?"

He stared at her, surprised to silence for a moment, then: "But I did write. You never answered."

She pushed away from him, her features contorted by a scowl. "Ohhh!" She stamped her foot.

"Well, I see you found him." It was Dr. Piaget in the doorway. He pushed the cart all the way into the room, closed the door.

Jenny whirled on him. "Uncle Larry! Did you keep Gil's letters from me?"

Piaget looked from her to Dasein. "Letters? What letters?"

"Gil wrote and I never got the letters!"

"Oh." Piaget nodded. "Well, you know how they are at the post office sometimes—valley girl, fellow from outside."

"Ohhh! I could scratch their eyes out!"

32

"Easy, girl." Piaget smiled at Dasein.

Jenny whirled back into Dasein's arms, surprised him with another kiss. He broke away slightly breathless.

"There," she said. "That's for being here. Those old biddies at the post office can't dump *that* in the trash basket."

"What old biddies?" Dasein asked. He felt he had missed part of the conversation. The warmth of Jenny's kisses, her open assumption nothing had changed between them, left him feeling defenseless, wary. A year had passed, after all. He'd managed to stay away from here for a year—leaning on his wounded masculine ego, true, fearful he'd find Jenny married . . . lost to him forever. But what had she leaned on? She could've come to Berkeley, if only for a visit.

And I could've come here.

Jenny grinned.

"Why're you grinning?" he demanded. "And you haven't explained this about the post office and the . . . "

"I'm grinning because I'm so happy," she said. "I'm grinning because I see the wheels going around in your head. Why didn't one of us go see the other before now? Well, *you're* here as I knew you would be. I just *knew* you would be." She hugged him impulsively, said: "About the post office . . . "

"I think Gilbert's breakfast is getting cold," Piaget said. "You don't mind if I call you Gilbert?"

"He doesn't mind," Jenny said. Her voice was bantering, but there was a sudden stiffness in her body. She pushed away from Dasein.

Piaget lifted a cover from one of the plates on the cart, said: "Jaspers omelette, I see. *Real* Jaspers."

Jenny spoke defensively with a curious lack of vitality: "I made it myself in Johnson's kitchen."

"I see," Piaget said. "Yes . . . well, perhaps that's best." He indicated the plate. "Have at it, Gilbert."

The thought of food made Dasein's stomach knot with hunger. He wanted to sit down and bolt the omelette . . . but something made him hesitate. He couldn't evade the nagging sense of danger.

"What's this Jaspers business?" he asked.

33

"Oh, that," Jenny said, pulling the cart over to the chair by the desk. "That just means something made with a product from the Co-op. This is our cheddar in the omelette. Sit down and eat."

"You'll like it," Piaget said. He crossed the room, put a hand on Dasein's shoulder, eased him into the chair. "Just let me have a quick look at you." He pinched Dasein's left ear lobe, studied it, looked at his eyes. "You're looking pretty fit. How's the head?"

"It's better now. It was pretty fierce when I woke up."

"Okay. Eat your breakfast. Take it easy for a day or two. Let me know if you feel nauseated again or have any general symptoms of lethargy. I suggest you eat liver for dinner and I'll have Jenny bring you some more iron pills. You weren't in there long enough to cause you any permanent trouble."

"When I think of that Mr. Johnson's carelessness, I want to take one of his cleavers to him," Jenny said.

"We *are* bloodthirsty today, aren't we," Piaget said.

Dasein picked up his fork, sampled the omelette. Jenny watched him, waiting. The omelette was delicious—moist and with a faint bite of cheese. He swallowed, smiled at her.

Jenny grinned back. "You know," she said, "that's the first food I ever cooked for you."

"Don't rush him off his feet, girl," Piaget said. He patted her head, said: "I'll leave you two for now. Why don't you bring your young man along home for dinner? I'll have Sarah make what he needs." He glanced at Dasein. "That all right with you?"

Dasein swallowed another bite of the omelette. The cheese left a tangy aftertaste that reminded him of the unpasteurized beer Burdeaux had served. "I'd be honored, sir," he said.

"Honored, yet," Piaget said. "We'll expect you around seven." He glanced at his wristwatch. "It's almost eight-thirty, Jenny. Aren't you working today?"

"I called George and told him I'd be late."

"He didn't object?"

34

"He knows . . . I have a friend . . . visiting." She blushed.

"Like that, eh? Well, don't get into any trouble." Piaget turned, lumbered from the room with a head-down purposeful stride.

Jenny turned a shy, questioning smile on Dasein. "Don't mind Uncle Larry," she said. "He darts around like that—one subject then another. He's a very real, wonderful person."

"Where do you work?" Dasein asked.

"At the Co-op."

"The cheese factory?"

"Yes. I'm . . . I'm on the inspection line."

Dasein swallowed, reminded himself he was here to do a market study. He was a spy. And what would Jenny say when she discovered that? But Jenny posed a new puzzle. She had a superior talent for clinical psychology—even according to Dr. Selador whose standards were high. Yet . . . she worked in the cheese factory.

"Isn't there any work . . . in your line here?" he asked.

"It's a good job," she said. She sat down on the edge of the desk, swung her legs. "Finish your breakfast. I didn't make that coffee. It's out of the hotel urn. Don't drink it if it's too strong. There's orange juice in the metal pitcher. I remembered you take your coffee black and didn't bring any . . ."

"Whoa!" he said.

"I'm talking too much I know it," she said. She hugged herself. "Oh, Gil, I'm so happy you're here. Finish your breakfast and you can take me across to the Co-op. Maybe I can take you on the guided tour. It's a fascinating place. There are lots of dark corners back in the storage cave."

Dasein drained his coffee, shook his head. "Jenny, you are incorrigible."

"Gil, you're going to love it here. I know you are," she said.

Dasein wiped his lips on his napkin. She was still in love with him. He could see that in every look. And he . . . he felt the same way about her. It was still *love me love my valley,* though. Her words betrayed it. Dasein sighed. He

35

could see the blank wall of an unresolvable difference looming ahead of them. If her love could stand the discovery of his true role here, could it also stand breaking away from the valley? Would she come away with him?

"Gil, are you all right?" she asked.

He pushed his chair back, got up. "Yes. I'm . . . "

The telephone rang.

Jenny reached behind her on the desk, brought the receiver to her ear. "Dr. Dasein's room." She grinned at Dasein. The grin turned to a scowl. "Oh, it's you, Mr. Pem Johnson, is it? Well, I'll tell you a thing or two, Mr. Johnson! I think you're a criminal the way you almost killed Dr. Dasein! If you'd . . . No! Don't you try to make excuses! Open gas jets in the rooms! I think Dr. Dasein ought to sue you for every cent you have!"

A tinny, rasping noise came from the phone. Dasein recognized only a few words. The grin returned to Jenny's face. "It's Jenny Sorge, that's who it is," she said. "Don't you . . . well, I'll tell you if you'll be quiet for a minute! I'm here bringing Dr. Dasein what the doctor ordered for him—a good breakfast. He doesn't dare eat anything you'd have prepared for him. It'd probably have poison in it!"

Dasein crossed to a trunk stand where his suitcase had been left, opened it. He spoke over his shoulder. "Jenny, what's he want, for heaven's sake?"

She waved him to silence.

Dasein rummaged in the suitcase looking for his briefcase. He tried to remember what had been done with it in the confusion of the previous night, looked around the room. No sign of it. Someone had gone to the other room for his things. Maybe whoever it was had missed the briefcase. Dasein thought of the case's contents, wet his lips with his tongue. Every step of his program to unravel the mystery of the Santaroga Barrier was outlined there. In the wrong hands, that information could cause him trouble, throw up new barriers.

"I'll tell him," Jenny said.

"Wait a minute," Dasein said. "I want to talk to him." He took the phone from her. "Johnson?"

"What do you want?" There was that twangy belliger-

36

ency, but Dasein couldn't blame him after the treatment he'd received from Jenny.

"My briefcase," Dasein said. "It was in the other room. Would you send up someone with a key and . . ."

"**Your** damned briefcase isn't in that room, mister! I cleaned the place out and I ought to know."

"Then where is it?" Dasein asked.

"If it's that case you were so touchy about last night, I saw Captain Marden leave with something that looked like it last night after all the commotion you caused."

"I caused?" Outrage filled Dasein's voice. "See here, Johnson! You stop twisting the facts!"

After only a heartbeat of silence, Johnson said: "I was, wasn't I? Sorry."

Johnson's abrupt candor disarmed the psychologist in Dasein. In a way, it reminded him of Jenny. Santarogans, he found, displayed a lopsided reality that was both attractive and confusing. When he'd collected his thoughts, all Dasein could say was: "What would Marden be doing with my case?"

"That's for him to say and you to find out," Johnson said with all his old belligerence. There was a sharp click as he broke the connection.

Dasein shook his head, put the phone back on its hook.

"Al Marden wants you to have lunch with him at the Blue Ewe," Jenny said.

"Hmmm?" He looked up at her, bemused, her words taking a moment to register. "Marden . . . lunch?"

"Twelve noon. The Blue Ewe's on the Avenue of the Giants where it goes through town . . . on the right just past the first cross street."

"Marden? The Highway patrol captain?"

"Yes. Johnson just passed the message along." She slipped down off the desk, a flash of knees, a swirl of the red skirt. "Come along. Escort me to work."

Dasein picked up his suitcoat, allowed himself to be led from the room.

That damn' briefcase with all its forms and notes and letters, he thought. *The whole show!* But it gave him a perverse feeling of satisfaction to know that everything would be out in the open. *I wasn't cut out to be a cloak and dagget type.*

There was no escaping the realization, though, that revelation of his real purpose here would intensify Santaroga's conspiracy of silence. And how would Jenny react?

2

Dasein's first impression of the Jasper Cheese Cooperative with the people at work in and around it was that the place was a hive. It loomed whitely behind its fence as Jenny led him from the Inn. He found it an odd companion for the Inn, just across the road, nestled against a steep hill, poking odd squares and rectangles up onto an outcropping. The previous night's brooding look had been replaced by this appearance of humming efficiency with electric carts buzzing across the yard, their platforms loaded with oblong packages. People walked with a leaning sense of purpose.

A hive, Dasein thought. There must be a queen inside and these were the workers, guarding, gathering food.

A uniformed guard, a police dog on a leash beside him, took Dasein's name as Jenny introduced him. The guard opened a gate in the chain-link fence. His dog grinned wolfishly at Dasein, whined.

Dasein remembered the baying he'd heard when he'd first looked down into the valley. That had been less than fourteen hours ago, Dasein realized. The time felt stretched out, longer. He asked himself why dogs guarded the Co-op. The question bothered him.

The yard they crossed was an immaculate concrete surface. Now that he was close to the factory, Dasein saw that it was a complex of structures that had been joined by filling the between areas with odd additions and covered walkways.

Jenny's mood changed markedly once they were well inside the grounds. Dasein saw her become more assertive, sure of herself. She introduced Dasein to four persons while crossing the yard—Willa Burdeaux among them.

Willa turned out to be a small husky-voiced young woman with a face that was almost ugly in its tiny, concise sharpness. She had her father's deeps-of-darkness skin, a petite figure.

"I met your father last night," Dasein said.

"Daddy told me," she said. She turned a knowing look on Jenny, added: "Anything I can do, just tell me, honey."

"Maybe later," Jenny said. "We have to be running."

"You're going to like it here, Gilbert Dasein," Willa said. She turned away with a wave, hurried across the yard.

Disturbed by the undertones of the conversation, Dasein allowed himself to be led down a side bay, into a wide door that opened onto an aisle between stacked cartons of Jaspers Cheese. Somewhere beyond the stacks there was a multiplexity of sounds—hissings, stampings, gurgling water, a clank-clank-clank.

The aisle ended in a short flight of wide steps, up to a loading bay with hand trucks racked along its edge. Jenny led him through a door marked "Office."

It was such an ordinary place—clips of order forms racked along a wall, two desks with women seated at them typing, a long counter with a gate at one end, windows opening onto the yard and a view of the Inn, a door labeled "Manager" beyond the women.

The door opened as Dasein and Jenny stopped at the counter. Out stepped one of the card players from the Inn's dining room—the balding sandy hair, the deeply cleft chin and wide mouth—George Nis. The heavily lidded blue eyes swept past Dasein to Jenny.

"Problems in Bay Nine, Jenny," Nis said. "You're needed over there right away."

"Oh, darn!" Jenny said.

"I'll take care of your friend," Nis said. "We'll see if we can't let you off early for your dinner date."

Jenny squeezed Dasein's hand, said: "Darling, forgive me. Duty and all that." She blinked a smile at him, whirled and was back out the door, the red skirt swirling.

The women at their typewriters looked up, seemed to take in Dasein with one look, went back to their work. Nis came to the gate in the counter, opened it.

40

"Come on in, Dr. Dasein." He extended a hand. The handshake was firm, casual.

Dasein followed the man into an oak-paneled office, unable to get his mind off the fact that Nis knew about the dinner date with Jenny. How could the man know? Piaget had extended the invitation only a few minutes before.

They sat down separated by a wide desk, its top empty of papers. The chairs were padded, comfortable with sloping arms. In large frames behind Nis hung an aerial photograph of the Co-op and what appeared to be a ground plan. Dasein recognized the layout of the yard and front of the building. The back became heavy dark lines that wandered off into the hill like the tributaries of a river. They were labeled with the initial *J* and numbers—*J-5* . . . *J-14* . . .

Nis saw the direction of Dasein's gaze, said: "Those are the storage caverns—constant temperature and humidity." He coughed discreetly behind a hand, said: "You catch us at an embarrassing moment, Dr. Dasein. I've nobody I can release to show you through the plant. Could Jenny bring you back another day?"

"At your convenience," Dasein said. He studied Nis, feeling oddly wary, on guard.

"Please don't wear any cologne or hair dressing or anything like that when you come," Nis said. "You'll notice that our women wear no makeup and we don't allow female visitors from outside to go into the cave or storage areas. It's quite easy to contaminate the culture, give an odd flavor to an entire batch."

Dasein was suddenly acutely aware of the aftershave lotion he'd used that morning.

"I'll be pure and clean," he said. He looked to the right out the windows, caught suddenly by motion there on the road between the Co-op and the Inn.

A peculiar high-wheeled vehicle went lurching past. Dasein counted eight pairs of wheels. They appeared to be at least fifteen feet in diameter, big ballooning doughnuts that hummed on the pavement. The wheels were slung on heavy arms like insect legs.

In an open cab, high up in front, four leashed hounds

41

seated behind him, rode Al Marden. He appeared to be steering by using two vertical handles.

"What in the devil is that?" Dasein demanded. He jumped up, crossed to the window to get a better look at the machine as it sped down the road. "Isn't that Captain Marden driving it?"

"That's our game warden's bush buggy," Nis said. "Al acts as game warden sometimes when the regular man's sick or busy on something else. Must've been out patroling the south hills. Heard there were some deer hunters from outside messing around there this morning."

"You don't allow outsiders to hunt in the valley, is that it?" Dasein asked.

"*Nobody* hunts in the valley," Nis corrected him. "Too much chance of stray bullets hitting someone. Most of the people around this area know the law, but we occasionally get someone from down south who blunders in. There're very few places the buggy can't get to them, though. We set them straight in a hurry."

Dasein imagined that giant-wheeled monstrosity lurching over the brush, descending on some hapless hunter who'd blundered into the valley. He found his sympathies with the hunter.

"I've never seen a vehicle like that before," Dasein said. "Is it something new?"

"Sam, Sam Scheler, built the bush buggy ten, twelve years ago," Nis said. "We were getting some poachers from over by Porterville then. They don't bother us anymore."

"I imagine not," Dasein said.

"I hope you'll forgive me," Nis said. "I do have a great deal of work and we're short-handed today. Get Jenny to bring you back later in the week . . . after . . . well, later in the week."

After what? Dasein wondered. He found himself strangely alert. He'd never felt this clearheaded before. He wondered if it could be some odd after effect of the gas.

"I'll, ah, let myself out," he said, rising.

"The gate guard will be expecting you," Nis said. He remained seated, his gaze fixed on Dasein with an odd intensity until the door closed between them.

42

The women in the outer office glanced up as Dasein let himself through the counter gate, went back to their work. A gang of men was loading hand trucks on the ramp when Dasein emerged. He felt their eyes boring into him as he made his way down the dock above them. A sliding door off to the left opened suddenly. Dasein glimpsed a long table with a conveyor belt down its middle, a line of men and women working along it, sorting packages.

Something about the people in that line caught his attention. They were oddly dull-eyed, slow in their actions. Dasein saw their legs beneath the table. The legs appeared to be held in stocks.

The door closed.

Dasein continued out into the sunshine, disturbed by what he had seen. Those workers had appeared . . . mentally retarded. He crossed the yard wondering. Problems in Bay 9? Jenny was a competent psychologist. More than competent. What did she do here? What did she *really* do?

The gate guard nodded to him, said: "Come again, Dr. Dasein." The man went into his little house, lifted a telephone, spoke briefly into it.

'The gate guard will be expecting you,' Dasein thought.

He crossed to the Inn, ran lightly up the steps and into the lobby. A gray-haired woman sat behind the desk working at an adding machine. She looked up at Dasein.

"Could I get a line out to Berkeley?" he asked.

"All the lines are out," she said. "Some trouble with a brush fire."

"Thanks."

Dasein went outside, paused on the long porch, scanned the sky. Brush fire? There wasn't a sign or smell of smoke.

Everything about Santaroga could appear so natural, he thought, if it weren't for the underlying sense of strangeness and secrecy that made his neck hairs crawl.

Dasein took a deep breath, went down to his truck, nursed it to life.

This time, he took the turn to 'City Center.' The Avenue of the Giants widened to four lanes presently with homes and business mixed at seeming random on both sides. A park opened on the left—paved paths, central bandstand, flower borders. Beyond the park, a stone church lifted an imposing spire into the sky. The sign on its lawn read: "Church of All Faiths . . . Sermon: 'Intensity of God response as a function of anxiety.' "

Intensity of God response? Dasein wondered. It was quite the oddest sermon announcement he had ever seen. He made a mental note to try and catch that sermon on Sunday.

The people on the streets began to catch Dasein's attention. Their alertness, the brisk way they moved, was a contrast to the dullness of the line he'd seen in the Co-op. Who were those dull creatures? For that matter, who were these swiftly striding folk on the streets?

There was vitality and a happy freedom in the people he saw, Dasein realized. He wondered if the mood could be infectious. He had never felt more vital himself.

Dasein noted a sign on his right just past the park: A gamboling sheep with the letters "Blue Ewe" carved in a rolling script. It was a windowless front faced with blue stone, an impersonal façade broken only by wide double doors containing one round glass port each.

So Marden wanted to have lunch with him there. Why? It seemed obvious the partrol captain had taken the briefcase. Was he going to pull the 'go-and-never-darken-my-door' routine he'd used on the hapless salesman in the dining room of the Inn? Or would it be something more subtle designed for 'Jenny's friend from the school'?

At the far end of the town, the street widened once more to open a broad access to a twelve-sided service station. Dasein slowed his truck to admire the structure. It was the largest service station he had ever seen. A canopy structure jutted from each of the twelve sides. Beneath each canopy were three rows of pumps, each row designed to handle four vehicles. Just beyond it, separated from the giant wheel of the station, stood a building containing rows of grease racks. Behind the station was a football-field-sized parking area with a large building at the far end labeled "Garage."

Dasein drove into the station, stopped at an outside row of pumps, got out to study the layout. He counted twenty

44

grease racks, six cars being serviced. Cars were coming and going all around him. It was another hive. He wondered why none of the datum-data mentioned this complex. The place swarmed with young men in neat blue-gray uniforms.

One of the neat young men came trotting up to Dasein, said: "What grade, sir?"

"Grade?"

"What octane gas do you want?"

"What do you have?"

"Eighty, ninety and a hundred-plus."

"Fill it with ninety and check the oil."

Dasein left the young man to his labors, walked out toward the street to get a better perspective on the station. It covered at least four acres, he estimated. He returned to the truck as the young man emerged from beneath the hood holding the dipstick.

"Your oil's down a bit more than a quart," the young man said.

"Put in thirty-weight detergent," Dasein said.

"Excuse me," he said, "but I heard this clunker drive in. We carry an aircraft grade of forty weight. I'd recommend you use it. You won't burn quite as much."

"What's it cost?"

"Same as all the others—thirty-five cents a quart."

"Okay." Dasein shook his head. Aircraft grade at that price? Where did *Mr. Sam* buy it?

"How do you like Santaroga?" the young man asked, his voice bright with the invitation for a compliment.

"Fine," Dasein said. "Beautiful little town. You know, this is the biggest service staton I've ever seen. It's a wonder there haven't been any newspaper or magazine articles about it."

"Old Sam doesn't cotton to publicity," the attendant said.

"Why's it so damn' big?" Dasein asked.

"Has to be big. It's the only one in the valley." The young man worked his way around the engine, checking the water in the radiator, the level in the battery. He grinned at Dasein. "Kinda surprises most outsiders. We find it handy. Some of the farmers have their own pumps

45

and there's service at the airport, but they all get their supplies through Sam." He closed the hood.

"And where does Old Sam get *his* supplies?"

The attendant leveled a probing stare at Dasein. "I sure hope you haven't taken on a sideline with one of the big oil companies, sir," he said. "If you're thinking of selling to Sam, forget it."

"I'm just curious," Dasein said. The attendant's choice of words was puzzling. *Sideline?* Dasein chose to ignore it for the moment, intent on the larger question.

"Sam orders his supplies once a year on open bid," the attendant said. He topped off the truck's gas tank, returned the hose to its holder. "This year it's a little company in Oklahoma. They truck it up here in convoys."

"That so?"

"I wouldn't say it if it weren't so."

"I wasn't questioning your word," Dasein said. "I was registering surprise."

"Don't see much to get surprised about. Person ought to buy where he gets the most value for his money. That'll be three dollars and three cents."

Dasein counted out the change, said: "Is there a pay phone around here?"

"If you're making a local call, there's a phone inside you can use, Dr. Dasein," the attendant said. "The pay phones are over there beside the rack building, but no sense wasting your time if you're calling outside. Lines are down. There was a fire over on the ridge."

Dasein went to full alert, glared at the attendant. "How'd you know my name?" he demanded.

"Heck, mister, it's all over town. You're Jenny's fellow from the city. You're the reason she sends all the locals packing."

The grin that went with this statement should have been completely disarming, but it only made Dasein more wary.

"You're going to like it here," the attendant said. "Everybody does." The grin faded somewhat. "If you'll excuse me, sir. I've other cars to service."

Dasein found himself staring at a retreating back. *He suspected I might represent an oil company,* Dasein

46

thought, *but he knows my name . . . and he knows about Jenny.* It was a curious disparity and Dasein felt it should tell him something. It could be the simple truth, though.

A long green Chrysler Imperial pulled into the empty space on the other side of the pumps. The driver, a fat man smoking a cigarette in a holder, leaned out, asked: "Hey! This the road out to 395?"

"Straight ahead," Dasein said.

"Any gas stations along the way?"

"Not here in the valley," Dasein said. "Maybe something outside." He shrugged. "I've never been out that way."

"You damn' natives," the driver growled. The Imperial shot ahead in a surge of power, swerved out onto the avenue and was gone.

"Up yours," Dasein muttered. "Who the hell you calling a native?"

He climbed into his truck, turned back the way he had come. At the fork, he headed up the mountain toward Porterville. The road climbed up, up—winding its way out of the redwoods and into a belt of oaks. He came at last to the turn off where he'd taken his first long look at the valley. He pulled out and parked.

A light smokey haze obscured details, but the Co-op stood out plainly and the slash burner of a sawmill off to the left. The town itself was a patch of color in the trees—tile roofs—and there was a serpentine river line out of the hills straight across from him. Dasein glanced at his wristwatch—five minutes to ten. He debated going out to Porterville and placing his call to Selador there. That would crowd him on the date with Marden, though. He decided to post a letter to Selador, have the "burned out phone lines" story checked from that end.

Without his briefcase and notes, Dasein felt at a disadvantage. He rummaged in the glove compartment, found a small gas-record notebook and stub of pencil, began setting down his observations for later formal entry in his report.

"The township itself is small," he wrote, "but it appears to serve a large market area. There are a great many people

47

about during the day. Note twelve double pumps in service station. Transients?

"Odd alertness about the natives. Sharpness of attitude toward each other and *outsiders*.

"Question local use of Jaspers products. Why won't the cheese travel? What's the reason for the decided local preference? It tastes different than what I bought outside. What about aftertaste? Subjective? What relationship to the beer?

"Investigate use of Jaspers as a label. Adjective?"

Something big was moving through the trees on the hill beyond the Co-op. The movement caught Dasein's attention. He studied it a moment. Too many trees intervened to permit a clear look.

Dasein went around to the camper back, found his binoculars there. He focused them on the movement in the trees. The donut-wheeled bush buggy leaped into view. Marden was driving. It threaded its way through trees and buck brush. The thing appeared to be herding something . . . or someone. Dasein scanned ahead for a clearing, found one, waited. Three men in hunting clothes emerged, hands clasped over their heads. Two dogs flasked them, watchful, guarding. The hunters appeared angry, frightened.

The group angled down into a stand of redwoods, was lost to view. Dasein climbed back into the cab, made a note on what he had seen.

It was all of a pattern, he thought. These were things that could be resolved by natural, logical explanations. A law enforcement officer had picked up three illegal hunters. That was what law enforcement officers were supposed to do. But the incident carried what Dasein was coming to recognize as a Santaroga twist. There was something about it out of phase with the way the rest of the world operated.

He headed his truck back into the valley, determined to question Marden about the captive hunters.

3

The Blue Ewe's interior was a low-key grotto, its walls painted in varying intensities of pastel blue. Rather ordinary banquette booths with tables flanked an open area of tables and chairs. A long bar with a mirror decorated by dancing sheep occupied the back wall.

Marden awaited him in one of the booths. A tall iced drink stood in front of him. The patrol captain appeared relaxed, his red hair neatly combed. The collar tabs of his uniform shirt carried the double bars of a captain. He wore no coat. His eyes followed Dasein's approach with an alert directness.

"Care for a drink?" he asked as Dasein sat down.

"What's that you're having?" Dasein nodded at the iced drink.

"Kind of an orange beer with Jaspers."

"I'll try it," Dasein said.

Marden raised a hand toward the bar, called: "Another ade, Jim." He returned his attention to Dasein. "How's your head today?"

"I'm fine," Dasein said. He found himself feeling edgy, wondering how Marden would bring up the subject of the briefcase. The drink was put in front of him. Dasein welcomed it as a distraction, sipped it. His tongue encountered a sharp orange flavor with the tangy, biting overtone of Jaspers.

"Oh, about your briefcase," Marden said.

Dasein put down his drink with careful deliberation, met Marden's level, measuring stare. "Yes?"

"Hope it hasn't inconvenienced you, my taking it."

49

"Not too much."

"I was curious about technique mostly," Marden said. "I already knew why you were here, of course."

"Oh?" Dasein studied Marden carefully for a clue to the man's mood. How could he know about the project?

Marden took a long swallow of the orange beer, wiped his mouth. "Great stuff, this."

"Very tasty," Dasein agreed.

"You've laid out a pretty routine approach, really," Marden said. He stared at Dasein. "You know, I've the funny feeling you don't realize how you're being used."

There was amusement in Marden's narrow face. It touched off abrupt anger in Dasein, and he struggled to hide his reaction. "What's that supposed to mean?" he asked.

"Would it interest you to know you've been a subject of discussion before our Town Council?" Marden asked.

"Me?"

"You. Several times. We knew they'd get to you sooner or later. Took 'em longer than we expected." Marden shook his head. "We circulated a photograph of you to key people—waiters, waitresses, bartenders, clerks . . . "

"Service station attendants," Dasein said. The pattern was becoming clear. He made no attempt to conceal his anger. How dared they?

Marden was sweet reasonableness. "They were bound to get wind of the fact that one of our girls was sweet on you," he said. "That's an edge, you understand. You use any edge you can find."

"Who's this *they* you keep referring to?" Dasein demanded.

"Hmmmm," Marden said.

Dasein took three deep breaths to calm himself. He had never really expected to hide his purpose here indefinitely, but he had hoped for more time before exposure. What the devil was this crazy patrol captain talking about?

"You pose quite a problem," Marden said.

"Well, don't try tossing me out of the valley the way you did that stupid salesman last night or those hunters you got today," Dasein said. "I'm obeying the law."

50

"Toss you out? Wouldn't think of it. Say, what would you like to eat? We did come here for lunch."

Dasein found himself psychologically off balance, his anger diverted by this sudden change of subject, his whole attitude hampered by feelings of guilt.

"I'm not hungry," he growled.

"You will be by the time the food gets here. I'll order for both of us." Marden signaled the waiter, said: "Two salads Jaspers on the special lunch."

"I'm not hungry," Dasein insisted.

"You will be." Marden smiled. "Hear a big two-fisted outsider in a Chrysler Imperial called you a native today. Did that tick you off?"

"News certainly gets around here," Dasein said.

"It certainly does, Doc. Of course, what that fellow's *mistake* says to me is that you're just a natural Santarogan. Jenny didn't make any mistake about *you*."

"Jenny has nothing to do with this."

"She has everything to do with it. Let's understand each other, Doc. Larry needs another psychologist and Jenny says you're one of the best. We can make a good place here in the valley for a fellow like you."

"How big a place?" Dasein asked, his mind on the two investigators who'd died here. "About six feet long and six feet deep?"

"Why don't you stop running away from yourself, Dasein?"

"I learned early," Dasein said, "that a good run was better than a bad stand."

"Huh?" Marden turned a puzzled frown on him.

"I'm not running away from myself," Dasein said. "That's what I mean. But I'm not going to stand still while you order my life for me the way you ordered those salads."

"You don't like the food you don't have to eat it," Marden said. "Am I to understand you won't consider the job Larry's offering?"

Dasein looked down at the table, absorbing the implications of the offer. The smart thing would be to play along, he knew. This was his opportunity to get behind the San-

51

taroga Barrier, to find out what really went on in the valley. But he couldn't escape the thought of the Town Council at its meetings, questioning Jenny about him, no doubt, discussing *preparations* for the Dasein invasion! The anger wouldn't stay down.

"You and Jenny and the rest, you have it all figured out, eh?" he asked. "Throw the poor sucker a bone. Buy him off with a . . . "

"Slack off, Doc," Marden said. The voice was level and still with that tone of amusement. "I'm appealing to your intelligence, not to your greed. Jenny says you're a very sharp fellow. That's what we're counting on."

Dasein gripped his hands into fists beneath the table, brought himself under control. So they thought he was a poor innocent jerk to be maneuvered by a pretty female and money!

"You think I'm being used," he said.

"We *know* you're being used."

"You haven't said by whom."

"Who's behind it? A group of financiers, Doc, who don't like what Santaroga represents. They want in and they can't get in."

"The Santaroga Barrier," Dasein said.

"That's what they call it."

"Who are *they*?"

"You want names? Maybe we'll give them to you if that suits our purposes."

"You want to use me, too, is that it?"

"That isn't the way Santaroga runs, Dasein."

The salads came. Dasein looked down into an inviting array of greens, diced chicken and a creamy golden dressing. A pang of hunger gripped him. He sampled a bite of chicken with the dressing, tasted the now familiar tang of a Jaspers cheese in it. The damned stuff was ubiquitous, he thought. But he had to admit it was delicious. Perhaps there was something in the claim that it wouldn't travel.

"Pretty good, isn't it?" Marden asked.

"Yes, it is." He studied the patrol captain a moment. "How does Santaroga run, Captain?"

"Council government with Town Meeting veto, annual

52

elections. Every resident above age eighteen has one vote."

"Basic Democracy," Dasein said. "Very nice when you have a community this size, but . . . "

"We had three thousand voters and fifty-eight hundred proxies at the last Town Meeting," Marden said. "It can be done if people are interested in governing themselves. We're interested, Dasein. That's how Santaroga's run."

Dasein gulped the bite of salad in his mouth, put down his fork. Almost nine thousand people over age eighteen in the valley! That was twice as many as he'd estimated. What did they all do? A place like this couldn't exist by taking in each others' wash.

"You want me to marry Jenny, settle here—another voter," Dasein said. "Is that it?"

"That's what Jenny appears to want. We tried to discourage her, but . . ." He shrugged.

"Discourage her—like interfering with the mails?"

"What?"

Dasein saw Marden's obvious puzzlement, told him about the lost letters.

"Those damn' biddies," Marden said. "I guess I'll have to go down there and read them the riot act. But that doesn't change things, really."

"No?"

"No. You love Jenny, don't you?"

"Of course I love her!"

It was out before Dasein could consider his answer. He heard his own voice, realized how basic this emotion was. Of course he loved Jenny. He'd been sick with longing for her. It was a wonder he'd managed to stay away this long—testimony to wounded masculine pride and the notion he'd been rejected.

Stupid pride!

"Well, fine," Marden said. "Finish your lunch, go look around the valley, and tonight you talk things over with Jenny."

He can't really believe it's that simple, Dasein thought.

"Here," Marden said. He brought Dasein's briefcase from the seat, put it on the table between them. "Make your market study. They already know everything you can

53

find out. That's not really how they want to use you."

"How *do* they want to use me?"

"Find out for yourself, Doc. That's the only way you'll believe it."

Marden returned to his salad, eating with gusto.

Dasein put down his fork, asked: "What happened to those hunters you picked up today?"

"We cut off their heads and pickled them," Marden said. "What'd you think? They were fined and sent packing. You want to see the court records?"

"What good would that do?"

"You know, Doc," Marden said, pointing a fork at Dasein, "you're taking this much the same way Win did—Win Burdeaux."

Taking what? Dasein wondered. But he asked: "*How* did Win take it?"

"He fought it. That's according to pattern, naturally. He caved in rather quickly, though, as I remember. Win was tired of running even before he got to Santaroga."

"You amateur psychologists," Dasein sneered.

"That's right, Doc. We could use another good professional."

Dasein felt baffled by Marden's unassailable good nature.

"Eat your salad," Marden said. "It's good for what ails you."

Dasein took another bite of the chicken drenched in Jaspers sauce. He had to admit the food was making him feel better. His head felt clear, mind alert. Hunger crept up on one at times, he knew. Food took off the pressures, allowed the mind to function.

Marden finished eating, sat back.

"You'll come around," he said. "You're confused now, but if you're as sharp as Jenny says, you'll see the truth for yourself. I think you'll like it here."

Marden slid out of the booth, stood up.

"I'm just supposed to take your word for it that I'm being used," Dasein said.

"I'm not running you out of the valley, am I?" Marden asked.

"Are the phone lines still burned out?" Dasein asked.

"Darned if I know," Marden said. He glanced at his watch. "Look, I have work to do. Call me after you've talked to Jenny."

With that, he left.

The waiter came up, started collecting dishes.

Dasein looked up into the man's round face, took in the gray hair, the bent shoulders. "Why do you live here?" he asked.

"Huh?" The voice was a gravelly baritone.

"Why do you live in Santaroga?" Dasein asked.

"You nuts? This is my home."

"But why this place rather than San Francisco, say, or Los Angeles?"

"You are nuts! What could I get there I can't get here?" He left with the dishes.

Dasein stared at his briefcase on the table. Market study. On the seat beyond it, he could see the corner of a newspaper. He reached across the table, captured the paper. The masthead read: "Santaroga Press."

The left-hand column carried an international news summary whose brevity and language startled Dasein. It was composed of paragraph items, one item per story.

Item: "Those nuts are still killing each other in Southeast Asia."

It slowly dawned on Dasein that this was the Vietnam news.

Item: "The dollar continues to slip on the international money market, although this fact is being played down or suppressed in the national news. The crash is going to make Black Friday look like a picnic."

Item: "The Geneva disarmament talks are disarming nobody except the arrogant and the complacent. We recall that the envoys were still talking the last time the bombs began to fall."

Item: "The United States Government is still expanding that big hidey hole under the mountain down by Denver. Wonder how many military bigshots, government officials and their families have tickets into there for when the blowup comes?"

55

Item: "France thumbed its nose at the U.S. again this week, said to keep U.S. military airplanes off French airbases. Do they know something we don't know?"

Item: "Automation nipped another .4 percent off the U.S. job market last month. The bites are getting bigger. Does anyone have a guess as to what's going to happen to the excess population?"

Dasein lowered the paper, stared at it without seeing it. The damned thing was subversive! Was it written by a pack of Communists? Was that the secret of Santaroga?

He looked up to see the waiter standing beside him.

"That your newspaper?" the man asked.

"Yes."

"Oh. I guess Al must've given it to you." He started to turn away.

"Where does this restaurant buy its food?" Dasein asked.

"From all over the valley, Dr. Dasein. Our beef comes from Ray Allison's ranch up at the head of the valley. Our chickens come from Mrs. Larson's place out west of here. The vegetables and things we get at the greenhouses."

"Oh. Thanks." Dasein returned to the newspaper.

"You want anything else, Dr. Dasein? Al said to give you anything you want. It's on his bill."

"No, thank you."

The waiter left Dasein to the paper.

Dasein began scanning through it. There were eight pages, only a few advertisements at the beginning, and half the back page turned over to classified. The display ads were rather flat announcements: "Brenner and Sons have a new consignment of bedroom furniture at reasonable prices. First come, first served. These are all first quality local.

"Four new freezer lockers (16 cubic feet) are available at the Lewis Market. Call for rates." The illustration was a smiling fat man holding open the door of a freezer locker.

The classified advertisements were mostly for trades: "Have thirty yards of hand-loomed wool (54 inches wide)—need a good chain saw. Call Ed Jankey at Number One Mill.

"That '56 Ford one-ton truck I bought two years ago is still running. Sam Scheler says its worth about $50 or a good heifer. William McCoy, River Junction."

Dasein began thumbing back through the paper. There was a garden column: "It's time to turn the toads loose in your garden to keep down the snails."

And one of the inside pages had a full column of meeting notices. Reading the column, Dasein was caught by a repetitive phrase: "Jaspers will be served."

Jaspers will be served, he thought. *Jaspers . . . Jaspers . . .* It was everywhere. Did they really consume that much of the stuff? He sensed a hidden significance in the word. It was a unifying thing, something peculiarly Santarogan.

Dasein turned back to the newspaper. A reference in a classified ad caught his eye: "I will trade two years' use of one half of my Jaspers Locker (20 cubic feet in level five of the Old Section) for six months of carpenter work. Leo Merriot, 1018 River Road."

What the devil was a Jaspers Locker? Whatever it was, ten cubic feet of it for two years was worth six months' carpentry—no small item, perhaps four thousand dollars.

A splash of sunlight brought his head up in time to see a young couple enter the restaurant. The girl was dark haired with deeply set brown eyes and beautiful, winged eyebrows, her young man fair, blue-eyed, a chiseled Norman face. They took the booth behind Dasein. He watched them in the tilted bar mirror. The young man glanced over his shoulder at Dasein, said something to the girl. She smiled.

The waiter served them two cold drinks.

Presently, the girl said: "After the Jaspers, we sat there and listened to the sunset, a rope and a bird."

"Sometime you should feel the fur on the water," her companion said. "It's the red upness of the wind."

Dasein came to full alert. That haunting, elusive quality of almost-meaning—it was schizophrenic or like the product of a psychedelic. He strained to hear more, but they had their heads together, whispering, laughing.

Abruptly, Dasein's memory darted back more than three years to his department's foray into LSD experiments

57

and he recalled that Jenny Sorge, the graduate student from Santaroga, had demonstrated an apparent immunity to the drug. The experiments, abandoned in the glare of sensational LSD publicity, had never confirmed this finding and Jenny had refused to discuss it. The memory of that one report returned to plague Dasein now.

Why should I recall that? he wondered.

The young couple finished whatever they'd ordered, got up and left the restaurant.

Dasein folded the newspaper, started to put it into his briefcase. A hand touched his arm. He looked up to find Marden staring down at him.

"I believe that's my paper," he said. He took it from Dasein's hand. "I was halfway to the forks before I remembered it. See you later." He hurried out, the paper tucked under his arm.

The casual bruskness, the speed with which he'd been relieved of that interesting publication, left Dasein feeling angry. He grabbed up his briefcase, ran for the door, was in time to see Marden pulling away from the curb in a patrol car.

To hell with you! he thought. *I'll get another one.*

The drugstore on the corner had no newspaper racks and the skinny clerk informed him coldly that the local newspaper could be obtained "by subscription only." He professed not to know where it was published. The clerk in the hardware store down the street gave him the same answer as did the cashier in the grocery store across from where he'd parked his truck.

Dasein climbed into the cab, opened his briefcase and made notes on as many of the paper's items as he could recall. When his memory ran dry, he started up the truck began cruising up and down the town's streets looking for the paper's sign or a job printing shop. He found nothing indicating the *Santaroga Press* was printed in the town, but the signs in a used car lot brought him to an abrupt stop across the street. He sat there staring at the signs.

A four-year-old Buick bore the notice in its window: "This one's an oil burner but a good buy at $100."

58

On a year old Rover: "Cracked block, but you can afford to put a new motor in it at this price: $500."

On a ten-year-old Chevrolet: "This car owned and maintained by Jersey Hofstedder. His widow only wants $650 for it."

His curiosity fully aroused, Dasein got out and crossed to Jersey Hofstedder's Chevrolet, looked in at the dash. The odometer recorded sixty-one thousand miles. The upholstery was leather, exquisitely fitted and tailored. Dasein couldn't see a scratch on the finish and the tires appeared to be almost new.

"You want to test drive it, Dr. Dasein?"

It was a woman's voice and Dasein turned to find himself face to face with a handsome gray-haired matron in a floral blouse and blue jeans. She had a big, open face, smooth tanned skin.

"I'm Clara Scheler, Sam's mother," she said. "I guess you've heard of my Sam by now."

"And you know me, of course," Dasein said, barely concealing his anger. "I'm Jenny's fellow from the city."

"Saw you this morning with Jenny," she said. "That's one fine girl there, Dr. Dasein. Now, if you're interested in Jersey's car, I can tell you about it."

"Please do," Dasein said.

"Folks around here know how Jersey was," she said. "He was a goldanged perfectionist, that's what. He had every moving part of this car out on his bench. He balanced and adjusted and fitted until it's just about the sweetest running thing you ever heard. Got disc brakes now, too. You can see what he did to the upholstery."

"Who was Jersey Hofstedder?" Dasein asked.

"Who . . . oh, that's right, you're new. Jersey was Sam's chief mechanic until he died about a month ago. His widow kept the Cord touring car Jersey was so proud of, but she says a body can only drive one car at a time. She asked me to sell the Chevvy. Here, listen to it."

She slipped behind the wheel, started the motor.

Dasein bent close to the hood. He could barely hear the engine running.

"Got dual ignition," Clara Scheler said. "Jersey bragged he could get thirty miles to the gallon with her and I wouldn't be a bit surprised."

"Neither would I," Dasein said.

"You want to pay cash or credit?" Clara Scheler asked.

"I . . . haven't decided to buy it," Dasein said.

"You and Jenny couldn't do better than starting out with Jersey's old car," she said. "You're going to have to get rid of that clunker you drove up in. I heard it. That one isn't long for this world unless you do something about those bearings."

"I . . . if I decide to buy it, I'll come back with Jenny," Dasein said. "Thank you for showing it to me." He turned, ran back to his truck with a feeling of escape. He had been strongly tempted to buy Jersey Hofstedder's car and found this astonishing. The woman must be a master salesman.

He drove back to the Inn, his mind in a turmoil over the strange personality which Santaroga presented. The bizarre candor of those used car signs, the ads in the *Santaroga Press*—they were all of the same pattern.

Casual honesty, Dasein thought. *That could be brutal at the wrong time.*

He went up to his room, lay down on the bed to try to think things through, make some sense out of the day. Marden's conversation over lunch sounded even more strange in review. A job with Piaget's clinic? The hauntingly obscure conversation of the young couple in the restaurant plagued him. Drugged? And the newspaper which didn't exist—except by subscription. Jersey Hofstedder's car —Dasein was tempted to go back and buy it, drive it out to have it examined by an *outside* mechanic.

A persistent murmuring of voices began to intrude on Dasein's awareness. He got up, looked around the room, but couldn't locate the source. The edge of sky visible through his window was beginning to gray. He walked over, looked out. Clouds were moving in from the northwest.

The murmur of voices continued.

Dasein made a circuit of the room, stopped under a tiny ventilator in the corner above the dresser. The desk chair gave him a step up onto the dresser and he put his ear to the ventilator. Faint but distinct, a familiar television jingle advertising chewing gum came from the opening.

Smiling at himself, Dasein stepped down off the dresser. It was just somebody watching TV. He frowned. This was the first evidence he'd found that they even had TV in the valley. He considered the geography of the area—a basin. To receive TV in here would require an antenna on one of the surrounding hills, amplifiers, a long stretch of cable.

Back onto the dresser he went, ear to the ventilator. He found he could separate the TV show (a daytime serial) from a background conversation between three or four women. One of the women appeared to be instructing another in knitting. Several times he heard the word "Jaspers" and once, very distinctly, "A vision, that's all; just a vision."

Dasein climbed down from the dresser, went into the hall. Between his door and the window at the end with its "Exit" sign there were no doors. Across the hall, yes, but not on this side. He stepped back into his room, studied the ventilator. It appeared to go straight through the wall, but appearances could be deceiving. It might come from another floor. What was in this whole rear corner of the building, though? Dasein was curious enough now to investigate.

Downstairs he trotted, through the empty lobby, outside and around to the back. There was the oak tree, a rough-barked patriarch, one big branch curving across a second-floor window. That window must be his, Dasein decided. It was in the right place and the branch confirmed it. A low porch roof over a kitchen service area angled outward beneath the window. Dasein swept his gaze toward the corner, counted three other windows in that area where no doors opened into a room. All three windows were blank with drawn shades.

No doors, but three windows, Dasein thought.

He set a slower pace back up to his room. The lobby was still empty, but there were sounds of voices and the switchboard from the office behind the desk.

Once more in his room, Dasein stood at the window,

61

looked down on the porch roof. The slope was shallow, shingles dry. He eased open the window, stepped out onto the roof. By leaning against the wall, he found he could work his way sideways along the roof.

At the first window, he took a firm grip on the ledge, looked for a gap in the curtain. There was no opening, but the sound of the TV was plain when he pressed his ear against the glass. He heard part of a soap commercial and one of the women in the room saying: "That's enough of this channel, switch to NBC."

Dasein drew back, crept to the next window. There was a half-inch gap at the bottom of the shade. He almost lost his balance bending to peer in it, caught himself, took a firm grip on the ledge and crouched to put his eyes to the gap.

The swimming wash of cathode gray in a shadowy room met his gaze. He could just make out a bank of eight TV receivers against the wall at his right. Five women sat in comfortable arm chairs at a good viewing distance from the screens. One of the women he noted with some satisfaction was knitting. Another appeared to be making notes on a shorthand pad. Yet another was operating some sort of recorder.

There was a businesslike women-at-work look about the group. They appeared to be past middle age, but when they moved it was with the grace of people who remained active. A blonde woman with a good figure stood up on the right, racked a clip-board across the face of the top right-hand screen, turned off the set. She flopped back into her chair with an exaggerated fatigue, spoke loudly:

"My God! Imagine letting that stuff pour uncensored into your brain day after day after day after . . . "

"Save it for the report, Suzie!" That was the woman with the recorder.

Report? Dasein asked himself. *What report?*

He swept his gaze around the room. A row of filing cabinets stood against the far wall. He could just see the edge of a couch directly under the window. A pull-down stairway of the type used for access to attics occupied the corner at the left. There were two typewriters on wheeled stands behind the women.

Dasein decided it was one of the most peculiar rooms he had ever seen. Here were all the fixtures of normalcy, but with that odd Santaroga twist to them. Why the secrecy? Why eight TV receivers? What was in the filing cabinets? What report?

From time to time, the women made notes, used the recorder, switched channels. All the time, they carried on casual conversations only parts of which were audible to Dasein. None of it made much sense—small talk: "I decided against putting in pleats; they're so much trouble." "If Fred can't pick me up after work, I'll need a ride to town."

His exposed position on the roof began to bother Dasein. He told himself there was nothing else to be learned from a vigil at the window. What explanation could he give if he were caught here?

Carefully, he worked his way back to his room, climbed in, closed the window. Again, he checked the hall. There just was no door into that strange room at this level. He walked down to the exit sign, opened a narrow door onto a back landing. An open stairway with doweled railing wound up and down from the landing. Dasein peered over the railing, looked down two stories to a basement level. He looked up. The stairwell was open to a skylight above the third floor.

Moving quietly, he climbed to the next level, opened the landing door onto another hall. He stepped in, looked at the wall above the secret room. Two steps from the landing there was another door labeled "Linen Supplies." Dasein tried the handle—locked.

Frustrated, he turned back to the landing. As he stepped from the hall, his right foot caught on a loose edge of carpeting. In one terrifying instant, Dasein saw the railing and the open stairwell flash toward him. His right shoulder hit the rail with a splintering crash, slowing his fall but not stopping it. He clutched at the broken rail with his left hand, felt it bend out, knew then that he was going over—three stories down to the basement. The broken rail in his hand made a screeching sound as it bent outward. It all seemed to be happening in a terrible slow motion. He could see the edges of the descending stairway where they had been painted and the paint had run in little yellow lines. He saw a cobweb beneath one of the risers, a ball of maroon lint caught in it.

The broken rail came free in one last splintering crack and Dasein went over. In this deadly instant, as he saw in his mind his own body splattered on the concrete three floors down, strong hands grabbed his ankles. Not quite realizing what had happened, Dasein swung head down, released the broken rail and saw it turn and twist downward.

He felt himself being pulled upward like a doll, dragged against the broken edges of the railing, turned over onto his back on the landing.

Dasein found himself looking up into the scowling black face of Win Burdeaux.

"That were a mighty close one, sir," Burdeaux said.

Dasein was gasping so hard he couldn't answer. His right shoulder felt like a giant ball of pain. The fingers of his left hand were bent inward with an agonizing cramp from the strength with which he had gripped the rail.

"I heard someone try the supply closet door," Burdeaux said. "I was in there, sir, and I came out. There you were going through the railing, sir. How did that happen?"

"Carpet," Dasein gasped. "Tripped."

Burdeaux bent to examine the area at the landing door. He straightened, said: "I'll be blessed if that carpet isn't torn there, sir. That's a very dangerous situation."

Dasein managed to straighten his cramped fingers. He took a deep breath, tried to sit up. Burdeaux helped him. Dasein noted that his shirt was torn. There was a long red scratch on his stomach and chest from being dragged across the broken rail.

"You best take it easy for a few minutes, sir," Burdeaux said. "You want for me to call the doctor?"

"No . . . no, thank you."

"It wouldn't take but a minute, sir."

"I'll . . . be all right."

Dasein looked at the torn carpet, a jagged edge of maroon fabric. He remembered the piece of railing as it had tumbled away into the stairwell and found it strange that he had no recollection of hearing the thing hit the bottom. There was another picture in his mind, equally disturbing: the fatal accidents of the two previous investigators. Dasein pictured himself dead at the bottom of that stairwell, the investigation—all very natural, regrettable, but natural. Such things happened.

But were they accidents?

His shoulder was beginning to throb.

"I'd better get down to my room . . . and change," Dasein said. The pain in his shoulder, intense now, told him he had to have medical attention. He could feel some instinct in himself fighting the idea, though, even as he struggled upright.

Burdeaux reached out to help him to his feet, but Dasein pulled away, knowing the irrationality of the act as he did it.

"Sir, I mean you no harm," Burdeaux said. There was a gentle chiding in the tone.

Was my fear of him that obvious? Dasein asked himself.

He remembered then the strong hands grabbing his ankles, the lifesaving catch at the brink of the stairwell. A feeling of apology overcame Dasein.

"I . . . know you don't," he said. "You saved my life. There aren't words to thank you for that. I . . . was thinking about the broken rail. Shouldn't you see about fixing that?"

Using the wall as a support, Dasein gained his feet. He stood there panting. The shoulder was a massive agony.

"I will lock this door here, sir," Burdeaux said, his voice gentle, but firm. "I am going to call the doctor, sir. You are favoring your shoulder. I suspect there is much pain in it. Best the doctor see you, sir."

Dasein turned away, wondering at his own ambivalence. A doctor had to see the shoulder—yes. But did it have to be Piaget? Hugging the wall for support, Dasein moved down the steps. Piaget . . . Piaget . . . Piaget. Had Piaget been called on the two fatal *accidents?* Movement sent

65

fiery pain through the shoulder. Piaget . . . Piaget . . . How could this incident on the stairs have been anything except an accident? Who could have predicted he'd be in that particular place at that particular moment?

There came the sound of the door being closed and latched above him. Burdeaux's heavy footsteps sounded on the stairs. The vibration sent more pain through the aching shoulder. Dasein clutched the shoulder, paused on the second floor landing.

"Sir?"

Dasein turned, looked up at the dark Moorish face, noting the expression of concern.

"It will be best, sir," Burdeaux said, "if you do not go out on the roof again. You may be subject to falls, sir. A fall from that roof would be very dangerous."

4

The rain storm hit the valley just before dark. Dasein was settled into a heavy old-fashioned chair in the Piaget house by then, his shoulder immobilized by a firm bandage, Jenny sitting across from him on a hassock, an accusing look on her face.

A gentle, unswerving Burdeaux had driven him to the clinic adjoining Piaget's house and had seen him into the antiseptic atmosphere of a tiled emergency room before leaving.

Dasein didn't know what he'd expected—certainly not the cold professional detachment with which Piaget had set about treating the shoulder.

"Torn ligaments and a slight dislocation," Piaget had said. "What were you trying to do—commit suicide?"

Dasein winced as a bandage was drawn tightly into place. "Where's Jenny?"

"Helping with dinner. We'll tell her about your damn' foolishness after we have you repaired." Piaget secured the end of a bandage. "You haven't told me what you were up to."

"I was snooping!" Dasein growled.

"Were you now?" He adjusted a sling around Dasein's neck, set it to immobilize the arm. "There, that should hold you for awhile. Don't move that arm any more than you have to. I guess I don't have to tell you that. Leave your coat off. There's a covered walkway to the house—right through that door. Go on in and I'll send Jenny to entertain you until dinner."

The covered walkway had glass sides and was lined with

potted geraniums. The storm struck as Dasein was making his way between the pots and he paused a moment to look out at a new-mown lawn, rows of standard roses, a lowering blue-gray sky. The wind whipped rain down a street beyond the roses, bending the branches of a line of white birches. There were people hurrying along the sidewalk beside the birches. The damp hems of their coats lashed their legs in each gust.

Dasein felt a bit light-headed, chilled in spite of the walk-way's protection. *What am I doing here?* he asked himself. He swallowed in a dry throat, hurried on to the door of the house and into a paneled living room full of big furniture. There was the faint smell of a coal fire in the room. His shoulder was a place of dull throbbing. He made his way across the room, past a sideboard full of massive cut-glass pieces, lowered himself carefully into a deep, soft chair of corded green upholstery.

The lack of movement and its temporary easing of pain filled him with a momentary sense of relief. Then the shoulder began throbbing again.

A door slammed—hurrying feet.

Jenny burst upon him through a wide archway to the left. Her face was flushed. A damp wisp of hair strayed at her temple. She was wearing a simple orange dress, a shocking splash of color in the dull tones of the big room. With an odd sense of detachment, Dasein remembered telling her once that orange was his favorite color. The memory filled him with an unexplainable wariness.

"Gil, for heavens sake!" she said, stopping in front of him, hands on hips.

Dasein swallowed.

Jenny looked at his open shirt, the edge of bandages, the sling. Abruptly, she dropped to her knees, put her head in his lap, clutching at him, and he saw she was crying—silent tears that spread shiny dampness across her cheeks.

"Hey!" Dasein said. "Jenny . . . " The tears, the lack of contortion in her face—he found it embarrassing. She filled him with a sense of guilt, as though he'd betrayed her in some way. The feeling overrode his pain and fatigue.

68

Jenny took his left hand, pressed her cheek against it. "Gil," she whispered. "Let's get married—right away."

Why not? he wondered. But the guilt remained . . . and the unanswered questions. Was Jenny bait in a trap that had been set for him? Would she even know it if she were? Did the worm know it was impaled on the hook to lure the trout?

A soft cough sounded from the archway to Dasein's left. Jenny pulled back, but still held his hand.

Dasein looked up to find Piaget there. The man had changed to a blue smoking jacket that made him look even more the mandarin. The big head was tipped slightly to the right with an air of amusement, but the dark eyes stared out speculatively.

Behind Piaget, amber wall sconces had been turned on in a dining room. Dasein could see a large oval table set with three places on white linen, the gleam of silver and crystal.

"Jenny?" Piaget said.

She sighed, released Dasein's hand, retreated to the green ottoman, sat down with her legs curled under her.

Dasein grew aware of the smell of roasting meat savory with garlic. It made him acutely aware of hunger. In the heightening of his senses, he detected an enticing tang, recognized the *Jaspers* odor.

"I think we should discuss your susceptibility to accidents," Piaget said. "Do you mind, Gilbert?"

"By all means," Dasein said. He sat watching the doctor carefully. There was an edge of caution in Piaget's voice, a hesitancy that went beyond a host's reluctance to engage in an embarrassing conversation.

"Have you had many painful accidents?" Piaget asked. He strode across the room as he spoke, crossing to a quilted leather chair behind Jenny. When he sat, he was looking across Jenny's shoulder at Dasein and Dasein had the abrupt suspicion that this position had been chosen with care. It aligned Piaget and Jenny against him.

"Well?" Piaget asked.

"Why don't we trade answers?" Dasein countered. "You

69

answer a question for me and I answer a question for you."

"Oh?" Piaget's face relaxed into the bemused smile of a private joke.

Jenny looked worried.

"What's your question?" Piaget asked.

"A bargain's a bargain," Dasein said. "First, an answer. You ask if I've been involved in many accidents. No, I have not. That is, not before coming here. I can recall one other—a fall from an apple tree when I was eight."

"So," Piaget said. "Now, you have a question for me."

Jenny frowned, looked away.

Dasein felt a sudden dryness in his throat, found his voice rasping when he spoke: "Tell me, Doctor—how did the two investigators die—the ones who came before me?"

Jenny's head snapped around. "Gil!" There was outrage in her voice.

"Easy, Jenny," Piaget said. A nerve began ticking on the broad plane of his left cheek. "You're on the wrong track, young man," he growled. "We're not savages here. There's no need. If we want someone to leave, he leaves."

"And you don't want me to leave?"

"Jenny doesn't want you to leave. And that's two questions from you. You owe me an answer."

Dasein nodded. He stared across Jenny at Piaget, reluctant to look at her.

"Do you love Jenny?" Piaget asked.

Dasein swallowed, lowered his gaze to meet a pleading stare in Jenny's eyes. Piaget knew the answer to that question! Why did he ask it now?

"You know I do," Dasein said.

Jenny smiled, but two bright tears beaded her eyelashes.

"Then why did you wait a year to come up here and tell her so?" Piaget asked. There was an angry, accusatory bite in his voice that made Dasein stiffen.

Jenny turned, stared at her uncle. Her shoulders trembled.

"Because I'm a damn' stubborn fool," Dasein said. "I don't want the woman I love to tell me where I have to live."

"So you don't like our valley," Piaget said. "Maybe

we can change your opinion about that. You willing to let us try?"

No! Dasein thought. *I'm not willing!* But he knew this answer, visceral and instinctive, would come out petulant, childish. "Do your damnedest," he muttered.

And Dasein wondered at himself. What were his instincts telling him? What was wrong with this valley that put him on guard at every turn?

"Dinner's ready."

It was a woman's voice from the archway.

Dasein turned to find a gaunt gray female in a gray dress standing there. She was a Grant Woods early American come to life, long-nosed, wary of eye, disapproval in every line of her face.

"Thank you, Sarah," Piaget said. "This is Dr. Dasein, Jenny's young man."

Her eyes weighed Dasein, found him wanting. "The food's getting cold," she said.

Piaget lifted himself out of his chair. "Sarah's my cousin," he said. "She comes from the old Yankee side of the family and absolutely refuses to dine with us if we eat at a fashionable hour."

"Damn' foolishness, the hours you keep," she muttered. "My father was always in bed by this time."

"And up at dawn," Piaget said.

"Don't you try to make fun of me, Larry Piaget," she said. She turned away. "Come to table. I'll bring the roast."

Jenny crossed to Dasein, helped him to his feet. She leaned close, kissed his cheek, whispered: "She really likes you. She told me so in the kitchen."

"What're you two whispering?" Piaget demanded.

"I was telling Gil what Sarah said about him."

"Oh, what'd Sarah say?"

"She said: 'Larry isn't going to browbeat that young man. He has eyes like Grandpa Sather.' "

Piaget turned to study Dasein. "By George, he has. I hadn't noticed." He turned away with an abrupt cutting-off motion, led the way into the dining room. "Come along, or Sarah will change her good opinion. We can't have that."

To Dasein, it was one of the strangest dinners of his life.

There was the pain of his injured shoulder, a steady throb that impelled him to an alertness that made every word and motion stand out in sharp relief. There was Jenny—she had never looked more warmly feminine and desirable. There was Piaget, who declared a conversational truce for the meal and plied Dasein with questions about his courses at the University, the professors, fellow students, his ambitions. There was Sarah, hovering with the food—a muttering specter who had soft looks only for Jenny.

With Sarah, it's what Jenny wants, Jenny gets, Dasein thought.

Finally, there was the food: a rib roast cooked to a medium rare perfection, the Jaspers sauce over peas and potato pancakes, the local beer with its palate-cleansing tang, and fresh peaches with honey for dessert.

Beer with dinner struck Dasein as strange at first until he experienced the play of tastes, a subtle mingling of flavor esters that made individual savors stand out on his tongue even as they were combining to produce entirely new sensations. It was a crossing of senses, he realized—smells tasted, colors amplifying the aromas.

At the first serving of beer, Piaget had tasted it, nodded. "Fresh," he said.

"Within the hour just like you ordered," Sarah snapped. And she'd cast a strange probing stare at Dasein.

It was shortly after 9:30 when Dasein left.

"I had your truck brought around," Piaget said. "Think you can drive it, or shall I have Jenny take you back to the hotel?"

"I'll be all right," Dasein said.

"Don't take those pain pills I gave you until you're safely in your room," Piaget said. "Don't want you running off the road."

They stood on the broad verandah at the front of the house then, street lights casting wet shadows of the birches onto the lawn. The rain had stopped, but there was a chilled feeling of dampness in the night air.

Jenny had thrown his coat around his shoulders. She stood beside him, a worried frown on her face. "Are you *sure* you'll be all right?"

"You ought to know I can steer with one hand," he said. He grinned at her.

"Sometimes I think you're a terrible man," she said. "I don't know why I put up with you."

"It's chemistry," he said.

Piaget cleared his throat. "Tell me, Gilbert," he said. "What *were* you doing on the hotel roof?"

Dasein felt an abrupt pang of fear, a sense of incongruity in the timing of that question.

What the hell! he thought. *Let's see what a straight answer does.*

"I was trying to find out why you're so all-fired secret about your TV," he said.

"Secret?" Piaget shook his head. "That's just a pet project of mine. They're analyzing the silly infantilisms of TV, producing data for a book I have in mind."

"Then why so secret?" Dasein felt Jenny clutching his arm, ignored the fear he sensed in her reaction.

"It's consideration for the sensibilities of others, not secrecy," Piaget said. "Most TV drives our people wild. We monitor the news, of course, but even that is mostly pap, sugar-coated and spoon-fed."

There was a ring of partial truth in Piaget's explanation, Dasein felt, but he wondered what was being left out. What else were those women *researching* in that room.

"I see," Dasein said.

"You owe me an answer now," Piaget said.

"Fire away."

"Another time," Piaget said. "I'll leave you two to say good night, now."

He went inside, closed the door.

Presently, Dasein was headed down the street in his truck, the tingling sensation of Jenny's kiss still warm on his lips.

He arrived at the wye intersection to the hotel shortly before ten, hesitated, then bore to the right on the road out of the valley to Porterville. There was an odd feeling of self-preservation in the decision, but he told himself it was just because he wanted to drive for awhile . . . and think.

What is happening to me? he wondered. His mind felt

73

abnormally clear, but he was enveloped by such a feeling of disquiet that his stomach was knotted with it. There was an odd broadening to his sense of being. It made him realize that he had forced himself inward with his concentration on psychology, that he had narrowed his world. Something was pushing at his self-imposed barriers now, and he sensed things lurking *beyond,* things which he feared to confront.

Why am I here? he asked himself.

He could trace a chain of cause and effect back to the university, to Jenny . . . but again he felt the interference of things outside this chain and he feared these things.

The night sped past his truck and he realized he was fleeing up the mountain, trying to escape the valley.

He thought of Jenny as she'd appeared this night: an elf in orange dress and orange shoes, lovely Jenny dressed to please him, her sincerity and love all transparent on her face.

Bits and pieces of the dinner conversation began coming back to him. *Jaspers.* "This is the old Jaspers—deep." That had been Jenny tasting the sauce. "Almost time to put down a new section of Jaspers in number five." That had been Sarah bringing in the dessert. And Piaget: "I'll talk to the boys about it tomorrow."

Now, recalling this, Dasein realized there'd been a faint, familiar tang even in the honey. He wondered then about the way *Jaspers* figured so often in their conversations. They never strayed far from it, seemed to find nothing unusual in the constancy of it. They talked Jaspers . . . and at the oddest moments.

He was at the pass out of the valley now, trembling with an ambivalent feeling of escape . . . and of loss.

There'd been a fire across the slopes through which Dasein was now descending. He smelled damp ashes on the wind that whipped through the ventilators, recalled the reported trouble with telephone lines. Clouds had begun to clear away here outside the valley. Dead trees stood out on the burned slopes like Chinese characters brushstroked on the moonlighted hills.

74

Abruptly, his mind clamped on a logical reason for coming out of the valley: *The telephone! I have to call Selador and confer. There are no lines out of the valley, but I can call from Porterville . . . before I go back.*

He drove steadily then, his being suspended, static, held in a curious lack of emotion—nothing on his mind. Even the pain of his shoulder receded.

Porterville loomed out of the night, the highway becoming a wide main street with a blue and white "Bus Depot" sign on the left over an all-night cafe—two big truck-trailer rigs there beside a little convertible and a green and white Sheriff's car. An orange glow across the street was "Frenchy's Mother Lode Saloon." The cars at the curb conveyed a general decrepit look, depressingly alike in their battered oldness.

Dasein drove past, found a lonely phone booth beneath a street light at the corner of a darkened Shell station. He turned in, stopped beside the booth. The truck's engine was hot and tried to go on running with a clunking, jerking motion after he shut off the ignition. He stopped the motion with the clutch, sat for a moment looking at the booth. Presently, he got out. The truck creaked with distress at his movement.

The Sheriff's car drove past, its headlights casting enormous shadows on a white fence behind the phone booth.

Dasein sighed, went into the booth. He felt strangely reluctant to make the call, had to force himself.

Presently, Selador's precise accent came on the line: "Gilbert? Is that you, Gilbert? Have they repaired the deuced telephone lines?"

"I'm calling from Porterville, just outside the valley."

"Is something wrong, Gilbert?"

Dasein swallowed. Even at long distance, Selador managed to remain perceptive. *Something wrong?* Dasein delivered a brief recital of his accidents.

After a prolonged silence, Selador said: "That's very odd, Gilbert, but I fail to see how you can construe these incidents as other than accidents. With the gas, for example, they put out a great effort to save you. And your tumble—how could anyone possibly have known you'd be the one to pass that way?"

"I just wanted you to know about them," Dasein said. "Piaget thinks I'm accident prone."

"Piaget? Oh, yes—the local doctor. Well, Gilbert, one should always discount pronouncements that go outside one's specialty. I doubt Piaget's qualified to diagnose an accident prone, even if there were such a syndrome—which I sincerely disbelieve." Selador cleared his throat. "You don't seriously think these people have malignant designs against you?"

Selador's sane, level tones had a soothing effect on Dasein. He was right, of course. Here, removed from the valley, the events of the past twenty-four hours took on a different shade of meaning.

"Of course not," Dasein said.

"Good! You've always struck me as a very level head, Gilbert. Let me caution you now that you may have intruded upon a situation where people are being genuinely careless. Under those circumstances, the Inn might be an extremely dangerous place, and you should leave."

"To go where?" Dasein asked.

"There must be other accommodations."

Carelessness at the Inn? Dasein wondered. Then why were no others injured? A dangerous place, yes—but only because it was part of the valley. He felt a strong reluctance to agree with Selador. It was as though his own reluctance were based on data unavailable to Selador.

Abruptly, Dasein saw how the loose carpet could have been aimed at him. He thought of a baited trap. The bait? That was the TV room, of course—an odd place certain to arouse his curiosity. Around the bait would be several traps, all avenues covered. He wondered what trap he had missed on the roof. As he thought about it, Dasein recalled how the stair rail had broken.

"Are you there, Gilbert?"

Selador's voice sounded thin and distant.

"Yes—I'm here."

Dasein nodded to himself. It was so beautifully simple. It answered all the vague uneasiness that had plagued him

76

about the accidents. So simple—like a child's drawing on a steamy window: no excess lines or unnecessary data. Bait and traps.

Even as he saw it, Dasein realized Selador wouldn't accept this solution. It smacked of paranoia. If the theory were wrong, it would be paranoic. It implied organization, the involvement of many people, many officials.

"Is there something else you wanted, Gilbert? We're paying for some rather costly silence."

Dasein came to himself suddenly. "Yes, sir. You recall Piaget's article about Santarogans and allergens?"

"Quite." Selador cleared his throat.

"I want you to query the public health officials and the department of agriculture. Find out if they have chemical analyses of the valley's farm products—including the cheese."

"Public health . . . agriculture . . . cheese," Selador said. Dasein could almost see him making notes. "Anything more?"

"Perhaps. Could you get to the attorneys for the real estate board and the chain store people? I'm sure they must've explored possibilities of legal recourse on the leased land they . . . "

"What're you driving at, Gilbert?"

"The chain stores leased the property and built their expensive installations before discovering the Santarogans wouldn't trade with them. Is this a pattern? Do Santaroga realtors trap unwary outsiders?"

"Conspiracy to defraud," Selador said. "I see. I'm rather inclined to believe, Gilbert, that this avenue already has been exhausted."

Hearing him, Dasein thought Selador's usual acuteness had been blunted. Perhaps he was tired.

"Most likely," Dasein said. "It wouldn't hurt, though, for me to see what the legal eagles were thinking. I might get some new clues on the scene."

"Very well. And, Gilbert, when are you going to send me copies of your notes?"

"I'll mail some carbons tonight from Porterville."

"Tomorrow will be all right. It's getting late and . . . "

77

"No, sir. I don't trust the Santaroga post office."

"Why?"

Dasein recounted Jenny's anger at the women in the post office. Selador chuckled.

"They sounded like a veritable band of harpies," Selador said. "Aren't there laws against tampering with the mails? But, of course, determined people and all that. I hope you found Miss Sorge in good health."

"As beautiful as ever," Dasein said, keeping his voice light. He wondered suddenly about Selador. *Miss* Sorge. No hesitation, no question at all about her being unmarried.

"We're exploring the source of their petrol supply," Selador said. "Nothing on that yet. Take care of yourself, Gilbert. I shouldn't want anything to happen to you."

"That makes two of us," Dasein said.

"Good-bye, then," Selador said. His voice sounded hesitant. A click signaled the breaking of the connection.

Dasein hung up, turned at a sound behind him. A Sheriff's car was pulling into the station. It stopped facing the booth. A spotlight flashed in Dasein's eyes. He heard a door open, footsteps.

"Turn that damn' light out of my eyes!" Dasein said.

The light was lowered. He discerned a bulky shape in uniform standing outside the booth, the gleam of a badge.

"Anything wrong?" It was an oddly squeaky voice to come from that bulk.

Dasein stepped out of the booth, still angry at the way they had flashed the light in his eyes. "Should there be?"

"You damn' Santarogans," the deputy muttered. "Must be important for one of you to come over to make a phone call."

Dasein started to protest he wasn't a Santarogan, remained silent as his mind was caught by a flow of questions. What made outsiders assume he was a Santarogan? The fat man in the Chrysler and now this deputy. Dasein recalled Marden's words. What was the identifying tag?

"If you're through, you best be getting home," the deputy said. "Can't park here all night."

Dasein saw an abrupt mental image of his gas gauge—it

78

was faulty and registered almost empty even when the tank was full. Would they believe he had to wait for the station to open in the morning? What if they roused an attendant and found his tank took only a few gallons?

Why am I debating petty deceptions? Dasein wondered.

It occurred to him that he was reluctant to return to Santaroga. Why? Was living in the valley turning him into a Santarogan?

"That's a real artistic bandage you're wearing," the deputy said. "Been in an accident?"

"Nothing important," Dasein said. "Strained some ligaments."

"Good night, then," the deputy said. "Take it easy on that road." He returned to his car, said something in a low voice to his companion. They chuckled. The car pulled slowly out of the station.

They mistook me for a Santarogan, Dasein thought, and he considered the reactions which had accompanied that mistake. They'd resented his presence here, but with an odd kind of diffidence . . . as though they were afraid of him. They hadn't hesitated to leave him alone here, though—no question of his being a criminal.

Disturbed by the incident and unable to explain his disturbance, Dasein climbed back into his truck, headed for Santaroga.

Why had they assumed he was a Santarogan? The question kept gnawing at him.

A bump in the road made him acutely conscious of his shoulder. The pain had settled into a dull ache. His mind felt clear and alert, though, poised on a knife-edge peak of observation. He began to wonder about this sensation as he drove.

The road flowed beneath him, climbing . . . climbing . . .

As though part of the road's pattern, disconnected images began flowing through his mind. They came with words and phrases, madly jumbled, no thought of order. Meaning eluded him. Feeling suddenly light-headed, he tried to grapple with the sensations—

Cave . . . limping man . . . fire . . .

What cave? he wondered. *Where have I seen a limping*

79

man? What fire? Is it the fire that destroyed the telephone lines?

He had the sudden impression that he was the limping man. Fire and cave eluded him.

Dasein felt he wasn't reasoning, but was pawing through old thoughts. Images—labels summoned objects before his mind's eye: *Car.* He saw Jersey Hofstedder's polished old machine. *Fence.* He saw the chain-link fence around the Co-op. *Shadows.* He saw bodiless shadows.

What's happening to me?

He felt trembly with hunger . . . sweaty. Perspiration rolled off his forehead and cheeks. He tasted it on his lips. Dasein opened his window, allowed the cold wind to whip around him.

At the turn-off where he'd stopped the first evening, Dasein pulled onto the gravel, shut off engine and lights. The clouds were gone and an oblate silver moon rode low on the horizon. He stared down into the valley—widely spaced lights, blue-green from the greenhouses far to his left, the bustle and stir from the Co-op off to the right.

Up here, Dasein felt removed from all that, isolated. The darkness enclosed him.

Cave? he wondered.

Jaspers?

It was difficult to think with his body behaving in this oddly erratic fashion. His shoulder throbbed. There was a nodule of aching in his left lung. He was aware of a tendon in his left ankle—not pain, but knowledge of a weakness there. He could trace in his mind the fiery line of scratches down his chest where Burdeaux had dragged him across the broken bannisters.

A picture of the map on George Nis's wall flashed into his mind, was gone.

He felt *possessed.* Something had taken over his body. It was an ancient, frightening thought. Mad. He gripped the steering wheel, imagined that it writhed, jerked his hands away.

His throat was dry.

Dasein took his own pulse, staring at the luminous dial on his wristwatch. The second hand jumped oddly. It was

80

either that or his pulse was rapid and erratic. Something was distorting his time sense.

Have I been poisoned? he wondered. *Was there something in Piaget's dinner? Ptomaine?*

The black bowl of the valley was a forbidding hand that could reach up and grab him.

Jaspers, he thought. *Jaspers.*

What did it really mean?

He sensed a oneness, a collective solitude focusing on the cooperative. He imagined something lurking outside there in the darkness, hovering at the edge of awareness.

Dasein put a hand to the seat. His fingers groped across the briefcase with its notes and documents, all the things that said he was a scientist. He tried to cling to this idea.

I'm a scientist. This uneasiness is what Aunt Nora would've called "the vapors."

What the scientist had to do was very clear in Dasein's mind. He had to insinuate himself into the Santaroga world, find his place in their oneness, live their life for a time, think as they thought. It was the one sure way to plumb the valley's mystery. There was a Santaroga state of mind. He had to put it on like a suit of clothes, fit it to his understanding.

This thought brought the sensation that something intruded on his inner awareness. He felt that an ancient being had risen there and examined him. It filled his whole subconscious, peering, urgent, restless—sensed only by reflection, indistinct, blurred . . . but real. It moved within him, something heavy and blundering.

The sensation passed.

When it was gone, there was an emptiness in Dasein such that it explained the whole concept of being empty. He felt himself to be a floating chip lost on an endless sea, fearful of every current and eddy that moved him.

He knew he was projecting. He was afraid to go back down into the valley, afraid to run away.

Jaspers.

There was another thing he had to do, Dasein knew. Again, he pictured the map on George Nis's wall, the black tributary lines, the ganglia pattern.

Cave.

He shivered, stared toward the distant bustling that was the Co-op. What lay hidden there behind the chain fence, the guards, the dogs and the prowling bush buggy?

There could be a way to find out.

Dasein stepped from the truck, locked the cab. The only weapon he could find in the camper was a rusty hunting knife with a mildewed sheath. He slipped the sheath onto his belt, working clumsily one-handed, feeling more than a little foolish, but aware also of that inner sense of danger. There was a penlight, too. He pocketed it.

The movement set his shoulder throbbing. Dasein ignored the pain, telling himself it would be too easy to find ↑ physical excuse for not doing what he knew he had to do.

A narrow game trail led down the hill from the upper end of the guard fence. Dasein picked his way down the trail, marking the path in the moonlight until it descended into brush-choked shadows.

Branches pulled at his clothing. He bulled his way through, guiding himself by the moon and the bustle of the Co-op, which was visible whenever he topped a ridge. Whatever the Santaroga mystery, Dasein knew, the answer lay there behind that chain fence.

Once, he stumbled and slid down a hillside into a dry creekbed. Following the creekbed brought him out onto a tiny alluvial plain that opened onto a panoramic view of the Co-op and the valley beyond bathed in moonlight. Twice, he startled deer, which went bounding and leaping off into the night. There were frequent scampering sounds in the brush as small creatures fled his blundering approach.

Holding to a narrow game trail, he came at last to a rock ledge about a thousand yards from the Co-op's fence and five hundred feet above it. Dasein sat down on a rock to catch his breath and, in the sudden silence, heard a powerful engine laboring somewhere to his right. A light swept the sky. He crept back into a low copse of buck brush, crouched there.

The sound of the engine grew louder, louder. A set of

giant wheels climbed out against the stars to occupy a hill above him. From somewhere above the wheels, a light flashed on, swept across the brush, probing, pausing, darting back and forth.

Dasein recognized the bush buggy, a monster vehicle some two hundred feet away. He felt exposed, naked with only a shield of thin brush between him and that nightmare creation. The light washed over the leaves above him.

Here it comes, he thought. *It'll come right down the hill onto me.*

The sound of the engine had grown muter while the bush buggy paused to search its surroundings. It was so near Dasein heard a dog whining on it, remembered the dogs that had accompanied Marden.

The dogs will smell me, he thought.

He tried to draw himself into as tight a ball as possible.

The engine sounds grew suddenly louder.

Dasein moved a branch, ventured a look through the brush, preparing himself to leap up and run. But the big machine turned up the ridge upon which it had emerged. It passed across the hills above Dasein, the noise and light receding.

When it was gone, he took a moment to calm himself, crept out to the lip of the rock ledge. Dasein saw then why the buggy had not come down upon him. This was a dead end, no trail down from here. He would have to climb up where the machine had emerged upon the hill, backtrack on it to find a way down.

He started to turn away, paused at sight of a black gash in the floor of the ledge off to his right. Dasein crossed to the break in the rock, looked down into darkness. The break in the rock wasn't more than three feet across, opening out to the face of the ledge, narrowing to a point about twenty feet to his right. Dasein knelt, risked a brief flash of his penlight. The light revealed a smooth-walled rock chimney leading down to another ledge. What was more important, he could see a game trail down there in the moonlight.

Dasein slid his feet over the edge of the chimney, sat down there with his legs hanging into the darkness, considered the problem. The injured shoulder made him

83

hesitate. Without that, he'd have gone right over, worked his way down, back against one side, feet against the other. Dangerous, yes—but a thing he had done many times in mountains rougher than these. The other ledge was no more than fifty feet down there.

He looked around him, wondering if he dared risk it. In this instant, his mind offered up the datum that he had forgotten to mail off the carbons of his notes to Selador. It was like a cold dash of water in the face. He felt that his own body had betrayed him, that he had conspired against himself.

How could I have forgotten? he wondered. There was anger in the thought, and fear. Perspiration bathed his palms. He glanced at the luminous dial of his wristwatch: almost midnight. There came over him then the almost overpowering desire to retrace his way back to the road and the camper.

He was suddenly more afraid of what his own body might do to him than he was of any danger which could come out of the night or of the climb down this simple rock chimney. Dasein sat there trembling, recalling his feeling that he was *possessed*.

This was madness!

He shook his head angrily.

There was no turning back; he had to go down there, find a way into that Co-op, expose its secrets. While the strength of anger was upon him, Dasein probed across the chimney with his feet, found the other side, slid off his perch and began working his way down. At each movement of his back, his shoulder stabbed him with pain. He gritted his teeth, felt his way down through the darkness. Rock scraped across his back. Once, his right foot slipped and he strained with the left for purchase.

The floor of the chimney when he found it was almost an anticlimax, a slope of loose rock which slid from beneath his feet and cascaded him out onto the game trail he had seen from above.

Dasein lay there a moment regaining his breath, allowing the fire in his shoulder to subside to a dull throb.

Presently, he struggled to his feet, marked where the

moonlighted trail led down to his right. He picked his way down through a screen of brush onto a sloping meadow dotted with the dark shapes of oaks. Moonlight gleamed on the fence beyond the meadow. There it was, the boundary of the Co-op. He wondered if he could climb that fence one-handed. It would be galling to come this far only to be stopped by a fence.

As he stood there examining the meadow and the fence, a deep humming sound impressed itself on him. It came from off to his right. He searched for the source of the sound, eyes hunting through shadows. Was that a gleam of metal down there, something round emerging from the meadow? He crouched low in the dry grass. There was a heavy odor of mushrooms all around. He recognized it abruptly—the smell of *Jaspers*. It came over Dasein that he was staring at a ventilator.

Ventilator!

He lifted himself to his feet, trotted across the meadow toward the sound. There was no mistaking that sound nor the wash of Jaspers-saturated air that enveloped him. There was a big fan at work down there under the earth.

Dasein stopped beside the ventilator outlet. It was about four feet across, stood approximately the same distance above the meadow topped by a cone-shaped rain hood. He was about to examine the fastenings of the hood when he heard a snuffling sound and crackling of brush from the direction of the fence. He ducked behind the ventilator as two uniformed guards emerged from the brush beyond the fence, dogs sniffing hungrily ahead of them, straining at their leashes.

If they get my scent, Dasein thought.

He crouched behind the ventilator breathing softly through his mouth. There was a tickling sensation on the back of his tongue. He wanted to cough, clear his throat, fought down the impulse. Dogs and guards had stopped directly below him.

A glaring light washed across the ventilator, swept the ground on both sides. One of the dogs whined eagerly. There was a rattling sound, a sharp command from one of the guards.

85

Dasein held his breath.

Again, something rattled. The sounds of guards and dogs moved along the fence. Dasein ventured a quick glance around the ventilator. They were flashing a light along the base of the fence, looking for tracks. One of the guards laughed. Dasein felt the touch of a light breeze on his cheeks, realized he was downwind from the dogs, allowed himself to relax slightly. The rattling sound came once more. Dasein saw it was one of the guards dragging a stick along the fence.

The casual mood of the guards caused him to relax even more. He took a deep breath. They were going over a low hill now, down the other side. The night swallowed them.

Dasein waited until he no longer could hear them before straightening. His left knee was trembling and it took a moment for this to subside.

Guards, dogs, that big bush buggy—all spoke of something important here. Dasein nodded to himself, began examining the ventilator. There was a heavy screen beneath the rain cap. He ventured a flash of the penlight, saw hood and screen were a welded unit held to the ventilator by heavy sheet metal screws.

Dasein brought out his hunting knife, tried one of the screws. Metal screeched against metal as he turned it. He stopped, listened. His ears detected only the sounds of the night. There was an owl somewhere in the brush above him. Its mournful call floated across the night. Dasein returned to the screw. It came out in his hand and he pocketed it, moved on to the next one. There were four in all.

When the last screw was out, he tried the screen. It and the hood lifted with a rasping metallic protest. He flashed his penlight inside, saw smooth metal walls going straight down about fifteen feet before curving back toward the hills.

Dasein returned the screen and hood to their normal position, went searching under the oaks until he found a fallen branch about six feet long. He used this to prop the hood and screen, peered once more down the ventilator with the penlight.

It was going to take two hands getting in there, he realized. No other way. Gritting his teeth, he removed the sling, stuffed it into a pocket. Even without the sling, he knew the arm wasn't going to be much use . . . except perhaps in an emergency. He felt the rim of the ventilator—sharp, rough metal. *The sling,* he thought. He brought it out, rolled it into a pad for his hands. Using this pad, he hauled himself across the lip of the ventilator. The pad slipped and he felt metal bite his stomach. He grabbed the edge, swung himself inward. Metal ripped buttons off his shirt. He heard them clatter somewhere below. His good hand found a purchase over a bit of the sling; he dropped down, pain screaming in his injured shoulder, swung his feet to the opposite side, turned and braced himself. Feet and back held. He slipped the hunting knife out of its sheath, reached up, knocked the limb prop aside.

Screen and hood came down with a clang he felt must have been heard for a mile. He waited, listening.

Silence.

Slowly, he began inching his way down.

Presently, his feet encountered the curve. He straightened, used the penlight. The ventilator slanted back under the hill at a gentle slope of about twenty degrees. There was something soft under his left foot. The light revealed the sling. He picked it up. The front of his shirt was sticking to his skin. He turned the light on it, saw red wetness, a section of skin scraped off by the lip of the ventilator. The pain was as a minor scratch compared to his shoulder.

I'm a mess, he thought. *What the hell am I doing here?*

The answer was there in his mind, clear and disturbing. He was here because he had been maneuvered into a one-way passage as direct and confining as this ventilator tube. Selador and friends formed one side of the passage; Jenny and fellow Santarogans formed the other side.

And here he was.

Dasein lifted the sling. It was torn but still serviceable. He gripped one end in his teeth, managed to restore it to a semblance of its former position.

There was only one way to go now. He dropped to his knees, crawled backward down the ventilator, using his

87

light occasionally to probe the darkness.

The Jaspers odor filled the confined space. It was a tangy essence of mushrooms here. He received the distinct impression it cleared his head.

The tube went on and on and on . . . He took it one step at a time. It curved slowly toward what he felt was south and the slope steepened. Once, he slipped, slid downward for twenty feet, cutting his left hand on a rivet. He wasn't positive, but he thought the sound of the fan motor grew louder.

Again, the tube turned—and again. Dasein lost all sense of direction in the confining darkness. Why had they constructed this ventilator with so many turns? he wondered. Had they followed a natural fault in the rock? It seemed likely.

His left foot encountered an edge of emptiness.

Dasein stopped, used the penlight. Its feeble glow illuminated a flat metal wall about six feet away and a square of shadows beneath it. He turned the light downward, exposed a box-like opening about five feet deep with a heavy screen for one side. The sound of the fan motor came from somewhere behind the screen and it definitely was louder here.

Bracing himself with a hand in the screen, Dasein lowered himself into the box. He stood there a moment examining his surroundings. The wall opposite the screen appeared different from the others. There were six round-head bolts in it held by flanged metal keepers as though they'd been designed to stay in that position while nuts were tightened from the outside.

Dasein pried up one of the flanges with his knife, turned the bolt. It moved easily, too easily. He pulled back on it, turned it once more. That took more effort and he was rewarded by having the bolt work backward into his hand. The nut dropped outside with a sound of falling on wood.

He waited, listening for a response to that sound.

Nothing.

Dasein put his eye to the bolt hole, peered out into an eerie red gloom. As his eye grew accustomed to it, he made out a section of heavy screen across from him, packages piled behind the screen.

He drew back. Well, Nis had said this was a storage cave.

Dasein applied himself to the other bolts. He left the bolt in the upper right corner, bent the metal out and swung it aside. There was a wooden catwalk immediately below him with three wing nuts on it. He slipped out to the catwalk, scooped up the wing nuts. The other nuts obviously had dropped through the space between the boards of the walk. He looked around, studying what he saw with care, absorbing the implications of this place.

It was a troglodyte cave illuminated by dim red light. The light came from globes beneath the catwalk and above it, casting enormous shadows on a rock wall behind the ventilator panel and over stacked tiers of cage-walled compartments. The cages ware stuffed with packages and reminded Dasein of nothing more than a public freezer locker.

The richly moist odor of Jaspers was all around him.

A sign to his right down the catwalk labeled this area as "Bay 21 — D-1 to J-5."

Dasein returned his attention to the ventilator, restored three of the bolts, forcing the cover plate back into position. A crease remained in the metal where he had bent it, but he thought it would pass casual inspection.

He looked up and down the catwalk.

Where would he find one of these compartments he could open to examine the contents? He crossed to the one opposite the ventilator plate, looked for a door. Could he find a compartment left unlocked by a careless Santarogan ... provided he could find the door? There apparently was no door on the first compartment he inspected. The lack of a door filled Dasein with unease. There had to be a door!

He stepped back, studied the line of compartments, gasped as he saw the answer. The fronts of the compartments slid aside in wooden channels ... and there were no locks. Simple peg latches held them.

Dasein opened the front of a compartment, pulled out a

small cardboard box. Its label read: "Auntie Beren's spiced crab apples. Ex. April '55." He replaced the box, extracted a salami-shaped package. Its label read: "Limburger exposed early 1929." Dasein replaced the limburger, closed the compartment.

Exposed?

Methodically, Dasein worked his way down the line in Bay 21, examining one or two packages in each compartment. Most of the time it was written "Ex" with a date. The older packages spelled it out.

Exposed.

Dasein sensed his mind racing. *Exposed. Exposed to what? How?*

The sound of footsteps on the lower catwalk behind him brought Dasein whirling around, muscles tense. He heard a compartment door slide open. Papers rustled.

Softly, Dasein worked his way along the catwalk away from the sound. He passed steps, one set leading up, one down, hesitated. He couldn't be certain whether he was going deeper into the cave complex or out of it. There was another catwalk above him, a rock ceiling dimly visible above that. There appeared to be at least three tiers of catwalks below him.

He chose the steps going up, lifted his head slowly above the floor level of the next walk, glanced both ways.

Empty.

This level was like the one below except for the rock ceiling. The rock appeared to be a form of granite, but with oily brown veins.

Moving as silently as he could, Dasein climbed out onto the walk, moved back in the direction of the ventilator listening for the person he had heard on the lower level.

Someone was whistling down there, an idiot tune repeated endlessly. Dasein pressed his back against a cage, peered down through the openings in the walk. There came a scraping of wood against wood. The whistling went away to his left, receded into silence.

That probably was the way out, then.

He had heard the person down there but hadn't been able to see him—a fact which could work both ways.

90

Placing his feet carefully, Dasein moved along the walk. He came to a cross way, peered around it. Empty both ways. The gloom appeared a little thicker to the left.

It occurred to Dasein that up to this point he hadn't felt the need to worry about how he was going to get out of the cave complex. He had been too intent on solving the mystery. But the mystery remained . . . and here he was.

I can't just go marching out, he thought. *Or can't I? What could they do to me?*

His throbbing shoulder, memory of the gas jet, the knowledge that two previous investigators had died in this valley—these were sufficient answer to the question, he thought.

Wood slammed against wood off to the front and below. Footsteps pounded along a catwalk—at least two pair of feet, possibly more. The running stopped almost directly beneath him. There came a low-voiced conversation, mostly unintelligible and sounding like instructions. Dasein recognized only three words— " . . . back . . . " " . . . away . . ." and a third word which set him in motion running softly down the dim side passage to his left.

" . . . ventilator . . . "

A man beneath him had said "ventilator" sharply and distinctly.

The pounding of feet resumed down there spreading out through the catwalks.

Dasein searched frantically ahead for a place to hide. There was a sound of machinery humming somewhere down there. The catwalk turned left at about a fifteen degree angle, and he saw the cave walls were converging here—fewer tiers below and smaller compartments on each side. The walk angled more sharply to the right and there was only his walk and the one below, single compartments on each side.

He had put himself into a dead-end side passage, Dasein realized. Still, there was the sound of machinery ahead.

His catwalk ended in a set of wooden stairs going down. There was no choice; he could hear someone running behind him.

Dasein went down.

91

The stairs turned left into a rock passage—no compartments, just the cave. There was a louvered door on the right, loud sound of an electric motor in there. His pursuer was at the head of the steps above.

Dasein opened the door, slipped through, closed the door. He found himself in a rectangular chamber about fifty feet long, twenty feet wide and some fifteen feet to the ceiling. A row of large electric motors lined the left wall, all of them extending into round metal throats with fanblades blurring the air there. The far wall was one giant metal screen and he could feel air rushing out of it toward the fans.

The right wall was piled high with cardboard cartons, sacks and wood boxes. There was a space between the pile and the ceiling and it appeared darker up there. Dasein scrambled up the pile, crawled along it, almost fell into a space hollowed out of boxes and sacks near the far end. He slid into the hole, found himself on what felt like blankets. His hand encountered something metallic, which groping fingers identified as a flashlight.

The louvered door slammed open. Feet pounded into the room. Someone scrambled up the far end of the pile. A woman's voice said: "Nothing up here."

There came the sound of someone dropping lightly to the floor.

There'd been something familiar about the woman's voice. Dasein was willing to swear he'd heard it before.

A man said: "Why'd you run this way? Did you hear something?"

"I thought so, but I wasn't sure," the woman said.

"You sure there's nothing on top of the stores?"

"Look for yourself."

"Doggone, I wish we could use real lights in here."

"Now, don't you go doing something foolish."

"Don't worry about me. Doggone that Jenny anyway, getting herself mixed up with an outsider!"

"Don't pick on Jenny. She knows what she's doing."

"I guess so, but it sure makes a lot of stupid extra work, and you know what's liable to happen if we don't find him pretty soon."

92

"So let's hurry it up."

They went out, closed the door.

Dasein lay quietly absorbing the import of what they'd said. Jenny knew what she was doing, did she? What would happen if they didn't find him?

It felt good to stretch out on the blankets. His shoulder was a steady aching throb. He brought up the flashlight he'd found here, pressed its switch. The thing produced a dull red glow. The light revealed a tight little nest— blankets, a pillow, a canteen half full of water. He drank some of it thirstily, found it heavy with Jaspers.

He supposed nothing in the cave could escape that flavor.

A fit of shivering took over his muscles. The canteen's cap rattled as he replaced it. When the trembling passed, he sat staring at the canteen in the dim red light.

Nothing in the cave could escape the Jaspers flavor!

That was it!

Exposed!

Something that could exist in this cave—a mould or a fungus, something related to mushrooms and dark places, something that wouldn't travel . . . a *Jaspers* something invaded anything exposed to this environment.

But why was it so important to keep this fact secret? Why the dogs and the guards?

He heard the louvered door open, close, turned off the red flashlight. Someone ran lightly across the rock floor to a point just below him.

"Gilbert Dasein!" a voice hissed at him.

Dasein stiffened.

"It's Willa Burdeaux," the voice hissed. "It's Willa, Jenny's friend. I know you're in there, in the place Cal made for us. Now, you listen. Arnulf will be right back from the upper end and I have to be out of here before that. You don't have much time. There's too much Jaspers in here for someone who's not used to it. You're breathing it and it's going in your pores and everything."

What the hell? Dasein thought.

He crawled up out of the nest, leaned out and looked down at Willa Burdeaux's dark, harshly-beautiful face.

"Why can't I take too much of it?" he asked.

"Hasn't that Jenny explained anything to you?" she whispered. "Well, no time now. You have to get out of here. Do you have a watch?"

"Yes, but . . . "

"There's no time to explain; just listen. Give me fifteen mintues to get Arnulf out of the way. He's such a prig. In fifteen minutes you come out of this room. Turn left the way you came in, but go down instead of up. Take the second crossway to your left and after that keep to your left. It's easy to remember. Left turns only. You want the ramp out of Bay 2-G. I've left the ramp's door unlocked. Lock it after you. It'll be about twenty steps straight in front of that door to an emergency gate. The gate's unlocked. Go out and lock it after you. The Inn's right across the road. You ought to be able to make that on your own."

"Apparently, you've been rather busy."

"I was in the office when they sounded the alarm. Now, get down out of sight and do just what I told you."

Dasein ducked back into the nest.

Presently, he heard the door open and close. He looked at his wristwatch: five minutes to three a.m. Where had the time gone?

Could he believe Willa Burdeaux? he wondered.

There'd been something about that black pixie face, an intensity . . . Dasein thought of compartments loaded with valuable food, all unlocked. Why should this evidence of a basic honesty alarm him? Perhaps it wasn't honesty. Fear could control behavior, too.

Could he believe Willa? Did he have a choice?

So this was a trysting place Cal Nis had made for the two of them. Why not? People in love usually wanted to be alone together.

Jenny knew what she was doing.

What did she know?

His mind felt clear and oiled, working at a furious pace. What was the danger in exposure to Jaspers? He thought of that dull-eyed line he'd glimpsed up there in the Co-op.

Was that what happened?

Dasein fought down a seige of trembling.

94

Ten minutes after three, the moment of decision, came more quickly than he wanted. He had no choice and knew it. His shoulder had gone stiff and there was a painful burning along his scraped chest and stomach. Favoring his shoulder, Dasein eased himself down off the storage pile.

The ramp door was unlocked as Willa had promised. He let himself out into a darkened side yard, hesitated. The stars overhead looked cold and close. It *was* cold. He felt goose pimples along his arms. There was no sign of a guard out here, but he glimpsed lights and motion far up on the hillside.

Lock the ramp door, she'd said.

Dasein locked the door, darted across the yard. It was a narrow gate in the chain fence. The hinges creaked and he thought the latch unnaturally loud. There was a hasp and padlock. He closed the lock.

A narrow path led along the fence to the road. There was the Inn across the way—dark, but inviting. A dim yellow light glowed through the double doors. Using the light as a beacon, Dasein limped down the path and across to the Inn.

The lobby was empty, most of its lights turned off. There was the sound of snoring from the switchboard room behind the desk.

Dasein slipped quietly across the lobby, up the stairs and down the hall to his room.

The key—had he turned it in or left it in the truck? No . . . here it was in his pocket. He opened the door softly, stepped into the darkness of his room. He'd spent only one night in this room but it suddenly was a haven.

The truck! It was still up there on the road to Porterville. The hell with it. He'd hire a ride up tomorrow and drive it down.

That Willa Burdeaux! Why had she done this?

Dasein began slipping out of his clothes. He wanted nothing more than a hot shower and bed. It was slow work undressing in the dark, but he knew a light might tell someone what time he'd returned.

What difference does that make? he asked himself. His clothing, torn, smeared with dirt, still stinking of the cave, was evidence enough of where he'd been and what he'd done.

Abruptly, he felt he no longer could sneak around.

Angry at himself, he turned on the light.

Directly ahead of him on the bedstand was a bottle of beer with a note attached to it. Dasein lifted the note, read it: "This isn't much, but it's all I could get. You'll need it in the morning. I'll call Jenny and tell her you're all right. —Willa."

Dasein picked up the bottle, looked at the label. There was a blue stamp on it: "Exposed January 1959."

5

A steady, loud pounding invaded Dasein's dream.

He felt he was trapped inside a giant drum. Reverberations beat through his brain. Each drumbeat became a stab of pain along his temples, through his shoulders, across his stomach.

He was the drum! That was it!

His lips were dry. Thirst spread a scabby dustiness over his throat. His tongue was thick, fuzzy.

My God! Would the pounding never stop?

He awoke feeling he'd been caught in a caricature of a hangover. The blankets were twisted around his body, immobilizing his injured shoulder. The shoulder felt better, and that was a relief, but something had to be done about his head and that insane pounding.

His free arm was asleep. It tingled painfully when he tried to move it. Sunlight filtered through a tear in the curtain on the room's single window. One thin ray outlined in dust motes stabbed across the room. It dazzled him, hurt his eyes.

That damned pounding!

"Hey! Open up in there!"

It was a masculine voice from outside.

Dasein felt he knew that voice. Marden, the CHP captain? What was he doing here at this hour. Dasein lifted his wristwatch, stared at it—ten twenty-five.

The pounding resumed.

"Just a minute!" Dasein shouted. His own voice sent waves of pain through his head.

Blessedly, the pounding stopped.

Dasein gasped with relief, twisted himself out of the blankets, sat up. The room's walls began going around and around in a mad circle.

For the love of heaven! he thought. *I've heard of hangovers, but nothing like this.*

"Open the door, Dasein."

That definitely was Marden.

"Right with you," Dasein rasped.

What's wrong with me? he wondered. He knew he'd had no more than the beers with dinner. They couldn't possibly explain his present malaise. Could it be delayed reaction to the gas?

Beer.

There was something about beer.

Slowly so as not to dislocate his neck, Dasein turned his head toward the bedstand. Yes, there was a beer. Willa had thoughtfully provided an opener. He levered the cap off the bottle, drank hungrily.

Waves of soothing relief spread out from his stomach. He put down the empty bottle, stood up. *Hair of the dog.* he thought. *Hair of the Jaspers dog.* The bottle was redolent with the mushroom tang.

"Are you all right in there, Dasein?"

To hell with you, mister, Dasein thought. He tried to take a step, was rewarded with instant nausea and a wave of dizziness. He leaned against the wall breathing slowly, deeply.

I'm sick, he thought. *I've caught something.*

The beer felt as though it had begun to boil in his stomach.

"Open this door, Dasein! Now!"

All right—all right, Dasein thought. He stumbled to the door, unlocked it, stepped back.

The door was flung open to reveal Al Marden in uniform, the captain's bars glistening at his neck. His visored cap was pushed back to reveal a sweaty band of red hair.

"Well," he said. "Haven't we been the busy one?"

He stepped into the room, closed the door. He carried

something round and chromed in his left hand—a thermos. What the devil was he doing here at this hour with a thermos? Dasein wondered.

One hand against the wall to steady himself, Dasein made his way back to the bed, sat on the edge.

Marden followed.

"I hope you're worth all this trouble," he said.

Dasein looked up at the narrow, cynical face, remembering the glimpse he'd had of the high-wheeled bush buggy wheeling down the road out there with Marden steering, and the dogs beside him. That had been a proper setting for this man. There was an elevated look about him, a peering-down-at-the-world's-stupidity. What was it about him? Was it the Santaroga look? But what had the Porterville deputies seen, then? What had the man in the Chrysler seen.

Do I look that way? Dasein wondered.

"I brought you some coffee," Marden said. "You look like you could use it." He opened the thermos, poured steaming amber liquid into the cup-top.

A rich smell of Jaspers rode on the steam from the cup. The smell set Dasein trembling, sent a pulsing, throbbing ache through his head. The ache seemed timed to a wavering reflection on the surface of the coffee as Marden presented it.

Dasein took the cup in both hands, tipped his head back and drank with a gulping eagerness. The coffee produced the same sensation of soothing as the beer.

Marden refilled the cup.

Dasein held it beneath his nose, inhaled the Jaspers rich steam. His headache began to fade. There was a hunger in him for the coffee that he realized went beyond the cravings from a hangover.

"Drink up," Marden said.

Dasein sipped the coffee. He could feel it settling his stomach, his mind coming alert. Marden no longer appeared superior—only amused.

Why was a hangover amusing?

"The Jaspers, that's what gave me the screaming fantods, isn't it?" Dasein asked. He returned the cup.

Marden concentrated on restoring the cap to the thermos.

"A person can get too much of it, eh?" Dasein persisted, recalling what Willa Burdeaux had said.

"Overexposure too soon can cause a hangover," Marden admitted. "You'll be all right when you get used to it."

"So you came up to play the good Samaritan," Dasein said. He could feel the beginnings of anger.

"We found your truck up on the Porterville road and got worried about you," Marden said. "You can't abandon a vehicle like that."

"I didn't abandon it."

"Oh? What'd you do?"

"I went for a walk."

"And caused one helluva lot of trouble," Marden said. "If you wanted a tour of the Co-op and the storage caves, all you had to do was ask."

"And I'd have had a nice safe guided tour."

"Any kind of tour you wanted."

"So you came up to arrest me."

"Arrest you? Don't talk stupid."

"How'd you know where I was?"

Marden looked at the ceiling, shook his head. "You're all alike, you young folks," he said. "That Willa's too damn' romantic, but she doesn't lie worth git all. None of us do, I guess." He turned his glance full of cynical amusement on Dasein. "You feeling better?"

"Yes!"

"Aren't we the intense one." He pursed his lips. "By the way, we broke into your truck and hot-wired it to drive it down. It's parked out front."

"Gee, thanks."

Dasein looked down at his hands. Anger and frustration twisted through him. He knew Marden wasn't a fit object for this anger . . . nor Jenny . . . nor Piaget . . . No person or thing presented itself to him as an object for anger—yet the emotion remained. He trembled with it.

"You sure you're all right?" Marden asked.

"Yes, I'm all right!"

100

"Okay, okay," Marden murmured. He turned away, but not before Dasein saw the smile forming on his lips.

The smile, not the man, brought Dasein's anger to focus. That smile! It embodied Santaroga—self-satisfied, superior, secretive. He jumped to his feet, strode to the window, whipped up the curtain.

Blazing sunshine on a flower garden, a small stream, and beyond that the flat with its broken edge dropping down into the redwoods. It was a day of brassy heat with the oaks sitting motionless, sun-drenched on the hillsides. He counted three plumes of smoke hanging on the still air, glimpsed a serpentine track of blue-green river in the distance.

This vale of pastoral beauty that was Santaroga, this was a fitting object for his anger, Dasein decided: Santaroga, this island of people in the wilderness. He pictured the valley as a swarming place behind a façade like a pyramid: solid, faceless, enduring. In there, behind the façade, Santaroga did something to its people. They lost personal identity and became masks for something that was the same in all of them.

He sensed a one-pointedness here such that every Santarogan became an extension of every other Santarogan. They were like rays spreading out from a pinhole in a black curtain.

What lay behind the black curtain?

There, he knew, was the real substance against which his anger was directed. The valley existed within an evil enchantment. The Santarogans had been trapped by a black sorcery, transmuted into the faceless pyramid.

With this thought, Dasein's anger faded. He realized he, too, had a place in this pyramid. It was like an ecological pyramid planted in the wilderness except for this gnome-change. The base of the pyramid had been firmly imbedded in the earth, extending roots deep into a moist, dank cave.

He could see the shape of his problem.

One thing set this valley apart—Jaspers. It brought Santarogans back as though they were addicted. He thought of his own craving reaction. It was the substance of the cave, the thing the pores drank and the lungs inhaled.

Marden stirred in the room behind him.

Dasein turned, looked at the man.

Santarogans became extensions of that cave and its substance. There was a drug-effect at work in this valley. It was a material in a way similar to lysergic acid diethylamide—LSD.

How did it work? he wondered.

Did it shift the serotonin balance?

Dasein felt his mind working with remarkable clarity, sorting out possibilities, setting up avenues of investigation.

"If you're feeling all right now, I'll be running along," Marden said. "Before you get any more harebrained ideas for night excursions, let us know, huh?"

"Well, naturally," Dasein said.

For some reason, this provoked a fit of laughter in Marden. He was still laughing as he let himself out.

"To hell with you, wise-guy Santarogan," Dasein muttered.

He turned back to the window.

Objectivity was going to be a problem, he saw. He had no guinea pig except himself. What was the Jaspers effect on himself? An impression of heightened awareness? Could it be an actual heightened awareness in the pattern of LSD? This would require careful evaluation. What was the source of the morning-after symptoms? Withdrawal?

He began to focus on the Santaroga personality pattern, their alertness, their abrupt mannerisms, their apparent honesty. If awareness actually were heightened, would that explain the honest advertising? Could you be anything but bluntly honest with a wide-awake human being?

Avenues of attack opened all around. Barriers collapsed like sand walls before the waves of his new awareness, but the exposed vistas contained their own mysteries.

Jenny.

Again, Dasein recalled how she'd been dropped from the university's attempt to evaluate LSD. *No apparent reaction.* The ones running the tests had wanted to explore this phenomenon, but Jenny had refused. Why? She'd been written off, of course—"a curious anomaly." The evaluation had gone on to its natural end in the publicity fiasco.

Jenny.

Dasein went into the shower, humming to himself, his mind busy. His shoulder felt remarkably improved in spite of the way he'd mistreated it during the night . . . or perhaps because of that—the exercise.

I'll call Jenny, he thought, as he dressed. *Maybe we can meet for lunch.*

The prospect of seeing Jenny filled him with a wondering delight. He sensed his own protectiveness toward her, the mutual emotional dependence. Love, that was what it was. It was a sensation that wouldn't submit to analysis. It could only be experienced.

Dasein sobered.

His love for Jenny required that he save her from the Santaroga enchantment. She'd have to help him whether she knew it or not, whether she wanted it or not.

A brisk double knock sounded on his door.

"Come in," he called.

Jenny slipped in, closed the door.

She wore a white dress, red scarf, red handbag and shoes. The outfit made her skin appear dark and exotic. She paused a moment at the door, her hand resting lightly on the knob, eyes wide and probing.

"Jen!" he said.

All in one swift dash, she was across the room into his arms, hugging him. Her lips were warm and soft on his. There was a clean spicy smell about her.

She pulled back, looked up at him. "Oh, darling, I was so frightened. I kept imagining you driving off a cliff somewhere, your car wrecked, you in the wreckage. Then Willa called. Why would you do such a thing?"

He put a finger on the tip of her nose, pressed gently. "I'm perfectly capable of taking care of myself."

"I don't know about that. Do you feel all right now? I met Al in the lobby. He said he brought you some Jaspers coffee."

"I've had my hair of the dog."

"Your hair of . . . Oh. But why would you . . . "

103

"But me no buts. I'm sorry I worried you, but I have a job to do."

"Oh, that!"

"I'm going to do the job I'm being paid to do."

"You gave your word, I suppose?"

"That's only part of it."

"Then they'll have to get something from you."

"More than *something*, Jenny, m'love."

She grinned. "I like it when you call me your love."

"Stop changing the subject."

"But it's such a nice subject."

"Agreed. Another time, though, eh?"

"How about tonight?"

"You're a forward wench, aren't you."

"I know what I want."

Dasein found himself studying her there in his arms. What had Willa said? *"Jenny knows what she's doing."* Whatever it was, he couldn't doubt her love for him. It was there in her eyes and her voice, a radiance and vivacity that couldn't be mistaken.

Still, there was the certainty two men had died on this investigation—accidents! The fading pain in his shoulder and its implications couldn't be doubted either.

"You're so quiet suddenly," Jenny said, looking up at him.

He took a deep breath. "Can you get me some Jaspers?"

"I almost forgot," she said. She pulled away, rummaged in her handbag. "I brought you a square of cheese and some wheat crackers for your lunch today. They're from Uncle Larry's locker. I knew you'd need it because . . . " She broke off, produced a sack from the bag. "Here they are." She proffered a brown paper sack, stared at him. "Gil! You said *Jaspers*." There was a wary look in her eyes.

"Why not?" He took the bag. She was reluctant to part with it, her fingers trailing across the paper as he pulled it away.

"I don't want to trick you, darling," she said.

"Trick me? How?"

She swallowed and her eyes glistened with unshed tears.

"We gave you an awfully strong dose last night, and then you went down into that stupid cave. Was it bad this morning?"

"I had quite a hangover, if that's what you mean."

"I can just barely remember how it was when I was a child," she said. "When you're growing up, your body changing, there are some severe metabolic adjustments. At the school, when I took part in that crazy LSD test, I had a hangover the next morning." She ran a finger along his forehead. "Poor dear. I'd have been here this morning, but Uncle Larry needed me in the clinic. Anyway, he said you weren't in any danger; Willa got you out in time."

"What would've happened if she hadn't got me out?"

Her eyes clouded as though with pain.

"What?" he insisted.

"You mustn't think about that."

"About what?"

"It can't happen to you anyway. Uncle Larry says you're the wrong type."

"Wrong type for what—turning into a zombie like those I saw in the Co-op?"

"Zombies? What're you talking about?"

He described what he'd glimpsed through the wide door.

"Oh . . . them." She looked away from him, her manner suddenly distant. "Gilbert, are you going to put them in your report?"

"Maybe."

"You mustn't."

"Why not? Who are they? *What* are they?"

"We take care of our own," she said. "They're useful members of the community."

"But not quite all there."

"That's right." She looked up at him with a fierce intensity. "If the state takes them over, they'll be moved out of the valley—most of them. That can be very bad for Santarogans, Gilbert. Believe me."

"I believe you."

"I knew you would."

"They're the failures, eh? The ones Jaspers ruined."

"Gilbert!" she said. Then—"It's not what you think.

105

Jaspers is . . . something wonderful. We call it a 'Consciousness Fuel.' It opens your eyes and your ears, it turns on your mind, it . . ." She broke off, smiled at him. "But you already know."

"I know what it appears to be," he said. He glanced at the bag in his hand. What did he hold here? Was it a paradisical gift for all mankind or something out of hell? Was it the evil enchantment he'd pictured, or an ultimate freedom?

"It's wonderful and you know it by now," Jenny said.

"Then why aren't you all shouting it from the rooftops?" he demanded.

"Gil!" She stared at him accusingly.

Abruptly, Dasein thought of what Meyer Davidson's reaction would be . . . Davidson and his cohorts, the eager young executives and the hard-eyed older men.

What he held here in his hand was their enemy.

To those men in their oddly similar dark suits, their cold eyes weighing and dismissing everything, the people of this valley were a foe to be defeated. As he thought of it, Dasein realized all customers were "The Enemy" to these men. Davidson and his kind were pitted against each other, yes, competitive, but among themselves they betrayed that they were pitted more against the masses who existed beyond that inner ring of knowledgable financial operation.

The alignment was apparent in everything they did, in their words as well as their actions. They spoke of "package grab-level" and "container flash time"—of "puff limit" and "acceptance threshold." It was an "in" language of militarylike maneuvering and combat. They knew which height on a shelf was most apt to make a customer grab an item. They knew the "flash time"—the shelf width needed for certain containers. They knew how much empty air could be "puffed" into a package to make it appear a greater bargain. They knew how much price and package manipulation the customer would accept without jarring him into a "rejection pattern."

And we're their spies, Dasein thought. *The psychiatrists and psychologists—all the "social scientists"—we're the espionage arm.*

106

He sensed the vast maneuvering of these armies, the conspiracy to maintain "The Enemy" in a sleepy state of unawareness—malleable. Whatever the leaders of these armies did among themselves to each other, they maintained their inner code. No one betrayed the *real* war.

Dasein never before viewed the market-study world in quite this way. He thought of the brutal honesty in Santaroga's advertising, crumpled the neck of the paper bag in his hand.

What was this stuff doing to him? He turned away from Jenny to hide a surge of anger. It was making him imagine crazy things! Armies!

There was no way to avoid Jaspers here in Santaroga. The investigation required that he *not* avoid it.

I must insinuate myself into their minds, he reminded himself. *I must live their life, think as they think.*

He saw the situation then as Jenny and her fellow Santarogans must see it. They were involved in a form of guerrilla warfare. They had achieved a way of life which wouldn't be tolerated by the *outside.* Santaroga offered too much of a threat to the oligarchs of the money-industry world. The only hope for Santaroga lay in isolation and secrecy.

Shout it from the rooftops, indeed. No wonder she'd snapped at him in surprise.

Dasein turned, looked at Jenny standing there patiently waiting for him to think his way through the maze. She smiled encouragingly at him and he suddenly saw all Santarogans through her. They were the buffalo Indians, people who needed to get away by themselves, to live and hunt in the way their instincts told them. The trouble was, they lived in a world which couldn't be culturally neutral. That world out there would keep trying to make people—all people—be everywhere alike.

Straddling both worlds, thinking with the drug and thinking with his memories of the *outside,* he felt a deep sadness for Jenny. Santaroga would be destroyed—no doubt of that.

"I'm sure you see it," Jenny said.

"Jaspers would be equated with LSD, with narcotics,"

107

he said. "It'd be legislated against as the Santaroga hashish. You'd be sneered out of existence, destroyed."

"I never doubted you'd understand once you were exposed," she said. She moved into his arms, leaned against him, hugging him fiercely. "I trusted you, Gil. I knew I couldn't be wrong about you."

He couldn't find words to answer her. A profound sadness held him. *Exposed.*

"You'll still have to do your report, of course," she said. "It wouldn't solve anything if you failed. They'd just find somebody else. We're getting kind of tired of it."

"Yes—I'll have to do a report," he said.

"We understand."

Her voice sent a shudder through Dasein. *"We understand."* That was the *We* which had searched his bag, had almost killed him . . . had actually killed two men.

"Why are you shivering?" Jenny asked.

"Just a chill," he said.

He thought then of the *thing* he had sensed lurking just beyond his awareness, that restless, urgently peering ancient being which had risen within his consciousness like the neck of a dinosaur. It was still there, studying, waiting to judge.

"I only work half a day today," Jenny said. "Some of my friends have arranged a picnic at the lake. They want to meet you." She leaned back, peered up at him. "I want to show you off, too."

"I . . . don't think I can go swimming," he said.

"Your poor shoulder," she said. "I know. But the lake's beautiful this time of year. We'll have a bonfire tonight."

Which We is that? he asked himself.

"It sounds wonderful," he said.

And he wondered as he spoke why his stomach knotted with a congestion of fear. He told himself it wasn't Jenny he feared—not this warm and beautiful woman. It might be goddess-Jenny he feared, though . . . this was a thought that rose in his mind to leer at him.

Dasein sneered at himself then, thinking that he read too much into every nuance of this valley and its people. That was the psychoanalyst's disease, of course—seeing everything through a haze of reasoning.

"Get some rest and meet me downstairs at noon," Jenny said.

She pulled away, went to the door, turned there to stare at him. "You're acting very odd, Gil," she said. "Is something bothering you?"

Her voice carried a weighted probing that brought Dasein to sudden alertness. This wasn't the spontaneous Jenny worried about the man she loved. This was an . . . an *observer* probing for something personally dangerous.

"Nothing food and rest won't cure," he said. He tried to sound bantering, knew he'd failed.

"I'll see you in a little while," she said, still in that distant tone.

Dasein watched the door close behind her. He had the feeling he'd been playing to a special kind of camera, one that pursued irrelevancies. An untethered thought wove through his mind: . . . *the exposure of personality, method and character.*

Who wants to expose my personality, method and character? Dasein asked himself. He felt this was a dangerous question, full of charge and countercharge.

The sack of food felt heavy in his hand. Dasein stared down at it, aware of his hunger, equally aware of the threat in this package. Did the Jaspers create irreversible change?

He tossed the sack onto his bed, went to the door, peered out into the hall. Empty. He stepped out, looked down the expanse of wall that concealed the TV room. It took a moment for him to realize something was wrong with that wall. It was like a dislocation of reality—a door occupied a space in that wall where no door had been.

As though pulled by strings, Dasein went to the door, stared at it. The door was framed in the same worn, polished wood that framed the other doors. Well-preserved age, that was the effect. This was a door that had always been here, that's what it said. The number plate carried a slight dent and a touch of tarnish at the edges where the maids' polishing rags had missed. There was a patina of long wear about the handle.

Dasein shook his head. He was tempted to try the door,

109

resisted. He found himself frightened by what might lie beyond. Normalcy—a bed, a bath, desk and chairs—that would be the worst thing of all. The number plate—262—fascinated him. He toyed with the eerie sensation that he'd seen it before . . . right here. The door was too ordinary.

Abruptly, Dasein whirled back and into his room, threw open his window. A look through the windows from the porch roof would solve the mystery. He started to climb out, stopped. A man stood on a rose-bordered walk beyond the giant oak tree.

Dasein recognized Winston Burdeaux. He was pumping a hand sprayer that sent dust over the roses. As Dasein stared, Burdeaux looked up, waved.

Later, Dasein told himself. *I'll look later.*

He nodded to Burdeaux, withdrew, pulled the curtain.

So they'd cut a door through that wall, had they? What were they trying to do? Destroy his sense of reality?

The sack on the bed caught Dasein's attention. It drew him across the room. He saw it as an ultimate temptation. It was more than food. There was a hunger in him only the Jaspers could fulfill. Dasein felt abruptly that he was like Tennyson's Ulysses, his aim "to strive, to seek, to find and not to yield." Still, the thought of the Jaspers in that sack drew his hand. He felt the paper tear beneath his fingers.

Jaspers cheese. That tantalizing aroma lifted from it. With a feeling of spiritual helplessness, he found a bite of the cheese in his mouth. The food radiated a sensation of warmth as it went down his throat. He continued eating, hypnotized by his own actions.

Slowly, he sank back onto the bed, leaned against the pillow, gazed up at the ceiling. The wood grain in a beam wavered like the lifting and falling of the sea. It filled him with awe, undiluted and terrifying. He felt his own consciousness stood as a barrier opposing the external world, and that external world was a stupid mechanism without feeling or compassion.

His own identity became a narrowing beam of light, and he sensed a massive, streaming unconsciousness growing

110

larger, larger . . . larger . . . building up an intolerable weight.

It's a psychedelic, he told himself. *Don't let go.*

But there was no stopping the movement now. His awareness, exploding up and out, riding a geyser of sense revelation, lifted him into a state of floating consciousness.

There was no inwardness now, only a timeless sense of being that existed without anxiety. Dasein found himself reveling in the sensation. His mind quested.

Where are the children? he asked himself.

It was a shocking sense of revelation for him to realize he'd seen no children or schools in the valley.

Where are the children? Why haven't any of the other investigators remarked on this?

The other investigators are dead, he reminded himself.

Death—that was an oddly nonfrightening thought. He felt he had risen through a consciousness decompression into a zone beyond all power struggles. The valley, the Jaspers, had become a condition of his being. The room full of probing sunlight, the leaves of the oak outside his window—all was beauty, innocent, uncluttered. The external universe had become translated into a part of himself, wise, compassionate.

Dasein marveled at the feeling. The universe *out there* —it was as though he had just created that universe. *Nama-Rupa,* he thought. *I am Nama-Rupa—name and form, creator of the universe in which I live.*

The pain of his injured shoulder occupied his drifting attention momentarily. Pain, a brief crisis, something against which to project memories of pleasure. The pain faded.

There came the sound of tires on gravel. He heard a bird singing. The sounds were a moire playing against his awareness. They danced and scintillated.

He remembered Jenny's probing stare.

This was an ugly, shocking memory that jerked him up short, compressed him. He found difficulty breathing. There was a sensation that he had been caught up in history, but it was a kind of history he'd never experienced, peopled by goddesses and creatures of terrifying powers. It

111

was a history moving at an astonishing speed, defying all preconceived notions of slowness. It was like a series of events that he couldn't separate or distinguish. They flashed across his consciousness, leaving him irrevocably changed.

The Jaspers, he thought. *I cannot return . . . to . . . what . . . I was . . . before.*

Tears rolled down his cheeks.

He thought of the way his bag had been searched. A sob shook him. What did they want?

Dasein found himself believing there were demons around him, cunning, seeking his blood and being, hungry for his soul. They gibbered beyond the charmed circle of his lonely awareness. The sensation, primitive as a witch dance, refused to leave. They were robots, automata with grimacing malleable faces and headlight eyes.

He began to tremble, knew he was perspiring heavily, but it was a distant sensation, something happening to a foreign person.

Head whirling, Dasein heaved himself off the bed, lurched to his feet, stumbled across the room. At the wall, he turned, stumbled back—forth and back . . . back and forth. No hiding place existed for him. Sunlight streaming in the window took on grotesque forms—lizards with human faces, silvery gnomes, insects with clock-face wings . . .

He slumped to the floor, clawed at the rug. A red braided pattern extruded claws that reached for him. He retreated to the bed, fell across it. The ceiling undulated with inverted waves.

Somewhere, someone played a piano—Chopin.

Dasein felt abruptly that he was the piano. The sounds struck a crystal brilliance through him, plucking out his anguish. Glaring white clarity began to seep over him. He grew aware his clothes were soaked with perspiration. His palms were slippery. He sensed he had come a long distance through a dangerous passage. The journey had leeched all strength from him.

But he saw the room now with an uncluttered innocence. The ceiling beams were objects to be understood, their

grain receding back into trees . . . to seedlings . . . to seeds
. . . to trees. Every artifact that met his vision extended into
past and future for him. Nothing remained static.

All was motion and he was a part of that motion.

Waves of sleep began creeping from the back of his
mind—higher . . . higher . . . higher.

Sleep enveloped him.

In the darkness of his sleep, something laughed and
laughed and laughed and laughed . . .

Dasein awoke with a feeling he'd been asleep for a long
time—perhaps a lifetime. A chuckle lifted from his throat.
He heard the noise coming from himself as from a stranger
and it frightened him. A glance at his wristwatch told him
he'd been asleep more than two hours.

Again, the stranger-chuckle teased his throat.

He pushed himself off the bed, wondering at his
weakness. His shoulder felt better, though, the pain dimin-
ishing to a dull ache.

A rap sounded on his door.

"Yes?" Dasein called.

"It's Win Burdeaux, sir. Miss Jenny asked me to remind
you she'll be here for you in about a half hour."

"Oh . . . thank you."

"That's all right, sir. Hope you had a nice nap."

Dasein stood staring at the door for a moment. *How did
Burdeaux know I was asleep?*

Perhaps I snored.

No further sound came from the hall, but Dasein knew
Burdeaux had gone away.

Thoughtful, Dasein stripped out of his wrinkled clothes,
showered and changed. He felt angry, frustrated. They
were watching him every minute. It would be so easy, he
knew, to let his anger become rage. This was no time for
rage, though.

He wondered then if there was a season for rage.

A sensation of wetness drew his attention to his right
hand. He was surprised to find himself still holding a
washrag. Innocent thing with a green and white braided
edge. He threw it into the bathroom where it landed with a
wet slap.

113

Another rap sounded on his door and he knew it was Jenny.

Decision gripped Dasein.

He strode across the room, threw open the door. She stood there in an orange jumper dress with white blouse, a smile deepening the dimple on her left cheek.

"I'm glad you're ready," she said. "Hurry up or we'll be late."

As he allowed her to lead him out and down the stairs, Dasein wondered if imagination had played a trick on him, or had there been a brief moment of worry before she smiled?

Jenny carried on a continuing babble of unanswerable conversation as they went down the stairs, through the lobby onto the porch.

"You'll love the lake this time of year. I wish I could spend more time there. You're not favoring your shoulder as much as you did. I'll bet it's better. Uncle Larry wants you to stop by later for him to check you. All the gang are anxious to meet you. Here they are now."

The gang occupied a stake truck.

Dasein recognized Willa Burdeaux's pixie face in the cab. She sat beside a blonde, rather craggy-faced youth with large innocent blue eyes. As he looked at her, she winked slowly, deliberately. At least a dozen couples stood in the back of the truck . . . and there were odd singles: a tall, brown-haired man with fierce dark eyes—Walter Somebody; Dasein failed to catch the last name . . . a set of twin young women, plump with long sandy hair, round faces—Rachel and Mariella.

Jenny performed the introductions too fast for Dasein to catch all the names, but he did focus on the fact that the young man with Willa Burdeaux was her fiancé, Cal Nis.

Reaching hands helped him into the back of the truck, pulled Jenny up beside him. There were boxes around the edges for seats. Dasein found himself crowded onto a box with Jenny snuggled beside him. He began to absorb the carnival air of the people around him—uninhibited laughter, bantering private jokes.

The truck rumbled into motion. Wind whipped them.

114

Dasein had an impression of passing trees, patches of sky, lurching movement . . . and the omnipresent laughter.

It grew on him that he and Jenny were being excluded from the laughter.

Was it a sense of delicacy in the group? Were they allowing the stranger time to acclimate himself?

He tried to see the situation as a psychologist, but his own involvement kept intruding. There was no way to focus his analytical eye on details without finding his own shadow across the scene. To cap it, his injured shoulder began to ache where Jenny pressed against it. Jenny's wind-tossed hair brushed his face. Each lurch of the truck sent a twinge through his shoulder.

The situation began to take on a nightmare quality.

Jenny stretched up, spoke into his ear: "Oh, Gil—I've dreamed of this day . . . when you'd be here, one of us."

One of us, Dasein thought. *Am I really one of them?*

Walter Somebody obviously had mistaken Jenny's move toward Dasein's ear. He waved and shouted from across the truck: "Hey! No smooching before dark!"

This brought a short burst of laughter from the group, but no general shift in their attention. They continued to look and speak around Dasein and Jenny.

Smooching.

The word sent Dasein's mind into high gear. It was a word no longer in common use *outside,* a word out of its time and place. On this Walter's lips, though, it had carried the inflection of familiarity. It was a word they used here in the valley.

Dasein began to see Santaroga in a new light. They were conservatives here in the true sense of the word. They were clinging to the past, resisting change. He modified this thought: They resisted *some* change. They were people who had made a judgment that some things from the past should be maintained. This was what made them foreign. The world *outside* was moving away from them. The valley had become a preserve for conditions of another time.

The truck turned off onto another track through an avenue of overhanging sycamores. Great patches of maple-shaped leaves cast a green-gold aura over their world.

115

A jolting bump made Dasein wince with pain as Jenny lurched against his shoulder.

The truck emerged from the sycamores, passed through a stand of bull pine onto a grassy flat that merged into beach sand edging a cerulean lake.

Dasein stared out the open rear of the truck, hardly aware of the cascade of people leaping down to the grass, ignoring Jenny's urgings that they leave. Something about this lake—some sense of familiarity—had struck him with a feeling of beauty and menace.

A narrow floating walkway reached out from the beach to a float and diving platform—the wood all dark silver-gray from the sun. There were rowboats tied along one side of the diving float.

Beauty and menace.

The sensation passed and he wondered at himself. He was seeing phantoms, focusing too much inward.

"Is it your shoulder?" Jenny asked.

"It'll be all right," Dasein said.

He followed her down off the truck, wishing he could let himself go, become a laughing part of this group. They were having fun here—carrying boxes to tables set under the trees, preparing fires in rock pits. Some wandered off into the trees, returned in bathing suits.

Jenny had attached herself to a group laying out picnic lunches on the tables. Presently, she joined the scampering movement toward the water, shedding her dress to reveal an orange one-piece bathing suit beneath. She was a naiad, limbs flashing brown and lithe in the sun.

She waved to him from the float, shouted: "See you in a minute, darling!"

Dasein watched her dive into the lake with a feeling she was suddenly lost to him. He experienced an intense jealousy, imagining himself a decrepit old man surrounded by playing children, unable to join them in their happiness.

He looked around at lake and verging woods. There was a breeze across the water. The breeze had summer in it, fragrant with grass and evergreen needles. He wished suddenly for some drink with which to salute this breeze and day, some potion that would make him a part of the scene.

116

Slowly, Dasein walked down to the floating walk and out onto the boards. There were fleece clouds in the sky, and as he stared down at the water, he saw those clouds floating on the lake bottom. Waves shattered the illusion. Jenny swam up, leaned her elbows on the boards. Her face all dripping water, smiling, had never seemed more lovely.

"Darling, why don't you come out to the float and sun yourself while we swim?" she asked.

"All right," he said. "Maybe I can scull around in one of those boats."

"You go easy on that shoulder or I'll tell Uncle Larry," she said. She kicked away from the walk, swam lazily out toward the float.

Dasein followed, making his way through dripping swimmers running up and down the walk. It struck him as odd how this crowd saw him but didn't see him. They made way for him, but never looked at him. They shouted across him, but not to him.

He moved to the first boat in the line, untied its painter and prepared to get into it. Jenny was swimming some fifty feet out, a slow, smooth crawl that took her diagonally away from the float.

Dasein stood up, moved to step into the boat. As he stepped, something pushed him in the middle of the back. His foot kicked the gunwale, thrusting the boat out into the water. He saw he was going to fall into the lake, thought: *Oh, damn! I'll get my clothes all wet.* The stern of the boat was turning toward *him* and he thought of trying to reach for it, but his left foot on the dock slipped in a patch of wet wood. Dasein found himself turning sideways without any control over his motion.

The edge of the boat, seen out of the corner of an eye, rushed toward him. He tried to reach up, but that was the side of his bad shoulder. His arm wouldn't move fast enough.

There was an explosion of blackness in his head. Dasein felt himself sinking into an enveloping cold, soundless, all dark and inviting.

A part of his mind screamed: *Beauty! Menace!*

He thought that an odd combination.

There was a distant ache in his lungs and it was cold
—terrifyingly cold. He felt pressure . . . and the cold . . .
all distant and unimportant.

I'm drowning, he thought.

It was an unexciting thought—something that concerned
another person.

They won't see me . . . and I'll drown.

The cold grew more immediate—wet.

Something turned him violently.

Still, everything remained remote—all happening to that
other being which he knew to be himself, but which could
not concern him.

Jenny's voice broke on him like a thunderclap: "Help
me! Please! Someone help me! Oh, God! Won't someone
help me? I love him! Please help me!"

He grew aware suddenly of other hands, other voices.

"All right, Jen. We've got him."

"Please save him!" Her voice carried a sobbing intensity.

Dasein felt himself draped across something hard that
pressed into his abdomen. Warmth gushed from his mouth.
There was a blinding, terrible pain in his chest.

Abruptly, he began to cough—gasping, the pain tearing
at his throat and bronchia.

"He swallowed a lot of water." It was a man's voice, almost vacant of emotion.

Jenny's voice came pleading beside Dasein's ear: "Is he
breathing? Please don't let anything happen to him." Dasein felt wetness on his neck, and still Jenny's voice pleading there beside him: "I love him. Please save him."

That same unemotional male voice answered: "We understand, Jenny."

And another voice, husky, feminine: "There's only one
thing to do, of course."

"We're doing it!" Jenny screamed. "Don't you understand?"

Even as hands picked Dasein up, began carrying him,
Dasein wondered: *Doing what?*

His coughing had subsided, but the pain in his chest remained. It hurt when he breathed.

118

Presently, there was grass under his back. Something warm and confining was wrapped around him. It was an oddly womblike sensation.

Dasein opened his eyes, found himself staring up at Jenny, her dark hair framed by blue sky. She managed a trembling smile.

"Oh, thank God," she whispered.

Hands lifted his shoulders. Jenny's face went away. A cup full of steaming brown liquid was pressed against his lips. Dasein experienced the almost overpowering smell of Jaspers, felt hot coffee burn down his throat.

Immediately, a sense of warmth and well-being began to seep outward through his body. The cup was pulled away. returned when he moved his mouth toward it.

Someone laughed, said something that Dasein couldn't quite catch. It sounded like, "Take a full load." But that didn't make sense and he rejected it.

The hands eased him gently back to the grass. That vacant masculine voice said: "Keep him warm and quiet for awhile. He's okay."

Jenny's face returned. Her hand stroked his head.

"Oh, darling," she said. "I looked at the dock and you were gone. I didn't see you fall, but I knew. And no one was paying any attention. It took me so long to get there. Oh, your poor head. Such a bruise."

Dasein felt the throbbing then as though her words had turned it on—a pulsing ache at the temple and across his ear. *A blow like that—shouldn't I have X-rays?* he wondered. *How do they know I haven't a fractured skull . . . or concussion?*

"Cal says the boat must've been tipping away from you as you hit it," Jenny said. "I don't think you've broken anything."

Pain shot through him as she touched the bruise.

"It's just a bad bruise."

Just a bad bruise! he thought. He was filled with abrupt anger at her. How could they be so casual?

Still, that feeling of warmth spread out through him, and he thought: *Of course I'm all right. I'm young, healthy. I'll heal. And I have Jenny to protect me. She loves me.*

119

Something about this train of thought struck him as profoundly wrong then. He blinked. As though that were the creative mechanism, his vision blurred, resolved into flashes of gemlike light, red, orange, yellow, brown, green, violet, blue light with offshooting crystal shards.

The light resolved into a membranous inward sensation, a perception of perception that reached out through his mind. He *saw* then strong pulses of his own heart, the tender brain sheathing that rose and fell with the pulse, the damaged area—just a bruise, skull intact.

Dasein grew aware then why the Santarogans showed so little concern for his injury. They *knew* the injury through him. If he were like them, he would tell them when he needed help.

Then why didn't they try to rescue me until Jenny came? Dasein asked himself. And the answer lay there to wonder at: *Because I didn't cry out for help in my thoughts!*

"You shouldn't sleep now, I don't think," Jenny said.

She found his left hand, gripped it. "Isn't there something about not sleeping after a head injury?"

Dasein stared up at her, seeing the dark wings of her hair disarrayed from rescuing him, the way her eyes seemed to touch him, so intense was her concentration. There was dampness on her lashes and he felt that he might look behind her eyes and find the way to a magic land.

"I love you," he whispered.

She pressed a finger against his lips. "I know."

I am a Santarogan now, Dasein thought.

He lay there rolling the thought in his mind, filled by this odd awareness that let him reach out to Jenny even when she released his hand and left him alone there on the grass. There was nothing of telepathy in this awareness. It was more knowledge of mood in those around him. It was a lake in which they all swam. When one disturbed the water, the others knew it.

My God! What this Jaspers could do for the world! Dasein thought.

But this thought sent roiling waves through the lake of mutual awareness. There was storm in this thought. It was dangerous. Dasein recoiled from it.

120

He remembered then why he had come here and saw the conflict from a new perspective. The people who'd sent him—what did they want?

Proof, he thought.

He found he couldn't focus on what *they* wanted to prove. It was all tied up with Jersey Hofstedder's car and the blunt Yankee insularity of these people.

Jenny's friends were noticing him now, Dasein saw. They looked at him—directly at him. They spoke to him. And when he felt he wanted to get up and go to the big fire they'd built against the evening chill, strong hands came without bidding and helped him.

Night fell.

Dasein found himself seated on a blanket beside Jenny. Someone was playing a guitar in the darkness. Moon colored half the lake, leaving a great black stone of night against one side. Wind-wrinkled water lapped at the stone and he felt that if the blackness could only be moved it would blaze in light to reveal fairyland.

Jenny snuggled against him, murmured: "You're feeling better. I know it."

He agreed with her silently.

Torches flamed down by the lake—people securing the boats. Someone handed him a sandwich redolent with Jaspers. He ate, his attention on the torches and the fire— the trees around them gleaming red, grotesque shadows lurching, dove wings of smoke against the moon. Abruptly, Dasein secreted part of his sandwich in a pocket.

For no reason he could explain, Dasein remembered a time shortly after Jenny had left the school. It had rained. He remembered reaching out his window to feel the rain, seeing the wet sparkle of the lawn beneath a window, like a broken necklace scattered there.

Abruptly, the wind across the lake shifted, stung his eyes with smoke. He swallowed a mouthful of the smoke and it brought him to an intense awareness of the here and now, Jenny beside him . . . waiting.

As he thought about her, she reached up, pulled his lips down on hers. It was a long kiss, full of guitar music, remembered rain and the taste of smoke.

121

How can I ever explain this? Dasein wondered. *Selador would think me mad.*

Jenny stirred against him at this thought, stroked his neck.

"Let's get married soon," she whispered.

Why not? Dasein asked himself. *I'm a Santarogan now.*

But this thought brought a surge of fear that tightened his chest and made Jenny shiver. She pulled away, stared at him with worry in her eyes.

"Everything will be all right," she whispered. "You'll see."

The worry remained in her voice, though. And Dasein sensed menace in the night. The guitarist struck a sour note, fell silent.

Dasein saw that moonlight had moved into the black area of the lake . . . and it revealed no fairyland—only more lake, more trees.

The night was definitely cold now.

Once more, Jenny pressed her lips to his.

Dasein knew he still loved her. It was a real thing to which he could cling. But there was no more magic in this night. He felt that he had skirted madness and the thing had left its taint on him.

When she pulled away, he whispered: "I want to marry you, Jenny. I love you . . . but . . . I need time. I need . . ."

"I know, darling," she said. She stroked his cheek. "Take all the time you need."

Her voice carried a withdrawing note compounded as she pulled back. Dasein felt the night's coldness then, the stillness of their companions.

Abruptly, there was a stirring in the people around them. They began moving toward the truck.

"It's time to go back," Jenny said.

Back where? Dasein asked himself.

Jenny stood up, helped him to his feet. He stumbled in a brief spasm of dizziness. Jenny steadied him.

"Do you want Uncle Larry to look at your head tonight?" she asked.

Piaget, Dasein thought. That was the *back* at which he

was aimed. Piaget. They would continue their trade of truths. The Jaspers change was forcing it.

"I'll see him in the morning," Dasein said.

"Not tonight?"

In my own sweet time, Dasien thought. And he said: "Not tonight."

The answer seemed to trouble Jenny. She sat barely touching him on the ride back to town.

6

When they were gone, leaving Dasein standing alone
behind his truck in the Inn yard, he stared up at the darkness of the sky, lost in thought. Jenny's good-night
kiss—strained, trembling—still tingled on his lips. There
was a smell of exhaust gases and oil in the air. From
somewhere inside the building came the faint sound of
music—a radio. The gravel of the driveway felt hard and
immediate under his feet.

Slowly, Dasein brought his right hand from his pocket,
opened it to stare at the small ball of matter there—an object indistinctly seen in the light from the Inn sign. Now,
there was a strong smell of Jaspers around him.

Dasein studied the object in his hand—a compressed
ball of bread, cheese and ham, a bit of one of the sand-
wiches from the picnic.

Did they know I secreted this? he wondered.

He debated going inside and changing his clothes. The
pants and shirt he'd worn on the picnic, garments that had
been soaked and allowed to dry on him, felt wrinkled and
twisted against his body.

Dasein felt that his mind wandered around this decision:
to change or not to change, that was the question. The object in his hand was more immediate, though. Selador. Yes,
Selador had to get this and examine it.

I'm not thinking clearly, Dasein told himself.

He felt torn between extremes, between decisions of
enormous moment. *The head injury?* he wondered. But he
trusted the Jaspers-induced insight that told him the injury
wasn't serious. Still . . . decisions . . .   .

With intense concentration, Dasein forced himself to get into his truck. He leaned against the steering wheel, put the compressed ball of the Jaspers sandwich on the seat beside him. There was warm wetness at his seat and he pulled his wallet from his hip pocket, felt the water trapped in it. The wallet went beside the bit of sandwich.

Now, Dasein told himself. *Now, I will go.*

But it was several minutes before he could muster the strength of decision to start the motor and pull out of the parking area and onto the road toward Porterville. He drove slowly, conscious of the blocking dullness inhibiting his motions.

The headlights picked out a wedge of flowing roadway and bordering trees—yellow center line, guard rails, driveways. Dasein opened his window, leaned out into the wind trying to clear his head. Now, he was on the winding road up out of the valley and the slowness of his mind grew like a deadly weight.

Headlights came toward him, passed.

Dark mass of rock beside the road—yellow center lines, twisting scars of repair lines on the paving . . . stars overhead . . . He came at last to the notch that led out through the black skeletons of burned trees.

Dasein felt something was drawing him back, ordering him to turn around and return to Santaroga. He fought it. Selador had to get that bit of food and analyze it. Duty. Promises. Had to get out to Porterville.

Somewhere in his mind, Dasein sensed a looming black shape, anonymous, terrifying. It studied him.

With an inner snapping sensation, Dasein felt his mind clear. The thing was so abrupt he almost lost control of the wheel, swerved across the center line and back, tires squealing.

The road, the night, the steering wheel, his foot on the accelerator—all slammed against his senses with a confused immediacy. Dasein hit the brakes, slowed almost to a crawl. Every nerve end yammered at him. His head whirled. Dasein clung to the wheel, concentrated on steering. Slowly, his senses sorted themselves out. He took a deep, trembling breath.

125

Drug reaction, he told himself. *Have to tell Selador.*

Porterville was the same dull street he had remembered—cars parked at the tavern, the single light beating down on the darkened gas station.

Dasein pulled to a stop beside the telephone booth, remembering the deputies who'd questioned him there, mistaking him for a Santarogan. Had they been premature? he wondered.

He gave the operator Selador's number, waited impatiently, tapping his finger against the wall. A faint and reedy woman's voice came on the line—"Selador residence."

Dasein leaned into the phone. "This is Gilbert Dasein. Let me speak to Dr. Selador."

"I'm sorry. The Seladors are out for the evening. Is there a message?"

"Damn!" Dasein stared at the phone. He felt an irrational anger at Selador. It took a conscious effort of logic for Dasein to tell himself Selador had no real reason to hang around the telephone. Life went on its normal way back in Berkeley.

"Is there a message, sir?" the reedy voice repeated.

"Tell him Gilbert Dasein called," Dasein said. "Tell him I'm sending him a package for chemical analysis."

"A package for chemical analysis. Yes sir. Is that all?"

"That's all."

Dasein replaced the receiver on its hook with a feeling of reluctance. He felt abandoned suddenly—alone up here with no one outside really caring whether he lived or died.

Why not chuck them all? he asked himself. *Why not marry Jenny, tell the rest of the world to go to hell?*

It was an intensely inviting prospect. He could feel himself sinking into quiet security back in the valley. Santaroga beckoned to him with that security. It was *safe* there.

That very sense of safety, though, was edged with danger. Dasein sensed it . . . a lurking something in the outer darkness. He shook his head, annoyed at the tricks his mind was playing. The *vapors,* again!

He returned to the truck, found a jar in the back where he'd kept a store of matches. He dumped out the matches, put in the remains of the sandwich, sealed the jar, packaged it with the remnants of a cardboard grocery box and a scrap of wrapping paper, tied the whole thing with a length of fishline and addressed it to Selador. When it was done, he wrote a covering letter on a page from his notebook, listed his reactions there painstakingly—the drug effect, the *accident* at the lake and his own impressions of the group . . . the wall they threw up to keep him at a distance . . . Jenny's terror . . .

It all went into the letter.

The effort of recalling the incidents made his head ache where he'd hit the edge of the boat. He found an envelope in his case, addressed the letter and sealed it.

With a sense of satisfaction, Dasein started up the truck, found a dark side street and parked. He locked the cab, climbed into the back and lay down to wait for morning when the Porterville post office would open.

They won't control the mail over here, he told himself. *Let Selador get the sample of Jaspers . . . we'll soon know what it is.*

He closed his eyes and his lids became like a movie screen for a fantasy—Jenny cringing, crying out, pleading with him. Selador laughing. A gigantic Dasein figure stood bound like Prometheus, the eyes glazed . . . panting with exertion . . .

Dasein's eyes popped open.

Waking fantasy!

He was over the hill—around the bend!

Hesitantly, he closed his eyes. Only darkness . . . but there was sound in this darkness—Selador laughing.

Dasein pressed his hands over his ears. The sound changed to tolling bells, slow cadence . . . mournful. He opened his eyes. The sound stopped.

He sat up, pushed himself back into a corner, eyes open. It was cold in the camper and there was a musty smell. He found his sleeping bag, wrapped it around him, sat there with his eyes open. There were cricket sounds outside, faint creakings in the truck's metal.

Slowly, sleep crept up on him. His eyelids drooped, popped open.

127

How long would it take for the Jaspers effect to wear off? he wondered. Surely, this was drug effect.

His eyes closed.

Somewhere in an echoing box, Jenny whispered: "Oh, Gil—I love you. Gil, I love you . . . "

He went to sleep with her voice whispering to him.

7

Daylight found Dasein staring up at the camper's metal
ceiling with a sense of disorientation. He recognized the
ceiling, but couldn't locate it in space. His head and shoulder throbbed. Ceiling . . . familiar ceiling.

A car horn honked. It brought him to the present and
awareness. He threw off the twisted folds of his sleeping
bag, climbed out into a gray, overcast day. His chin felt
rough and stubbly. There was a sour taste in his mouth.

Two passing schoolboys stared at him, whispering.

I must look a sight, Dasein thought. He looked down at
his clothes. They were twisted and wrinkled as though he
had gone swimming in them and then slept in them until
they dried. Dasein smiled to himself, thinking that was ex-
actly what had happened.

He climbed into the cab, turned around and found the
main street, drove down it until he saw the Post Office sign
over the porch of a general store.

The postmaster had to finish selling candy to a girl
before he could come around behind his caged counter to
weigh Dasein's package and letter. The man was tall, pale
with thinning black hair, darting, wary blue eyes. He
sniffed once at Dasein, said: "That'll be eighty-four for the
package and five for the letter."

Dasein pushed a dollar bill under the cage.

The man made change, looked once more at the
package. "What's in the package, mister?"

"Specimens for analysis at our laboratory," Dasein said.

"Oh."

The man didn't appear curious about specimens of what. "Any return address?" he asked.

"Dr. Gilbert Dasein, general delivery, Santaroga," he said.

"Dasein," the man said with sudden interest. "Dasein ... seems I got a package for a Dasein. Just a minute."

He disappeared into the back, returned in a moment with a box about a foot square wrapped neatly and tied with heavy twine. Even from a distance, Dasein recognized Selador's precise script on the address.

Selador writing me here? Dasein wondered.

The air of conspiracy in this gave Dasein the abrupt sensation of being completely transparent to Selador. The man could send a package here and *know* it would be picked up. Immediately, Dasein told himself this was the simplest thing to figure—given the Santaroga Post Office situation as he'd described it to Selador.

There remained, though, the feeling he was a pawn and his every move was known to the masters of the game.

"Let's see your identification," the postmaster said.

Dasein showed it.

"Sign here," the man said.

Dasein signed, took the package. It felt heavy.

"Funny thing you Santarogans using my Post Office," the postmaster said. "Something wrong with your own?"

Santarogans ... plural, Dasein thought. He said: "Is some other ... Santarogan using your Post Office?"

"Well—used to be," the man said. "Negro fellow over there ... Burdeaux, as I recollect. He used to send some mail from here. Got a package here once from Louisiana. Long time ago that was."

"Oh, yes," Dasein said, not knowing how else to acknowledge this information.

"Haven't seen Burdeaux in quite a spell," the postmaster mused. "Nice fellow. Hope he's all right."

"Quite all right," Dasein said. "Well—thank you." He took his package, went out to the truck.

With a feeling of caution he couldn't explain, Dasein left

the package unopened on the seat beside him while he drove east on the road to Santaroga until he found a shady spot in which to pull off.

The box contained a .32 caliber automatic pistol with an extra clip and box of cartridges. Wired to the trigger guard was a note from Selador: "Gilbert—This has been gathering dust in my bureau drawer for many years and I'm probably an old woman for sending it to you, but here it is. I think I'm sending it in the hope you won't have to use it. The situation you describe, however, has filled me with the oddest sensations of disquiet that I can remember. I hope you're being extremely cautious."

On the reverse side of the note was a scrawled postscript: "No news yet on the investigations you requested. These things move slowly. You give me hope, though, that we'll get the goods on these people." It was signed: "S."

Dasein hefted the automatic, fought down an impulse to heave it out the window. The thing embodied ultimate menace. What had he said to prompt Selador to send it? Or was this part of some obscure motivational gambit Selador was setting up?

Could it be a reminder of duty? His bruised head ached with thought.

A line in Selador's note came back to him and he reread it: " . . . get the goods on these people."

Is that what I'm supposed to do? Dasein wondered. *Am I to set them up for prosecution?*

He remembered Marden alluding to the reasons an investigator had been sent.

Dasein swallowed. Selador's line, read once more, looked like a slip. Had the good doctor tipped his hand? Sending a gun wasn't like the man. In fact, Dasein realized if he'd been asked, he would've said Selador wasn't even the type to *own* a gun.

What to do with the damn' thing now that he had it?

Dasein checked it, found the clip full, no cartridge in the chamber. He resisted the impulse to shove it in the glove compartment and forget it. If the truck were searched . . . .

131

Damn Selador!

Feeling foolish as he did it, Dasein slipped the gun into a hip pocket, pulled his coat over it. He'd settle with Selador later. Right now there was Piaget . . . and Piaget had some answers to give.

8

Piaget was in his office with a patient when Dasein arrived. The gaunt, gray Sarah opened the door, allowed he could wait in the living room. With a grudging show of hospitality, she added that she would bring him some coffee if he wanted it.

With a stomach-gripping pang, Dasein realized he was ravenous with hunger. He wondered if he could mention this fact.

As though she'd read his mind, Sarah said. "I'll bet you haven't eaten breakfast." She looked him up and down. "You look like you'd slept in those clothes. You doctors are all alike. Never care how you look."

"As a matter of fact, I haven't eaten," Dasein said.

"You're going to lead Jenny some life," she said. But she softened her words with a smile.

Dasein stared in wonder at a double, whiteboned row of false teeth in the wrinkled face.

"Got a leftover apple roll and some Jaspers cream," Sarah said. "Bet you'd like that."

She turned away, went out through the dining room into a glistening white kitchen, which Dasein glimpsed once through a swinging door. The door went slap-slap behind her.

Dasein thought about that smile, recalled Jenny saying Sarah liked him. On impulse, he followed her into the kitchen.

"Bet you don't like feeding people in the living room," he said.

"Feed people wherever they have to be fed," she said.

133

She put a dish on an oval table beside windows looking onto a flower garden brilliant in the morning sun. "Sit here, young man," she said. She poured a thick flow of cream from a pitcher onto the golden mound of crust in the dish.

Dasein inhaled a strong smell of Jaspers. His hand trembled as he picked up the spoon Sarah placed within his reach. The trembling stopped at his first swallow of the food.

The pastry was sweet and soothing, rich with apples.

With a detached feeling of shock, Dasein watched his hand guide the spoon into the pastry for another bite, saw the food conveyed to his mouth, felt himself swallow it.

Soothing.

I'm addicted to the stuff, he thought.

"Something wrong?" Sarah asked.

"I . . ." He put down his spoon. "You've trapped me, haven't you?" he asked.

"What're you talking about?" Sarah asked.

"What's it . . ." He nodded toward the pastry. " . . . doing to me?"

"You feel strange?" Sarah asked. "Got a fluttery feeling behind your eyes?"

"I'm . . ." He shook his head. Her words sounded insane. *Fluttery feeling behind his eyes!*

"I'll bring Doctor Larry," Sarah said. She darted out a connecting door at the back of the kitchen and he saw her running along the covered walkway to the clinic.

Presently, she reappeared with Piaget in tow. The doctor's face wore a worried frown.

"What's this Sarah's telling me?" Piaget asked. He put a hand under Dasein's chin, stared into Dasein's eyes.

"What's she telling you what?" Dasein asked. The words sounded foolish as they spilled from his lips. He brushed Piaget's hand aside. The doctor's frown, the squinting eyes—he looked like an angry Buddha.

"You seem to be all right," Piaget said. "Any strange symptoms of . . ."

"You've trapped me," Dasein said. "That's what I told her. You've trapped me." He gestured at the plate in front of him. "With this."

134

"Ohhh," Piaget said.

"Is he just fighting it?" Sarah asked.

"Probably," Piaget said.

"Don't make sense," Sarah said.

"It happens," Piaget said.

"I know, but . . ."

"Will you two stop talking about me like I was a blob of something on a slide!" Dasein raged. He pushed away from the table, jumped to his feet. The motion sent his bowl of food sliding off the table with a crash.

"Now look what you've done!" Sarah said.

"I'm a human being," Dasein said, "not some sort of . . ."

"Easy, lad, easy," Piaget said.

Dasein whirled away, brushed past Piaget. He had to get away from this pair or be consumed by rage. Dasein's mind kept focusing on the weapon in his hip pocket.

Damn Selador!

"Here, now—wait a minute!" Piaget called.

Dasein paused in the kitchen door, turned to glare slit-eyed at Piaget.

"You can't leave like this," Piaget said.

"Don't try to stop me," Dasein growled. The gun felt large and cold against his hip.

Piaget fell silent—a stillness that Dasein imagined came up from the toes to stare out of measuring eyes. It was as though the man receded to become a figure seen through a reversed telescope—remote, secretive.

"Very well," Piaget said. His voice came from that far away.

Deliberately, Dasein turned, went out the door, through the living room—out of the house. He felt his feet hitting the concrete of the front walk, the grass parking strip. His truck's door handle was cold under his hand. He started the motor, wondering at his own sensations—dreamlike.

A street flowed past, receded—signposts . . . pavement crawling beneath his vision . . . the Inn. He parked facing the long porch, an old green car on his left, make indeterminate, unimportant.

As though awakening, Dasein found his right hand on

135

the Inn's front door—tugging, tugging. The door resisted. A sign on the center panel stared back at him.

"Closed."

Dasein peered at the sign. *Closed?*

"Your luggage is right there by the steps, Dr. Dasein."

The voice Dasein recognized immediately—the infuriating Al Marden: *Authority . . . Secrecy . . . Conspiracy.*

Dasein turned, feeling himself bundled into a tight ball of consciousness. There was Marden standing halfway down the porch: red-haired, the narrow face, the green eyes, the tight-lipped mouth drawn into a straight line that could have signified any emotion from anger to amusement.

"So you're turning me out," Dasein said.

"Hotel's closed," Marden said. "Health department."

"The Inn, the restaurant, too?" Dasein asked.

"All closed." It was a flat square of voice brooking no appeal.

"I can just go back where I came from, eh?" Dasein asked.

"Suit yourself."

"You have other hotels," Dasein said.

"Do we?"

"You must."

"Must we?"

Dasein stared at the patrol captain, experiencing the same sensation he'd had with Piaget. The man receded.

"You can leave or go back to Dr. Piaget's," Marden said. "He'll likely put you up." So far away, that voice.

"Back to Piaget's," Dasein said. "How'd you know I just came from there?"

Marden remained silent, eyes withdrawn . . . distant.

"You move fast around here," Dasein said.

"When we have to."

Back to Piaget's? Dasein asked himself. He smiled, husbanding his tight ball of consciousness. *No!* They hadn't thought of everything. They hadn't thought of *quite* everything.

Still smiling, Dasein scooped up his suitcase from beside

136

the steps, strode down to the truck, threw the bag into the cab, climbed behind the wheel.

"Best let people help you who know how," Marden called.

There was just a faint trace of worry in his voice now. It broadened Dasein's smile, stayed with him as a satisfying memory as he drove back toward the town.

In the rear-view mirror, Dasein saw the patrol car following him. They wouldn't let him park in town, Dasein knew, but he remembered the map posted on a window of Scheler's service station. The map had shown a state park on the road west—Sand Hills State Park.

Down the main street he drove, Marden's patrol car right behind. There was the giant service station directly ahead. Dasein saw the telephone kiosk beside the parking area, swerved in so suddenly that Marden went past, screeched to a stop, backed up. Dasein already was out of the truck and at the kiosk.

Marden stopped the patrol car on the street, waited, staring at Dasein. The patrol car's motor seemed to rumble disapprovingly. Dasein turned, looked back at the service station—such a strange normality to the activity there: cars pulling in, out . . . no one paying the slightest attention to Marden or to the object of his attention.

Dasein shrugged, went into the booth, closed the door.

He put a dime in the slot, dialed the operator, asked for the Cooperative's number.

"If you want Jenny, Dr. Dasein, she's already gone home." Dasein stared at the telephone mouthpiece in front of him, letting the import of that supercilious female voice sink home. Not only did they know who was calling, they knew what he wanted before he could say it!

Dasein stared out at Marden, attention focused on the green eyes, the cynical green eyes.

Anger boiled in Dasein. He put it down. Damn them! Yes, he wanted to talk to Jenny. He'd talk to her in spite of them.

"I don't have Dr. Piaget's number."

A distinctly audible sigh came over the line.

137

Dasein looked at the telephone directory chained to the kiosk wall, felt a wave of guilt, unreasonable, damning, instantly repressed. He heard the operator dialing, the ring.

Jenny's voice answered.

"Jenny!"

"Oh, hello, Gilbert."

Dasein experienced a cold sensation in his stomach. Her voice was so casual.

"You know they're trying to run me out of the valley, Jenny?" he asked.

Silence.

"Jenny?"

"I heard you." Still that casual . . . distance in her tone.

"Is that all you have to say?" His voice betrayed hurt anger.

"Gilbert . . ." There was a long pause, then: ". . . maybe it'd be . . . better . . . if you . . . just for a while, just for a while, went . . . well . . . outside."

He sensed strain beneath the casual tone now.

"Jenny, I'm driving out to the Sand Hills Park and live in my camper. They're not running me out."

"Gilbert, don't!"

"You . . . want me to leave?"

"I . . . Gilbert, please come back and talk to Uncle Larry."

"I talked to Uncle Larry."

"Please. For me."

"If you want to see me, come out to the park."

"I . . . don't dare."

"You don't dare?" He was outraged. What pressure had they applied to her?

"Please don't ask me to explain."

He hesitated, then: "Jenny, I'm setting up camp in the park. To make my point. I'll be back after I make my point."

"For the love of heaven, Gilbert—please be careful."

"Careful of what?"

"Just . . . careful."

Dasein felt the gun in his pocket, a heavy weight that brought his mind to bear on the nameless threats of this

138

valley. That was the thing—the threats were nameless. They lacked form. What use was a gun against a formless target?

"I'll be back, Jenny," he said. "I love you."

She began crying. He heard the sobs distinctly before she broke the connection.

His muscles stiff with anger, Dasein marched back to his truck, pulled it around the police car and headed out the east road, Marden right behind.

Let the son-of-a-bitch follow, Dasein told himself. He could feel the reckless inanity of his actions, but there remained a driving current underneath that told him he had to do this. This was asking for a showdown. That was the thing. A showdown. Perhaps a showdown was needed to provide answers.

He crossed the river on a concrete bridge, glimpsed rows of greenhouses off to the left through the trees. The road climbed up through the trees, emerged into scrub country—madrone and mesquite. It twisted down through the scrub and again the land changed. In the distance there were tree-covered heights, but in between stretched low mounds of hills topped by gnarled bushes, scattered weedy growths with bare gray dirt and pools of black water, miasmic water untouched by growing things, in the low spots.

A smell of sulfur, dank and suffocating, hung over the land.

With almost a sense of recognition, Dasein realized these must be the sand hills. A broken sign came into view on the right. It dangled from one post. Another post leaned at a crazy angle.

Sand Hills State Park. Public camp ground.

Twin ruts led off through the sand to the right toward a fenced area with a doorless outhouse at one end and crumbling stone fireplaces spaced around the edge.

Dasein turned into the ruts. The truck lurched and growled its way to the parking area. He stopped beside one of the stone fireplaces, stared around. The place was outrageously drab.

A sound of wheels and laboring car engine brought Da-

139

sein's attention to the left. Marden pulled the patrol car to a stop beside him, leaned across to the open window.

"What're you stopping here for, Dasein?" There was just a touch of petulance in Marden's tone.

"This is a state park isn't it?" Dasein asked. "Any law says I can't camp here?"

"Don't get smart with me, Dasein!"

"Unless you have a legal objection, I'm going to camp here," Dasein said.

"Here?" Marden gestured at the desolation of the place.

"I find it relatively friendly after Santaroga," Dasein said.

"What're you trying to prove, Dasein?"

Dasein answered him with a silent stare.

Marden pulled back into the patrol car. Dasein could see the man's knuckles white on the steering wheel. Presently, the patrol captain leaned back, glared up at Dasein. "Okay, mister. It's your funeral."

The patrol car leaped ahead, made a sand-spewing turn around the parking area, roared out to the highway and headed back toward town.

Dasein waited for the dust to settle before getting out. He climbed into the camper, checked his emergency larder—beans, powdered milk and powdered eggs, canned frankfurters, two bottles of ketchup, a can of syrup and a half empty box of prepared pancake mix . . . coffee, sugar . . . He sighed, sat down on the bunk.

The window opposite framed a view of the sand hills and the doorless outhouse. Dasein rubbed his forehead. There was an ache behind his eyes. The bruise on his head throbbed. The pitiless light beating down on the drab hills filled him with a sense of self-accusation.

For the first time since pointing his truck down into the valley, Dasein began to question his own actions. He felt there was an air of insanity around everything he had done. It was a mad pavane—Jenny . . . Marden . . . Burdeaux, Piaget, Willa, Scheler, Nis . . . It was mad, yet with its own kind of sense. His brushes with disaster became a part of the stately nonsense.

And there was Jersey Hofstedder's car—somehow the most significant thing of all.

He felt he had been down once more beneath the lake, rising now into a brutal honesty with himself. Jenny's *"We"* lost some of its terrors. That was the *We* of the cave and the Jaspers, the *We* that waited patiently for him to make his decision.

The decision was his, he saw. No matter what the substance out of that dim red cave did to the psyche, the decision was his. It had to be his decision or the mad pavane lost all meaning.

I'm still fighting it, he thought. *I'm still afraid I'll wind up "fluttery behind the eyes" and standing on a wrapping line at the Co-op.*

Restlessly, he climbed down out of the camper, stood on the sand absorbing the mid-afternoon heat. A single crow flew overhead so close he heard the rushing harp sound of wind through its plumage.

Dasein gazed after the bird thinking how strange to see only one crow. They were not a solitary bird. But here was this one—alone as he was alone.

What was I before that I cannot return to? he wondered. And he thought if he made the decision against Santaroga he'd be like that solitary crow, a creature without its own kind anywhere.

The problem, he knew, lay in a compulsion somewhere within him to make an honest report to those who'd hired him. The Jaspers clarity-of-being urged it. His own remembered sense of duty urged it. To do anything less would be a form of dishonesty, an erosion of selfdom. He felt a jealous possessiveness about this self. No smallest part of it was cheap enough to discard.

This self of his, old but newly seen, precious beyond anything he'd ever imagined, placed a terrifying burden on him, Dasein saw. He remembered the wildness of the Jaspers revelation, the gamut he'd run to come through to this peak.

The *had-I-but-known* quality of his immediate past settled on him then like a fog that chilled him in spite of the

141

afternoon's heat. Dasein shivered. How pleasant it would be, he thought, to have no decisions. How tempting to allow that restlessly stirring *something* within his consciousness lift up its ancient snake's head and devour the disturbing parts of his awareness.

His view of the valley's people took on an Olympian cast. They stood beside him for a moment in ghostly ranks, godlike, masters of the primitive.

Are they testing me? he wondered.

Then why would Jenny say she dared not come here to him?

And where are the children?

A coldly rational part of his mind weighed his thinking and found the balance uncertain. *How much of what's in my mind is the drug thinking?* he asked himself.

At the fulcrum of any decision, that was the essential question. Where could he find solid ground upon which to stand and say, "The things I'm to decide about are there ... and there ... and there ... ?"

No one could help him find this ground, he knew. It must be a lonely search. If he made an honest report to Meyer Davidson's crew, that would doom Santaroga. But to make a false report would be to plant a cancer within himself.

He had separated himself from Santaroga in a definite way, like a knife stroke, Dasein realized. The Jaspers package he'd sent for analysis to Selador loomed in his mind. The cutting off had begun there.

It had been a gesture, nothing more. Symbolic. Some part of him had known even as he mailed it that the package would arrive with whatever Jaspers it had contained completely dissipated. He'd been sending a gesture of defiance to the Santaroga part of himself, Dasein realized.

Had Burdeaux done that? he wondered. What packages had Burdeaux exchanged with Louisiana?

The package to Selador—it had been like a thrown rock that could not reach its mark. He remembered as a child throwing a rock at a cat too far away to hit. Gray cat. He remembered the sudden bird silence in his aunt's garden,

142

the gray cat slinking into view . . . the rock landing short.

Piaget was the gray cat.

The cat in the garden had looked up, momentarily surprised by the sound, weighed the situation, and returned to its hunting with an insulting disdain for distant boys with distant rocks.

What had Piaget done?

Dasein experienced a sudden *deitgrasp,* an act of self-discovery in which the sky appeared to shimmer. He realized in this instant why he felt so terrifyingly lonely.

He had no group, no place in a hive of fellow-activity, nothing to shield him from personal decisions that might overwhelm him. Whatever decision he made, no matter the consequences, that was *his* decision. Selador might face the shame of his agent's failure. The school might lose its munificent grant. The unique *thing* that was Santaroga might be dissipated.

All because of a decision, a gesture really, by a lone man standing in a patch of barren sand hills, his mind caught up in fantasies about a solitary crow and a gray cat.

It was a moment for positive action, and all he could think to do was re-enter the camper and eat.

As he moved in the confining space preparing himself a powered-egg mess in the frying pan, the truck emitted protesting creaks. Hunger gnawed at him, but he didn't want this food. He knew what he wanted—what he had fled here to escape, what his body craved until it was an ache at the core of him—

Jaspers.

9

At full dark, Dasein switched on the camper's wall light, retreated into his notes. He felt he had to keep his mind occupied, but the fetid smell of the campground intruded. The camper was a tiny world with sharp boundaries, but it couldn't hold off the universe out there. Dasein peered out a window at stars: bright holes punched in blackness. They amplified his sense of loneliness. He jerked his gaze away.

The notes . . .

Always the same items floated to the surface:

Where were the children?

What failure of the Jaspers change produced zombies?

How could a whole community be ignited with the unconscious desire to kill a person?

What was the Jaspers essence? What was it? What did it do to the body's chemistry?

Dasein sensed the danger in putting his hand to these questions. They were questions and at the same time an answer. This probing—this was what ignited the community.

He had to do it. Like a child poking at a sore, he had to do it. But once he had done it, could he turn then and tell the whole story to Meyer Davidson's crowd?

Even if he did find the answers and decided to make a full and honest report, would Santaroga permit it?

There were forces at work out there, Dasein realized, against which he was but a candle flickering in a gale.

He grew aware of footsteps crunching on the sand, turned off the light, opened the door and peered out.

A ghostly blur of a figure in the starlight, a woman in a

light dress or a small man in a coat, was approaching along the tracks from the highway.

"Who's there?" Dasein called.

"Gil!"

"Jenny!"

He jumped down, strode to meet her. "I thought you couldn't come out here. You told me . . . "

"Please don't come any closer," she said. She stopped about ten paces from him.

Such an oddly brittle quality to her voice—Dasein hesitated.

"Gil, if you won't come back to Uncle Larry's you must leave the valley," she said.

"You want me to leave?"

"You must."

"Why?"

"I . . . they want you to go."

"What have I done?"

"You're dangerous to us. We all know it. We can feel it. You're dangerous."

"Jen . . . do you think I'd hurt you?"

"I don't know! I just know you're dangerous."

"And you want me to leave?"

"I'm ordering you to leave."

"Ordering me?" He heard hysteria in her voice.

"Gil, please."

"I can't go, Jen. I can't."

"You must."

"I can't."

"Then come back to Uncle Larry's. We'll take care of you."

"Even if I turn into a zombie?"

"Don't say that!"

"It could happen, couldn't it?"

"Darling, we'll take care of you whatever happens!"

"You take care of your own."

"Of course we do."

"Jenny, do you know I love you?"

"I know," she whispered.

"Then why are you doing this to me?"

145

"We're not doing anything to you." She was crying, speaking through sobs. "It's you who're doing . . . whatever it is you're doing."

"I'm only doing what I have to do."

"You don't have to do anything."

"Would you have me be dishonest . . . lie?"

"Gil, I'm begging you. For my sake . . . for your own sake, leave."

"Or come back to Uncle Larry's?"

"Oh, please."

"What'll happen to me if I don't?"

"If you really love me . . . Oh, Gil, I couldn't stand it if . . . if . . . "

She broke off, crying too hard to speak.

He moved toward her. "Jen, don't."

The crying stopped abruptly and she began backing away, shaking her head at him. "Stay away from me!"

"Jenny, what's wrong with you?"

She retreated even faster.

"Jenny, stop it."

Suddenly, she whirled, began running down the track. He started to run after her, stopped. What was the use?

Her voice came back to him in a hysterical scream: "Stay away from me! I love you! Stay away!"

He stood in shocked silence until he heard a car door slam out there on the highway. Lights came on; a car raced back toward town.

He remembered the soft moon of her face in the starlight, two black holes for eyes. It had been like a mask. He trudged back to the camper, his mind in turmoil. "*I love you! Stay away!*"

What do I really know about Jenny? he asked himself.

Nothing . . . except that she loved him.

Stay away?

Could that have been Jenny demanding, begging, ordering?

This speared his mind with a touch of madness. It transcended the irrationality of people in love.

"*You're dangerous. We all know it.*"

Indeed, they must.

146

In the Jaspers oneness he'd experienced at the lake, they must know him for a danger. If he could stay away from the stuff, kick it—would they know him then?

How could they help but know him then? His action would be the ultimate betrayal.

He thought of Santaroga then as a deceptive curtain of calmness over a pool of violence. Olympian-like, they'd surmounted the primitive—yes. But the primitive was still there, more explosive because it could not be recognized and because it had been held down like a coiled spring.

Jenny must sense it, he thought. Her love for him would give her a touch of clarity.

"*Stay away from me!*"

Her cry still rang in his ears.

And this was how the other investigators had died —releasing the explosion that was Santaroga.

Voices intruded on Dasein's reverie. They came from the other side of the camper away from the road. One voice definitely was that of a woman. He couldn't be sure about the other two. Dasein stepped around the camper, stared off toward the dank pools and sand hills. It was a shadowed starlit landscape with a suggestion of a glow in it.

A flashlight came into view across the hills. It wavered and darted. There were three black, lurching figures associated with the light. Dasein thought of Macbeth's witches. They walked and slid down a hill, skirted a pool and came on toward the campground.

Dasein wondered if he should call out. Perhaps they were lost. Why else would three people be out here in the night?

There was a burst of laughter from the group, vaguely childlike. The woman's voice came clearly out of the dark then: "Oh, Petey! It's so good to have you with us."

Dasein cleared his throat, said: "Hello." Then, louder: "Hello!"

The light stabbed toward him. The lilting woman's voice said: "Someone's in the campground."

There was a masculine grunt.

"Who is it?" she asked.

"Just a camper," Dasein said. "Are you lost?"

147

"We've just been out frogging." It sounded very like the voice of a young boy.

The trio came on toward him.

"Pretty poor place to camp," the woman said.

Dasein studied the approaching figures. That was a boy on the left—definitely a boy. He appeared to be carrying a bow and a quiver of arrows. The woman had a long gigging pole, a bulky bag of some kind on one shoulder. The men carried the flashlight and a string of bullfrogs. They stopped beside the camper and the woman leaned against it to remove a shoe and pour sand from it.

"Been out to the pond," she said.

"Hunh!" the man grunted.

"We got eight of them," the boy said. "Mom's gonna fry 'em for breakfast."

"Petey had his heart set on it," the woman said. "I couldn't say no, not on his first day home."

"I passed," the boy said. "Pop didn't pass, but I did."

"I see," Dasein said. He studied the man in the light reflected off the aluminum side of the camper. He was a tall man, slim, rather gawky. Wisps of blonde hair protruded from a stocking cap. His eyes were as vacant as two pieces of blue glass.

The woman had put the shoe back on, now had the other one off emptying it. She was wrapped in a heavy coat that gave her the appearance of having been molded in a corrugated barrel. She was short, wouldn't stand any taller than the man's shoulder, but there was a purposeful air about her that reminded Dasein of Clara Scheler at the used-car lot.

"Bill's the first one in his family in eight generations didn't make it," she said, restoring the shoe and straightening. "They think it was something in his mother's diet before he was born. We were engaged before . . . Why'm I telling you all this? I don't think I know you."

"Dasein . . . Gilbert Dasein," he said. And he thought: *So this is how they take care of their own.*

"Jenny's fellow!" the woman said. "Well, now."

Dasein looked at the boy. *Petey.* He appeared to be no more than twelve, almost as tall as the woman. His face

148

when the flashlight beam brushed it was a carbon copy of the man's. No denying parenthood there.

"Turn the light over here, Bill," the woman said. She spoke carefully and distinctly as one might to a very young child. "Over here, hon."

"Over there, Pop." The boy directed the man's uncertain hand.

"That's it, love," the woman said. "I think I got the gigging hook caught in my coat." She fussed with a length of line at her side.

"Hunh," the man said.

Dasein stared at him with a cold feeling of horror. He could see himself there, Jenny "taking care" of him, their children helping.

"There," the woman said, pulling the line free and attaching it to the gigging pole. "Turn the light down toward the ground now, Bill. Toward the ground, hon."

"Down this way, Pop," the boy said, helping.

"That's a love," the woman said. She reached out, patted the man's cheek.

Dasein felt something obscene in the gesture, wanted to turn away, couldn't.

"He's real good, Bill is," the woman said.

The boy began playing with his bow, drawing it, releasing it.

"What you doing out here, Dr. Dasein?" the woman asked.

"I . . . wanted to be . . . alone for awhile." He forced himself to look at her.

"Well, this is a place to be alone all right," she said. "You feel all right? No . . . *flutters* . . . or anything?"

"Quite all right," Dasein said. He shuddered.

The boy had knocked an arrow into the bow, was waving it about.

"I'm Mabel Jorick," the woman said. "This is Bill, my husband; our son, Petey. Petey's been . . . you know, with Doc Piaget. Just got his bill of health."

"I passed," the boy said.

"Indeed you did, love." She looked at Dasein. "He's going outside to college next year."

"Isn't he kind of young?" Dasein asked.

"Fifteen," she said.

"Hunh," the man said.

The boy had drawn the bow to its full arc, Dasein saw. The arrow tip glittered in the light from the flash.

Up, down . . . right, left the arrow pointed.

Dasein moved uneasily as the tip traversed his chest—across, back. Sweat started on his forehead. He felt menace in the boy.

Instinctively, Dasein moved to put the man between himself and Petey, but Jorick moved back, stared off toward the highway.

"I think he hears the car," the woman said. "My brother, Jim, coming to pick us up." She shook her head wonderingly. "He has awful good hearing, Bill has."

Dasein felt a crisis rushing upon him, dropped to his hands and knees. As he fell, he heard the bow twang, felt the wind of an arrow brush the back of his neck, heard it slam into the side of the camper.

"Petey!" the woman shouted. She snatched the bow from him. "What're you doing?"

"It slipped, Ma."

Dasein climbed to his feet studying these people narrowly.

"Hunh," the man said.

The mother turned toward Dasein, the bow in her hand.

"He tried to kill me," Dasein whispered.

"It was just an accident!" the boy protested.

The man lifted the flashlight, a menacing gesture.

Without looking at him, the woman said: "Point it toward the ground, hon." She pushed the light down, stared at Dasein. "You don't think . . . "

"It was an accident," the boy said.

Dasein looked at the arrow. It had penetrated halfway through the camper's wall on a level with his chest. He tried to swallow in a dry throat. If he hadn't ducked at just that instant . . . An accident. A regrettable accident. The boy was playing with a bow and arrow. It slipped.

Death by misadventure.

150

What warned me? Dasein wondered.

He knew the answer. It lay there in his mind, clearly readable. He had come to recognize the Santaroga pattern of menace. The means might differ, but the pattern carried a sameness—something lethal in an apparently innocent context.

"It was just an accident," the woman whispered. "Petey wouldn't harm a fly."

She didn't believe it, Dasein saw.

And that was another thing. He was still connected by a tenuous thread to the Jaspers oneness. The warning message along that line was unmistakable. She'd received it, too.

"Wouldn't he?" Dasein asked. He looked once more at the arrow protruding from the camper.

The woman turned, grabbed her son's shoulder in one hand, shook the bow at him. "You want to go back?" she demanded. "Is that it?"

"Hunh," the man said. He shuffled his feet uneasily.

"It was an accident," the boy said. He obviously was near tears.

The woman turned a pleading look on Dasein. "You wouldn't say anything to Doctor Larry, would you?"

"Say anything?" Dasein stared at her stupidly.

"He might . . . you know, misunderstand."

Dasein shook his head. What was she talking about?

"It's so hard," the woman said. "After Bill, I mean. You know how it is over there." She gestured vaguely with her head. "The way they keep such a close watch on you, picking at every little symptom. It's so hard having a son there . . . knowing, seeing him only at visiting hours and . . . and never really being sure until . . . "

"I'm all right, Mom," the boy said.

"Of course you are, love." She kept her eyes on Dasein.

"I wouldn't deliberately hurt anyone," Petey said.

"Of course you wouldn't, love."

Dasein sighed.

"I passed," the boy said. "I'm not like Pop."

"Hunh," the man said.

Dasein felt like crying.

"You wouldn't say anything, would you?" the woman pleaded.

So Piaget had rewarding work for him here in the valley, Dasein thought. A clinic job . . . working with young people. And it was tied up with Jaspers, of course.

"Are they going to send me back?" Petey asked. There was fear in his voice.

"Dr. Dasein, please . . ." the woman begged.

"It was an accident," Dasein said. He knew it had not been an accident. The woman knew it. The arrow had been meant to kill. He said: "Perhaps you'd better take the bow and arrows away from him for awhile."

"Oh, don't you worry about that," she said. There was a deep sighing of relief in her tone.

A car pulled to a stop on the highway at the entrance to the campground.

"There's Jim now," the woman said. She turned away, her shoulder bag swinging toward Dasein. A rich aroma of Jaspers wafted across Dasein. It came from the bag.

Dasein stopped his right hand as it automatically reached toward the bag.

Mabel Jorick glanced back at him. "I want to thank you for being so understanding," she said. "If there's ever anything . . ." She broke off, noting Dasein's attention on the bag. "Bet you smelled the coffee," she said. "You want it?"

Dasein found himself unable to keep from nodding.

"Well, here." She swung the bag around in front of her. "Thermos is almost full. I just had one cup out at the pond. Spilled most of that. Petey, you run along, help your dad out to the car."

"All right, Mom. Good night, Dr. Dasein."

Dasein was unable to take his gaze from the woman's hands pulling a shiny metal thermos from the bag.

"Take the thermos," she said, holding it toward him. "You can return it when you come back to town. We're only half a block from the clinic on Salmon Way."

Dasein felt his fingers close around the corrugated sides of the thermos. He began trembling.

"You sure you're all right?" the woman asked.

152

"I'm . . . it's the aftereffect . . . shock, I guess," he said.

"Sure. I'm so sorry." She moved behind Dasein to the camper, broke off the protuding arrow. "I'm going to give this to Petey as a reminder of how careful he should be."

Dasein tore his attention away from the thermos, looked along the sand track. Petey and his father were almost halfway to the highway. The car's lights carved out a funnel of brilliance there. A horn honked once.

"If you're sure you're all right," the woman said. "I better be going." She looked at the camper, glanced once more at Dasein. "If there's ever anything we can do . . . "

"I'll . . . bring your thermos back as soon as I can," Dasein said.

"Oh, no hurry; no hurry at all." She pulled her coat tightly around her, trudged off toward the highway. About twenty paces away, she paused, turned. "That was real sweet of you, Dr. Dasein. I won't forget it."

Dasein watched until the car turned back toward town. Before the car was out of sight, he was in the camper, the lid off the thermos, pouring himself a steaming cup of the coffee.

His hands trembled as he lifted the cup.

All the time and matter had been reduced to this moment, this cup, this Jaspers rich steam enveloping him. He drained the cup.

It was a sensation of rays spreading out from a pinhead spot in his stomach. Dasein groped his way to his bunk, wrapped the sleeping bag around him. He felt supremely detached, a transitory being. His awareness moved within a framework of glowing nets.

There was terror here. He tried to recoil, but the nets held him. *Where is the self that once I was?* he thought. He tried to hold onto a *self* that bore some familiarity, one he could identify. The very idea of a self eluded him. It became an ear-shaped symbol he interpreted as mind-in-action.

For a flickering instant he felt he had encountered the solid ground, a core of relative truth from which he could make his decisions and justify all his experiences. His eyes flew open. In the faint starlight reflected into the camper he

153

saw something glittering on the wall, recognized the head of Petey's arrow.

There it was—the relative truth: an arrowhead. It had originated; it had ceased.

Everything with origin has cessation, he told himself.

He sensed the stirring in his consciousness then, the ancient *thing* abiding there, the mind eater. *Sleep,* Dasein told himself. There was an *atman* of sleep within him. It resisted awakening. It was infinite, circular. He lay spread on its rim.

Dasein slept.

10

Dawn light awakened him.

The coffee in the thermos was cold and had lost its
Jaspers savor. He sipped it anyway to ease the dryness in
his throat.

There will be a place like a school, he thought. *A board-
ing school . . . with visiting hours. It will have the Santaroga difference. It will be something besides a school.*

He stared at the thermos. It was empty. The bitter taste
of its contents remained on his tongue, a reminder of his
weakness in the night. The Jaspers had immersed him in
nightmares. He remembered dreaming of glass houses, a
shattering of glass that tumbled about him . . . screaming.

House of glass, he thought. *Greenhouses.*

The sound of an approaching car intruded. Dasein
stepped outside into chilly morning air. A green Chevrolet
was bumping up the track toward him. It looked familiar.
He decided the car either was Jersey Hofstedder's machine
or its double.

Then he saw the beefy, gray-haired woman driving the
car and he knew. It was Sam Scheler's mother—Clara, the
car dealer.

She pulled to a stop beside Dasein, slid across the seat
and got out his side.

"They told me you were here and by golly you are," she
said. She stood facing Dasein, a covered dish in her hands.

Dasein looked at the car. "Did you drive clear out here
to try to sell me that car again?" he asked.

"The car?" She looked around at the car as though it
had appeared there by some form of magic. "Oh, Jersey's

car. Plenty of time for that . . . later. I brought you some hair of the dog." She presented the dish.

Dasein hesitated. Why should she bring him anything?

"Petey's my grandson," she said. "Mabel, my daughter, told me how nice you were last night." She glanced at the stub of the arrow in the side of Dasein's camper, returned her attention to Dasein. "Occurred to me maybe your problem's you don't realize how much we want you to be one of us. So I brought you some of my sour cream stew—plenty of Jaspers."

She thrust the dish at him.

Dasein took it. Smooth, warm china under his hands. He fought down an unreasonable impulse to drop the dish and smash it. He was afraid suddenly. Perspiration made his palms slippery against the dish.

"Go on, eat it," she said. "It'll set you up for the day."

I must not do it, Dasein told himself.

But that was irrational. The woman was just being kind, thoughtful . . . Petey's grandmother. Thought of the boy brought the incident of the night flooding back into his mind.

School . . . observation . . . Jaspers . . .

A whuffling noise from the green Chevrolet distracted him. A gray-muzzled old black-and-white border collie eased itself over onto the front seat, climbed down to the sand. It moved with the patient pain of old age, sniffed at Clara's heels.

She reached down, patted the dog's head. "I brought Jimbo," she said. "He doesn't get out in the country much anymore. Dang nigh thirty-five years old and I think he's going blind." She straightened, nodded to the dish in Dasein's hands. "Go ahead, eat it."

But Dasein was fascinated by the dog. Thirty-five? That was equivalent to more than two hundred years in a human. He put the dish on the camper's steps, bent to stare at the dog. *Jimbo.* Going blind, she said, but its eyes carried that same disturbing *Jaspers* directness he saw in all the humans.

"You like dogs?" Clara Scheler asked.

Dasein nodded. "Is he really thirty-five?"

156

"Thirty-six in the spring . . . if he lasts."

Jimbo ambled across to Dasein, aimed the gray muzzle at his face, sniffed. Apparently satisfied, he curled up at the foot of the camper's steps, sighed, stared off across the sand hills.

"You going to eat or aren't you?" Clara asked.

"Later," Dasein said. He was remembering how Jersey Hofstedder's car had figured in his thoughts—a key to Santaroga. Was it the car? he wondered. Or was the car just a symbol? Which was the important thing—the car or the symbol?

Seeing his attention on the car, Clara said: "It's still priced at $650 if you want it."

"I'd like to drive it," Dasein said.

"Right now?"

"Why not?"

She glanced at the dish on the camper's step, said: "That stew won't heat very well . . . and the Jaspers fades, you know."

"I had your daughter's coffee last night," Dasein said.

"No . . . aftereffects?"

It was a practical question. Dasein found himself probing his own bodily sensations—head injury fading, shoulder pain almost gone . . . a bit of latent anger over Petcy's arrow, but nothing time wouldn't heal.

"I'm fine."

"Well! You're coming around," she said. "Jenny said you would. Okay." She gestured toward the green Chevrolet. "Let's take a spin up the highway and back. You drive." She climbed into the right-hand seat, closed the door.

The dog raised his head from his paws.

"You stay there, Jimbo," she said. "We'll be right back."

Dasein went around, climbed behind the wheel. The seat seemed to mould itself to his back.

"Comfortable, huh?" Clara asked.

Dasein nodded. He had an odd feeling of *déjà vu*, that he'd driven this car before. It felt right beneath his hands. The engine purred alive, settled into an almost noiseless motion. He backed the car around, eased it over the ruts and out the track to the highway, turned right away from town.

A touch on the throttle and the old Chevrolet leaped ahead—fifty . . . sixty . . . seventy. He eased back to sixty-five. It cornered like a sports car.

"Got torsion bars," Clara said. "Doesn't roll worth a sweet damn. Isn't she pretty?"

Dasein touched the brakes—no fading and the nose strayed not an inch. It was as though the car rode on tracks.

"This car's in better shape right now than the day it came off the assembly line," Clara said.

Dasein silently agreed with her. It was a pleasure to drive. He liked the leather smell of the interior. The hand-finished wood of the dash glistened with a dull luster. There was no distraction from it, just a tight cluster of instruments set up high to be read easily without taking his eyes too long from the road.

"Notice how he padded the dash on this side," Clara said. "Inch-and-a-half thick and a thin roll of metal underneath. He cut the steering wheel about a third of the way back, offset it on a U-joint. Hit anything with this car and you won't have that wheel sticking out your back. Jersey was making safe cars before Detroit even heard the word."

Dasein found a wide spot at a turn, pulled off, turned around and headed back to the campground. He knew he had to have this car. It was everything this woman said.

"Tell you what," Clara said. "I'll deliver the car over to the Doc's when I get back. We'll figure out the details later. You won't find me hard to deal with, though I can't give you much for that clunker of a truck."

"I . . . don't know how I can pay for it," Dasein said. "But . . ."

"Say no more. We'll figure out something."

The track into the campground came into view. Dasein slowed, turned off onto the ruts, shifted down to second.

"You really ought to use the seatbelt," Clara said. "I noticed you . . ." She broke off as Dasein stopped behind the camper. "Something's wrong with Jimbo!" she said, and she was out of the car and across to the dog.

Dasein turned off the ignition, jumped out and ran around to her side.

The dog lay almost over on its back, feet stretched out stiff, neck curved backward, its mouth open and tongue extended.

"He's dead," Clara said. "Jimbo's dead."

Dasein's attention went to the dish on the steps. Its cover had been pushed aside and the contents disturbed. There was a splash of gravy beside the lid. Again, he looked at the dog. The sand was scratched in a wide swirl around Jimbo.

Abruptly, Dasein bent to the dish of stew, sniffed it. Beneath the heavy odor of Jaspers there was a bitter aroma that curled his nostrils.

"Cyanide?" he asked. He stared accusingly at Clara Scheler.

She looked at the dish. "Cyanide?"

"You were trying to kill me!"

She picked up the dish, smelled it. Her face went pale. She turned, stared wide-eyed at Dasein.

"Oh, my God! The paint bleach," she said. She dropped the dish, whirled away, dashed to the car before Dasein could stop her. The Chevrolet leaped to life, turned in a whirl of sand and roared out the track to the highway. It made a skidding turn onto the highway, raced back toward town.

Dasein stared after her.

She tried to kill me, he thought. *Cyanide. Paint bleach.*

But he couldn't shake the memory of her pale, wide-eyed stare. She'd been surprised, as shocked as he was. *Paint bleach.* He stared down at the dead dog. Would she have left the dish there near her dog if she'd known it contained poison? Not likely. Then why had she run?

Paint bleach.

There was contaminated food at her house, Dasein realized. She was racing back to get it before it killed anyone.

I would've eaten the stew, Dasein thought.

An accident . . . another bloody accident.

He kicked the fallen dish aside, dragged the dog out of the way, got behind the wheel of his camper. The Ford's

159

engine was a dismal, throbbing mess after Jersey's car. He maneuvered it gently out to the highway, turned toward town.

Accident, he thought.

A pattern was emerging, but he found it difficult to accept. There was a Holmesian flavor to his thought—". . . *when you have eliminated the impossible, whatever remains, however improbable, must be the truth.*"

Jenny had screamed: "Stay away from me. I love you."

That was consistent. She did love him. Therefore, he had to stay away from her.

For the time being.

The road forked and he turned right, following the direction by a sign labeled: "Greenhouses."

There was a bridge over the river—an old-fashioned bridge that crowned in the middle . . . heavy planks rattling under the wheels. The river foamed and bunched itself over the shell-backs of smooth stones under the bridge.

Dasein slowed the truck at the far side, taken suddenly by a warning sense of caution which he had learned to trust.

The road followed the river's right bank. He paced the current, glanced upstream toward the bridge, found it hidden by a stand of willows.

It came over Dasein that there was something sliding and treacherous about the river. He thought of a liquid snake, venomous, full of evil energy. It contained a concentration of malevolence as it slipped down the rapids beside the road. And the sound—it laughed at him.

Dasein drew a sigh of relief when the road turned away from the river, wound over two low hills and down into a shallow valley. He glimpsed the glass through trees. It was an expanse of glistening green and covered a much larger area than he'd expected.

The road ended at a paved parking lot in front of a long stone building. More stone buildings—tile roofs, curtained windows—stepped in ranks up the hill beside the greenhouses.

A great many cars waited in the parking lot, a fact Dasein found curious—at least a hundred cars.

And there were people—men walking between the greenhouses, white-coated figures behind the glass, briskly striding women coming and going.

Dasein drove down the line of cars looking for a place to park. He found a slot beyond the end of the long stone building, pulled in to a stop and stared around.

Chanting.

Dasein turned toward the sound; it came from the ranks of buildings beyond the greenhouses. A troop of children came marching into view down a path between the buildings. They carried baskets. Three adults accompanied them. They counted a marching cadence. The troop wound out of sight down into the greenhouse level.

A tight feeling gripped Dasein's chest.

Footsteps sounded on his left. Dasein turned to find Piaget striding down the line of cars toward him. The doctor's bulky figure was accented by a long white smock. He was hatless, his hair wind mussed.

Piaget turned into the slot beside Dasein, stopped to stand looking in the truck's open window.

"Well," he said. "Jenny said there'd be an arriving."

Dasein shook his head. There was almost meaning in Piaget's words, but the sense eluded him. He wet his lips with his tongue. "What?"

Piaget scowled. "Jenny knows rapport. She said you'd probably show up here." His voice sounded suddenly full of effort.

An arriving, Dasein thought.

It was a label for an event, a statement withholding judgment. He studied Piaget's wide, bland face.

"I saw children," Dasein said.

"What did you expect?"

Dasein shrugged. "Are you going to run me off?"

"Al Marden says the ones that run get the fever," Piaget said. "The ones that watch get the benefit."

"Count me among the watchers," Dasein said.

Piaget grinned, opened the truck door. "Come."

Dasein remembered the river, hesitated. He thought of the torn carpet in the Inn's hallway, the open gas jet, the lake, the arrow . . . the paint bleach. He thought of Jenny

161

running away from him— *"Stay away from me! I love you."*

"Come along," Piaget said.

Still hesitating, Dasein said: "Why're the children kept here?"

"We must push back at the surface of childhood," Piaget said. "It's a brutal, animate thing. But there's food growing." He gestured at the expanse of greenhouses. "There's educating. There's useful energy. Waste not; want not."

Again, Dasein shook his head. *Almost-meaning.*

Push back at the surface of childhood?

It was like schizophrenic talk and he recalled the incident in the Blue Ewe, the haunting conversation of the young couple.

How could one hear a sunset?

"You . . . you're not speaking English," Dasein complained.

"I'm speaking," Piaget said.

"But . . . "

"Jenny says you'll be an understander." Piaget scratched his cheek, a pensive look on his face. "You have the training, Dasein." Again, his voice took on that leaden effort. "Where's your *Weltanschauung?* You do have a world view? The whole is greater than the sum of its parts. What is it?"

Piaget's arm swept out to include the greenhouse complex and the entire valley, the world and the universe beyond.

Dasein's mouth felt dry. The man was insane.

"You contain the Jaspers experience," Piaget said. "Digest it. Jenny says you can do it. Reality shoots through her words."

The tight sensation was a pain in Dasein's chest. Thoughts tumbled through his mind without order or sense.

In a heavy voice, Piaget said: "For approximately one in five hundred, the Jaspers cannot . . . " He spread his arms, palms up. "You are not one of those few. I stake a reputation on it. You will be an opening person."

Dasein looked at the stone building, the hurrying people.

162

All that action and purpose. He sensed it all might be like the dance of bees—motions designed to show him a direction. The direction escaped him.

"I will try to put it in the words of *outside*," Piaget said. "Perhaps then . . ." He shrugged, leaned against the side of the door to bring his broad face close to Dasein. "We sift reality through screens composed of ideas. These idea systems are limited by language. That is to say: language cuts the grooves in which our thoughts must move. If we seek new validity forms, we must step outside the language."

"What's that have to do with the children?" Dasein nodded toward the greenhouses.

"Dasein! We have a common instinctive experience, you and I. What happens in the unformed psyche? As individuals, as cultures and societies, we humans reenact every aspect of the instinctive life that has accompanied our species for uncounted generations. With the Jaspers, we take off the binding element. Couple that with the brutality of childhood? No! We would have violence, chaos. We would have no society. It's simple, isn't it? We must superimpose a limiting order on the innate patterns of our nervous systems. We must have common interests."

Dasein found himself grappling with these ideas, trying to see through them to some sense in Piaget's earlier words. *Push back at the surface of childhood? World view?*

"We must meet the survival needs of individuals," Piaget said. "We know the civilization-culture-society outside is dying. They *do* die, you know. When this is about to happen, pieces break off from the parent body. Pieces cut themselves free, Dasein. Our scalpel—that was Jaspers. Think, man! You've lived out there. It's a Virgilian autumn . . . the dusk of a civilization."

Piaget stepped back, studied Dasein.

For his part. Dasein found himself suddenly fascinated by the doctor. There was a timeless essence in the man, powerful, intrusive on everything about him. Framed in the white smock's collar was an Egyptian head, strong cheeks and jaws, a nose out of Moses' time, white even teeth behind thin lips.

163

Piaget smiled, a deaf smile of ultimate stubbornness, let a honeyed look flow across the landscape around them, the greenhouses, the people.

Dasein knew then why he'd been sent here. No mere market report had prompted this. Marden had nailed it. He was here to break this up, smash it.

The Santarogans were working their children here, training them. Child labor. Piaget seemed not to care how much he revealed.

"Come along," Piaget said. "I'll show you our school."

Dasein shook his head. What would it be in there? An accidental push against broken glass? A child with a knife?

"I'm . . . I have to think," Dasein said.

"Are you sure?" Piaget's words dropped on the air like a challenge.

Dasein thought of a fortress abbey in the Dark Ages, warrior monks. All this was contained in Piaget and his valley, in the confidence with which Santarogans defied the *outside*. Were they really confident? he wondered. Or were they actors hypnotized by their own performance?

"You've been a swimmer on the surface," Piaget said. "You haven't even seen the struggle. You haven't yet developed the innocent eye that sees the universe uncluttered by past assumptions. You were programmed and sent here to break us up."

Dasein paled.

"To be programmed is to be prejudiced," Piaget said. "Because prejudice is selecting and rejecting and that is programming." He sighed. "Such pains we take with you because of our Jenny."

"I came here with an open mind," Dasein said.

"Not prejudiced?" Piaget raised his eyebrows.

"So you're contending with . . . groups outside over what's the right way . . . "

"Contending is too soft a word, Dasein. There's a power struggle going on over control of the human consciousness. We are a cell of health surrounded by plague. It's not men's minds that are at stake, but their consciousness, their awareness. This isn't a struggle over a market area. Make no mistake about it. This is a struggle over what's to be judged valuable in our universe. Outside, they value whatever can be measured, counted or tabulated. Here, we go by different standards."

Dasein sensed threat in Piaget's voice. There was no longer a veneer of pretense here. The doctor was setting up the sides in a war and Dasein felt caught in the middle. He was, he knew, on more dangerous ground than he'd ever been before. Piaget and his friends controlled the valley. An ex-post-facto accident would be child's play for them.

"The ones who hired me," Dasein said, "they're men who believe . . . "

"Men!" Piaget sneered. "Out there . . . " He pointed beyond the hills which enclosed the valley. " . . . they're destroying their environment. In the process, they're becoming not-men! We are men." He touched his chest. "They are not. Nature is a unified field. A radical change in environment means the inhabitants must change to survive. The not-men out there are changing to survive."

Dasein gaped at Piaget. That was it, of course. The Santarogans were conservatives . . . unchanging. He'd seen this for himself. But there was a fanatic intensity to Piaget, a religious fervor, that repelled Dasein. So it was a struggle over men's minds . . .

"You are saying to yourself," Piaget said, "that these fool Santarogans have a psycheletic substance which makes them inhuman."

It was so close to his thoughts that Dasein grew still with fear. Could they read minds? Was that a by-product of the Jaspers substance?

"You're equating us with the unwashed, sandaled users of LSD," Piaget said. "Kooks, you would say. But you are like them—unaware. We are aware. We have truly released the mind. We have a power medicine—just as whiskey and gin and aspirin and tobacco . . . and, yes, LSD, just as these are power medicines. But you must see the difference. Whiskey and the other depressants, these keep their subjects docile. Our medicine releases the animal that has never been tamed . . . up to now."

165

Dasein looked at the greenhouses.

"Yes," Piaget said. "Look here. That is where we domesticate the human animal."

With a shock of awareness, Dasein realized he had heard too much ever to be allowed out of the valley. They had passed a point of no return with him. In his present state of mind, there was only one answer for the Santarogans: they had to kill him. The only question remaining was: Did they know it? Was any of this conscious? Or did it truly operate at the level of instinct?

If he precipitated a crisis, Dasein knew he'd find out. Was there a way to avoid it? he wondered. As he hesitated, Piaget moved around the truck, climbed in beside him.

"You won't come with me," he said. "I'll go with you."

"You'll go with me?"

"To my house; to the clinic." He turned, studied Dasein. "I love my niece, you understand? I'll not have her hurt if I can prevent it."

"If I refuse?"

"Ahh, Gilbert, you would make the angels weep. We don't want weeping, do we? We don't want Jenny's tears. Aren't you concerned about her?"

"I've some anxiety about . . . "

"When anxiety enters, inquiry stops. You have a hard head, Gilbert. A hard head makes a sore back. Let us go to the clinic."

"What kind of death trap have you set up there?"

Piaget glared at him in outrage. "Death trap?"

Holding as reasonable a tone as he could manage, Dasein said: "You're trying to kill me. Don't deny it. I've . . ."

"I'm disgusted with you, Gilbert. When have we tried to kill you?"

Dasein took a deep breath, held up his right hand, enumerated the *accidents,* dropping a finger for each one until his hand was clenched into a fist. He had left out only the incident with Petey Jorick . . . and that because of a promise.

"Accidents!" Piaget said.

"As we both know," Dasein said, "there are very few real accidents in this world. Most of what we call accidents

166

are unconscious violence. You say you've opened your mind. Use it."

"Pah! Your thoughts are like muddy water!"

"Let the muddy water stand and it becomes clear," Dasein said.

"You can't be serious." He glared at Dasein. "But I see that you are." He closed his eyes momentarily, opened them. "Well, would you believe Jenny?"

Stay away from me! I love you! Dasein thought.

"Let's go to your clinic," Dasein said. He started the truck, backed out of the parking lot and headed toward town.

"Trying to kill you," Piaget muttered. He stared out at the landscape rushing past them.

Dasein drove in silence . . . thinking, thinking, thinking. The instant he headed toward Jenny, the old fantasies gripped him. Jenny and her valley! The place had enveloped him in its aura—crazy, crazy, crazy! But the pattern was emerging. It was going together with its own Santaroga kind of logic.

"So not everyone can take your . . . power medicine?" Dasein asked. "What happens to the ones who fail?"

"We take care of our own," Piaget growled. "That's why I keep hoping you'll stay."

"Jenny's a trained psychologist. Why don't you use her?"

"She does her tour of duty."

"I'm going to ask Jenny to leave with me," Dasein said. "You know that, don't you?"

Piaget sniffed.

"She can break away from your . . . Jaspers," Dasein said. "Men go into the service from here. They must . . . "

"They always come home when it's over," Piaget said. "That's in your notes. Don't you realize how unhappy they are out there?" He turned toward Dasein. "Is that the choice you'd offer Jenny?"

"They can't be all that unhappy about leaving," Dasein said. "Otherwise you clever people would've found another solution."

"Hmmph!" Piaget snorted. "You didn't even do your

167

homework for the people who hired you." He sighed. "I'll tell you, Gilbert. The draft rejects most of our young men—severe allergy reaction to a diet which doesn't include periodic administration of Jaspers. They can only get that here. The approximately six percent of our young people who go out do so as a duty to the valley. We don't want to call down the federal wrath on us. We have a political accommodation with the state, but we're not large enough to apply the same technique nationally."

They've already decided about me, Dasein thought. *They don't care what they tell me.*

The realization brought a tight sensation of fear in the pit of his stomach.

He rounded a corner and came parallel with the river. Ahead stood the clump of willows and the long, down-sweeping curve to the bridge. Dasein recalled his projection of evil onto the river, stepped on the throttle to get this place behind him. The truck entered the curve. The road was banked nicely. The bridge came into view. There was a yellow truck parked off the road at the far side, men standing behind it drinking out of metal cups.

"Look out!" Piaget shouted.

In that instant, Dasein saw the reason for the truck—a gaping hole in the center of the bridge where the planks had been removed. That was a county work crew and they'd opened at least a ten foot hole in the bridge.

The truck sped some forty feet during the moment it took Dasein to realize his peril.

Now, he could see a two-by-four stretched across each end of the bridge, yellow warning flags tied at their centers.

Dasein gripped the steering wheel. His mind shifted into a speed of computation he had never before experienced. The effect was to slow the external passage of time. The truck seemed to come almost to a stop while he reviewed the possibilities—

Hit the brakes?

No. Brakes and tires were old. At this speed, the truck would skid onto the bridge and into the hole.

Swerve off the road?

168

No. The river waited on both sides—a deep cut in the earth to swallow them.

Aim for a bridge abutment to stop the truck?

Not at this speed and without seat belts.

Hit the throttle to increase speed?

That was a possibility. There was the temporary barrier to break through, but that was only a two-by-four. The bridge rose in a slight arc up and over the river. The hole had been opened in the center. Given enough speed, the truck could leap the hole.

Dasein jammed the throttle to the floorboards. The old truck leaped ahead. There came a sharp cracking sound as they smashed through the barrier. Planks clattered beneath the wheels. There came a breathless instant of flying, a spring-crushing lurch as they landed across the hole, the "crack" of the far barrier.

He hit the brakes, came to a screeching stop opposite the workmen. Time resumed its normal pace as Dasein stared out at the crew—five men, faces pale, mouths agape.

"For the love of heaven!" Piaget gasped. "Do you always take chances like that?"

"Was there any other way to get us out of that mess?" Dasein asked. He lifted his right hand, stared at it. The hand was trembling.

Piaget reflected a moment, then: "You took what was probably the only way out . . . but if you hadn't been driving so damn' fast on a blind . . . "

"I will make you a bet," Dasein said. "I'll bet the work on that bridge wasn't necessary, that it was either a mistake or some sort of make-work."

Dasein reached for his door handle, had to grope twice to get it in his hand, then found it took a conscious surge of effort to open the door. He stepped out, found his knees rubbery. He stood a moment, took several deep breaths, then moved around to the front of the truck.

Both headlights were smashed and there was a deep dent stretching across both fenders and the grill.

Dasein turned his attention to the workmen. One, a

169

stocky, dark-haired man in a plaid shirt and dungarees stood a step ahead of the others. Dasein focused on the man, said: "Why wasn't there a warning sign back there around the corner?"

"Good God, man!" the fellow said. His face reddened. "Nobody comes down that road this time of day."

Dasein walked down the road toward a pile of planks, dirt and oil on them testifying that they'd been taken from the bridge. They looked to be three-by-twelve redwood. He lifted the end of one, turned it over—no cracks or checks. It gave off the sharp sound of an unbroken board when he dropped it back to the pile.

He turned to see the workman he'd addressed approaching. Piaget was several paces behind the man.

"When did you get the order to do this work?" Dasein asked.

"Huh?" The man stopped, stared at Dasein with a puzzled frown.

"When did you get orders to repair this bridge?" Dasein asked.

"Well . . . we decided to come up here about an hour ago. What the hell difference does it make? You've smashed the . . ."

"You decided?" Dasein asked. "Aren't you assigned to jobs?"

"I'm the road crew foreman in this valley, mister. I decide, not that it's any of your business."

Piaget came to a stop beside the man, said: "Dr. Dasein, this is Josh Marden, Captain Marden's nephew."

"Nepotism begins at home, I see," Dasein said, his tone elaborately polite. "Well, Mr. Marden, or may I call you Josh?"

"Now, you look here, Dr. Das . . . "

"Josh, then," Dasein said, still in that tone of calm politeness. "I'm very curious, Josh. These appear to be perfectly sound planks. Why'd you decide to replace them?"

"What the hell diff . . . "

"Tell him, Josh," Piaget said. "I confess to a certain curiosity of my own."

Marden looked at Piaget, back to Dasein. "Well . . . we

170

inspected the bridge . . . We make regular inpsections. We just decided to do a little preventive maintenance, put in new planks here and use the old ones on a bridge that doesn't get as much traffic. There's nothing unusual about . . ."

"Is there any *urgent* road work in this valley?" Dasein asked. "Is there some job you put off to come to this . . . "

"Now, look here, Mister!" Marden took a step toward Dasein. "You've no call to . . . "

"What about the Old Mill Road?" Piaget asked. "Are those pot holes still on the curve by the ditch?"

"Now, look, Doc," Marden said, whirling toward Piaget. "Not you, too. We decided . . . "

"Easy does it, Josh," Piaget said. "I'm just curious. What about the Old Mill Road?"

"Aw, Doc. It was such a nice day and the . . . "

"So that work still has to be done," Piaget said.

"I win the bet," Dasein said. He headed back toward his truck.

Piaget fell into step beside him.

"Hey!" Marden shouted. "You've broken county property and those boards you landed on are probably . . ."

Dasein cut him off without turning. "You'd better get that bridge repaired before somebody else has trouble here."

He slid behind the wheel of his truck, slammed the door. Reaction was setting in now: his whole body felt tense with anger.

Piaget climbed in beside him. The truck rattled as he closed his door. "Will it still run?" he asked.

"Accident!" Dasein said.

Piaget remained silent.

Dasein put the truck in gear, eased it up to a steady thirty-five miles an hour. The rear-view mirror showed him the crew already at work on the bridge, one of their number with a warning flag trudging back around the blind corner.

"Now, they send out a flagman," Dasein said.

A corner cut off the view in the mirror. Dasein concentrated on driving. The truck had developed new rattles and a front-end shimmy.

171

"They *have* to be accidents," Piaget said. "There's no other explanation."

A stop sign came into view ahead. Dasein stopped for the main highway. It was empty of traffic. He turned right toward town. Piaget's protestations deserved no answer, he thought, and he gave no answer.

They entered the outskirts of town. There was Scheler's station on the left. Dasein pulled in behind the station, drove back to the large shed-roofed metal building labeled "Garage."

"What're you doing here?" Piaget asked. "This machine isn't worth . . . "

"I want it repaired sufficiently to get me out of Santaroga," Dasein said.

The garage doors were open. Dasein nosed the truck inside, stopped, climbed out. There was a steady sound of work all around—clanging of metal, machinery humming. Lines of cars had been angled toward benches down both sides of the garage. Lights glared down on the benches.

A stocky, dark-skinned man in stained white coveralls came from the back of the garage, stopped in front of the truck.

"What the devil did you hit?" he asked.

Dasein recognized one of the quartet from the card game at the Inn—Scheler himself.

"Doctor Piaget here will tell you all about it," Dasein said. "I want some headlights put on this thing and you might have a look at the steering."

"Why don't you junk it?" Scheler asked.

The truck door slammed and Piaget came up on the right. "Can you fix it, Sam?" he asked.

"Sure, but it isn't worth it."

"Do it anyway and put it on my bill. I don't want our friend here to think we're trying to trap him in the valley."

"If you say so, Doc."

Scheler turned around, shouted: "Bill! Take that Lincoln off the rack and put this truck on. I'll write up a ticket."

A young man in greasy blue coveralls came around from

172

the left bench where he had been hidden by a Lincoln Continental lifted halfway up on a hoist. The young man had Scheler's build and dark skin, the same set of face and eyes: bright blue and alert.

"My son, Bill," Scheler said. "He'll take care of it for you."

Dasein felt a twinge of warning fear, backed against the side of his truck. The garage around him had taken on the same feeling of concentrated malevolence he had sensed in the river.

Scheler started through the space between the Lincoln and an old Studebaker truck, called over his shoulder: "If you'll sign the ticket over here, Dr. Dasein, we'll get right at it."

Dasein took two steps after him, hesitated. He felt the garage closing in around him.

"We can walk to the clinic from here," Piaget said. "Sam will call when your rig's ready."

Dasein took another step, stopped, glanced back. Young Bill Scheler was right behind him. The sense of menace was a pounding drumbeat in Dasein's head. He saw Bill reach out a friendly hand to guide him between the cars. There was no doubt of the innocent intention of that hand, the smiling face behind it, but Dasein saw the hand as the embodiment of danger. With an inarticulate cry, Dasein sprang aside.

The young mechanic, caught off balance with nothing ahead of his thrusting arm, lurched forward, stumbled, fell. As he fell, the hoist with the Lincoln on it came crashing down. It rocked twice, subsided. Bill Scheler lay halfway under it. One of his legs twitched, was still.

A pool of red began to flow from beneath the car.

Piaget dashed past him shouting for Scheler to raise the hoist.

A compressor began thumping somewhere in the background. The Lincoln jerked, began to rise. It exposed a body, its head smashed beyond recognition by one of the hoist's arms.

Dasein whirled away, ran out of the garage and was sick.

173

That could've been me, he thought. *That was meant for me.* He grew aware of a great bustle of activity, the sound of a siren in the distance.

Two mechanics emerged from the garage with a pale-faced, staggering Sam Scheler between them.

It was his son, Dasein thought. He felt that this was of the deepest significance, but his shocked mind gave no explanation for that feeling.

He heard one of the mechanics with Scheler say: "It was an accident, Sam. Nothing you could do."

They went into the station with him.

A siren began giving voice in the distance. Its wailing grew louder. Dasein backed off to the edge of the station's parking area, stood against a low fence.

His truck, nosed into the garage, lurched into motion, was swallowed by the building.

The ambulance droned its way into the parking area, turned, backed into the garage. Presently, it emerged, drove away with its siren silent.

Piaget came out of the garage.

He was an oddly subdued man, indecisive in his walk—short strides, soft of step. He saw Dasein, approached with an air of diffidence. There was a smear of blood down the right side of his white smock, black grease at the hem, grease on the left arm.

Blood and grease—they struck Dasein as an odd combination but things out of which an entire scene could be reconstructed. He shuddered.

"I . . . I need a cup of coffee," Piaget said. He closed his eyes briefly, opened them to stare pleadingly at Dasein. "There's a café around the corner. Would you . . . " He broke off to take a deep, trembling breath. "I brought that boy into the world." He shook his head. "Just when you think you're the complete doctor, immune to all personal involvement . . . "

Dasein experienced a surge of compassion for Piaget, stepped away from the fence to take the doctor's arm. "Where's this café? I could use something myself."

The café was a narrow brick building squeezed between

174

a hardware store and a dark little shop labeled "Bootery." The screen door banged behind them. The place smelled of steam and the omnipresent Jaspers. One of Scheler's station attendants—dark green jacket and white hat—sat at a counter on the left staring into a cup of coffee. A man in a leather apron, horn-callused hands, gray hair, was eating a sandwich at the far end of the counter.

Dasein steered Piaget into a booth opposite the counter, sat down across from him.

The station attendant at the counter, turned, glanced at them. Dasein found himself confronted by a face he knew to be another Scheler—the same set to the blue eyes, the same blocky figure and dark skin. The man looked at Piaget, said: "Hi, Doc. There was a siren."

Piaget lifted his gaze from the tabletop, looked at the speaker. The glaze left Piaget's eyes. He took two shallow breaths, looked away, back to the man at the counter.

"Harry," Piaget said, and his voice was a hoarse croak. "I . . . couldn't . . . " He broke off.

The man slid off the counter stool. His face was a pale, frozen mask. "I've been sitting here . . . feeling . . . " He brushed a hand across his mouth. "It was . . . Bill!" He whirled, dashed out of the café. The door slammed behind him.

"That's Scheler's other son," Piaget said.

"He knew," Dasein said, and he recalled the experience at the lake, the feeling of rapport.

Life exists immersed in a sea of unconsciousness, he reminded himself. *In the drug, these people gain a view of that sea.*

Piaget studied Dasein a moment, then: "Of course he knew. Haven't you ever had a tooth pulled? Couldn't you feel the hole where it had been?"

A slender red-haired woman in a white apron, lines of worry on her face, came up to the booth, stood looking down at Piaget. "I'll bring your coffee," she said. She started to turn away, hesitated. "I . . . felt it . . . and Jim next door came to the back to tell me. I didn't know how to tell Harry. He just kept sitting there . . . getting lower and lower . . . knowing really but refusing to face it. I . . . " She shrugged. "Anything besides coffee?"

Piaget shook his head. Dasein realized with a sense of shock the man was near tears.

The waitress left, returned with two mugs of coffee, went back to the kitchen—all without speaking. She, too, had sensed Piaget's emotions.

Dasein sighed, lifted his coffee, started to put the mug to his lips, hesitated. There was an odd bitter odor beneath the omnipresent Jaspers tang in the coffee. Dasein put his nose to the mug, sniffed. Bitter. A plume of steam rising from the dark liquid assumed for Dasein the shape of a hooded cobra lifting its fanged head to strike him.

Shakily, he returned the mug to the table, looked up to meet Piaget's questioning gaze.

"There's poison in that coffee," Dasein rasped.

Piaget looked at his own coffee.

Dasein took the mug from him, sniffed at it. The bitter odor was missing. He touched his tongue to it—heat, the soothing flow of Jaspers . . . coffee . . .

"Is something wrong?"

Dasein looked up to find the waitress standing over him. "There's poison in my coffee," he said.

"Nonsense." She took the mug from Dasein's hand, started to drink.

Piaget stopped her with a hand on her arm. "No, Vina—this one." He handed her the other mug.

She stared at it, smelled it, put it down, dashed for the kitchen. Presently, she returned carrying a small yellow box. Her face was porcelain white, freckles standing out across her cheeks and nose like the marks of some disease.

"Roach powder," she whispered. "I . . . the box was spilled on the shelf over the counter. I . . . " She shook her head.

Dasein looked at Piaget, but the doctor refused to meet his gaze.

"Another accident," Dasein said, holding his voice even. "Eh, doctor?"

Piaget wet his lips with his tongue.

Dasein slid out of the booth, pushing the waitress aside.

176

He took the mug of poisoned coffee, poured it deliberately on the floor. "Accidents will happen, won't they . . . Vina?"

"Please," she said. "I . . . didn't . . . "

"Of course you didn't," Dasein said.

"You don't understand," Piaget said.

"But I *do* understand," Dasein said. "What'll it be next time? A gun accident? How about something heavy dropped from a roof? Accidentally, of course." He turned, strode out of the cafe, stood on the sidewalk to study his surroundings.

It was such a *normal* town. The trees on the parking strip were so normal. The young couple walking down the sidewalk across from him—they were so normal. The sounds—a truck out on the avenue to his right, the cars there, a pair of jays arguing in the treetops, two women talking on the steps of a house down the street to his left—such an air of normalcy about it all.

The screen door slapped behind him. Piaget came up to stand at Dasein's side. "I know what you're thinking," he said.

"Do you, really?"

"I know how all this must look to you."

"Is that so?"

"Believe me," Piaget said, "all this is just a terrible series of coincidences that . . . "

"Coincidence!" Dasein whirled on him, glaring. "How far can you stretch credulity, doctor? How long can you rationalize before you have to admit . . ."

"Gilbert, I'd cut off my right arm rather than let anything happen to you. It'd break Jenny's heart to . . . "

"You actually don't see it, do you?" Dasein asked, his voice filled with awe. "You don't see it. You refuse to see it."

"Dr. Dasein?"

The voice came from his right. Dasein turned to find Harry—"Scheler's other son"—standing there, hat in hand. He looked younger than he had in the café—no more than nineteen. There was a sad hesitancy in his manner.

"I wanted to . . . " He broke off. "My father said to tell

177

you . . . We know it wasn't your fault that . . ." He looked into Dasein's eyes, a look that pleaded for help.

Dasein felt a pang of rapport for the young man. There was a basic decency at work here. In the midst of their own grief, the Schelers had taken time to try to ease Dasein's feelings.

They expected me to feel guilt about this, Dasein thought. The fact that he'd experienced no such feeling filled Dasein now with an odd questing sensation of remorse.

If I hadn't . . . He aborted the thought. *If I hadn't what? That accident was meant for me.*

"It's all right, Harry," Piaget said. "We understand."

"Thanks, Doc." He looked at Piaget with relief. "Dad said to tell you . . . the car, Dr. Dasein's truck . . . The new headlights are in it. That's all we can do. The steering . . . You'll just have to drive slow unless you replace the whole front end."

"Already?" Dasein asked.

"It doesn't take long to put in headlights, sir."

Dasein looked from the youth to Piaget. The doctor returned his stare with an expression that said as clearly as words: *"They want your truck out of there. It's a reminder . . ."*

Dasein nodded. Yes. The truck would remind them of the tragedy. This was logical. Without a word, he set off for the garage.

Piaget sped up, matched his pace to Dasein's.

"Gilbert," he said, "I must insist you come over to the house. Jenny can . . . "

"Insist?"

"You're being very pig-headed, Gilbert."

Dasein put down a surge of anger, said: "I don't want to hurt Jenny any more than you do. That's why I'm going to direct my own steps. I don't really want you to know what I'm going to do next. I don't want any of you waiting there in my path with one of your . . . accidents."

"Gilbert, you *must* put that idea out of your mind! None of us want to hurt you."

They were on the parking area between the station and

178

the garage now. Dasein stared at the gaping door to the garage, overcome suddenly by the sensation that the door was a mouth with deadly teeth ready to clamp down on him. The door yawned there to swallow him.

Dasein hesitated, slowed, stopped.

"What is it now?" Piaget asked.

"Your truck's just inside," Harry Scheler said. "You can drive it and . . ."

"What about the bill?" Dasein asked, stalling for time.

"I'll take care of that," Piaget said. "Go get your truck while I'm settling up. Then we'll go to . . ."

"I want the truck driven out here for me," Dasein said. He moved to one side, out of the path of anything that might come spewing from that mouth-door.

"I can understand your reluctance to go back in there," Piaget said, "but really . . ."

"You drive it out for me, Harry," Dasein said.

The youth stared at Dasein with an oddly trapped look. "Well, I have some . . ."

"Drive the damn' car out for him!" Piaget ordered. "This is nonsense!"

"Sir?" Harry looked at Piaget.

"I said drive the damn' car out here for him!" Piaget repeated. "I've had as much of this as I can stomach!"

Hesitantly, the youth turned toward the garage door. His feet moved with a dragging slowness.

"See here, Gilbert," Piaget said, "you can't really believe we . . ."

"I believe what I see," Dasein said.

Piaget threw up his hands, turned away in exasperation.

Dasein listened to the sounds from the garage. They were subdued in there—voices, only a few mechanical noises, the whirring buzz of some machine.

A door slammed. It sounded like the door to the truck. Dasein recognized the grinding of his starter. The engine caught with its characteristic banging, as drowned immediately in a roaring explosion that sent a blast of flame shooting out the garage door.

Piaget leaped back with an oath.

Dasein ran diagonally past him to look into the garage.

179

He glimpsed figures rushing out a door at the far end. His truck stood in the central traffic aisle at the core of a red-orange ball of flame. As he stared at the truck, a burning something emerged from the flames, staggered, fell.

Behind Dasein, someone screamed: "Harry!"

Without consciously willing it, Dasein found himself dashing through the garage door to grab into the flames and drag the youth to safety. There were sensations of heat, pain. A roaring-crackling sound of fire filled the air around him. The smell of gasoline and char invaded Dasein's nostrils. He saw a river of fire reach toward him along the floor. A blazing beam crashed down where the youth had lain. There were shouts, a great scrambling confusion.

Something white was thrown over the figure he was dragging, engulfed the flames. Hands eased him aside. Dasein realized he was out of the garage, that Piaget was using his white smock to smother the fire on Harry.

Someone appeared to be doing something similar to both Dasein's arms and the front of his jacket, using a coat and a car robe. The coat and robe were pulled away. Dasein stared down at his own arms—black and red flesh, blisters forming. The sleeves of his shirt and jacket ended at the elbows in jagged edgings of char.

The pain began—a throbbing agony along the backs of both arms and hands. Through a world hazed by the pain, Dasein saw a station-wagon screech to a rocking stop beside him, saw men carry the smock-shrouded figure of Harry into the back of the wagon. More hands eased Dasein into the seat beside the driver.

There were voices: "Easy there." "Get 'em to the clinic, Ed, and don't loiter." "Give us a hand here." "Here! Over here!"

There was a sound of sirens, the pounding throb of heavy truck engines.

Dasein heard Piaget's voice from the rear of the station-wagon: "Okay, Ed. Let's get going."

The wagon slipped into motion, dipped onto the street, turned, gathered speed. Dasein looked at the driver, recognized one of the station attendants, turned to peer into the back.

Piaget crouched there working over the injured youth.

"How bad is he?" Dasein asked.

"He was wearing long johns," Piaget said. "They helped. He seems to've protected his face by burying it in his cap, but his back is bad. So're his legs and arms and his hands."

Dasein stared at the injured youth.

"Will he . . . "

"I think we got to him in time," Piaget said. "I gave him a shot to put him out." He looked at Dasein's arms. "Do you want a needle?"

Dasein shook his head from side to side. "No."

What made me rush in there to save him? Dasein asked himself. It had been an instinctive reaction. Saving Harry had precipitated him into a semihelpless situation, needing medical attention himself, caught in a car with two Santarogans. Dasein probed at his embryo *Jaspers awareness*, the sixth sense which had warned him of danger. He found nothing. The threat appeared to have been withdrawn. *Is that why I acted to save Harry?* Dasein wondered. *Did I hope to propitiate Santaroga by saving one of their own even while they were trying to kill me?*

"Another accident," Piaget said, and his voice carried a questioning tone of self-doubt.

Dasein met the doctor's probing gaze, nodded.

The station-wagon turned onto a tree-lined street, and Dasein recognized the broad, brown-shingled front of Piaget's house. They drove past it and onto a graveled driveway that curved around to the rear through a tall board fence and under a portico jutting from a two-storey brick building.

In spite of his pain, Dasein realized this building lay concealed from the street by the fence and a border planting of evergreens, that it must be part of the complex which included Piaget's house. It all seemed hazily significant.

White-coated attendants rushed a gurney out of the building, eased the burned youth from the rear of the station wagon. Piaget opened Dasein's door, said: "Can you get out under your own power, Gilbert?"

"I . . . think so."

181

Dasein held his arms out in front of him, slid from the car. The pain and the motion required all his attention. There was a beginning ache along his forehead now and down the right side of his face. The brick building, a pair of swinging glass doors, hands gently guiding him—all seemed rather distant and receding.

I'm blacking out, he thought. He felt it might be extremely dangerous to sink into unconsciousness. With a start, he realized he had been eased into a wheelchair, that it was speeding down a green-walled hallway. The surge of awareness sent his senses crashing into the pain. He felt himself recoiling toward the blessed relief of unconsciousness. It was an almost physical thing, as though his body was bouncing between limiting walls—unconsciousness or pain.

Bright lights!

The light was all around him. He heard scissors snipping, looked down to see hands working the scissors. They were cutting the sleeves of his jacket and shirt, lifting the fabric away from seared flesh.

That's my flesh, Dasein thought. He tore his gaze away from it.

Dasein felt something cool at his left shoulder, a pricking sensation, a pulling. A hand holding a hypodermic moved across his plane of vision. The important thing to Dasein in this moment was that his vision was limited to a plane. There was light, a foggy glittering out of which hands moved and faces appeared. He felt himself being undressed. Something cool, soothing, sliding was being applied to his hands and arms, to his face.

They've given me a shot to put me out, he thought. He tried to think about danger then, about being totally helpless here. Consciousness refused to respond. He couldn't push his awareness through the glittering fog.

There were voices. He concentrated on the voices. Someone said: "For the love of heaven! He was carrying a gun." Another voice: "Put that down!"

For some reason, this amused Dasein, but his body refused to laugh.

He thought then of his camper as he'd last seen it—a

ball of orange flame. All his records had been in there, Dasein realized. Every bit of evidence he'd accumulated about Santaroga had gone up in that fire. *Evidence?* he thought. *Notes . . . speculations . . .* It was all still in his mind, subject to recall.

But memory is lost at death! he thought.

Fear galvanized a miniscule core of selfdom in him. He tried to shout. No sound came. He tried to move. Muscles refused to obey.

When the darkness came, it was like a hand that reached up and seized him.

11

Dasein awoke remembering a dream—a conversation with faceless gods.

"Dunghills rise and castles fall." In the dream, something with an echo-box voice had said that. *"Dunghills rise and castles fall."*

Dasein felt it important to remember all the dream. Yes. "I'm the man who woke up." That was what he'd tried to tell the faceless gods. "I'm the man who woke up."

The dream was a flowing pattern in his memory, a *process* that couldn't be separated from himself. It was full of pure deeds and anguish. There was a chronic frustration in it. He had tried to do something that was inherently impossible. What had he tried to do? It eluded him.

Dasein remembered the hand of darkness that had preceded the dream. He caught his breath and his eyes popped open. Daylight. He was in a bed in a green-walled room. Out a window at his left he could see a twisted red branch of madrone, oily green leaves, blue-sky. He felt his body then: bandages and pain along his arms, bandages across his forehead and his right cheek. His throat felt dry and there was a sourness on his tongue.

Still, the dream clung to him. It was a disembodied *thing*. Disembodied. Death! That was a clue. He knew it. Dasein recalled Piaget speaking of "a common instinctive experience." What did instinct have to do with the dream? Instinct. Instinct. What was instinct? An innate pettern impressed on the nervous system. Death. Instinct.

"Look inward, look inward, oh Man, on thyself," the

faceless gods of the dream had said. He recalled that now and felt like sneering.

It was the old know-thyself syndrome, the psychologist's disease. Inward, ever inward. The death instinct was in there with all the other instincts. Know thyself? Dasein sensed then he couldn't know himself without dying. Death was the background against which life could know itself.

A throat was cleared to Dasein's right.

He tensed, turned his head to look toward the sound.

Winston Burdeaux sat in a chair beside the door. The brown eyes staring out of Burdeaux's moorish face held a quizzical expression.

Why Burdeaux? Dasein wondered.

"I'm happy to see you're awake, sir," Burdeaux said.

There was a soothing sense of companionship in the man's rumbling voice. Was that why Burdeaux had been brought in? Dasein wondered. Had Burdeaux been picked to soothe and lull the victim?

But I'm still alive, Dasein thought.

If they'd wanted to harm him, what better opportunity had presented itself? He'd been helpless, unconscious . . .

"What time is it?" Dasein asked. The movement of speaking hurt his burned cheek.

"It's almost ten o'clock of a beautiful morning," Burdeaux said. He smiled, a flash of white teeth in the dark features. "Is there anything you wish?"

At the question, Daselin's stomach knotted in a pang of hunger. He hesitated on the point of asking for breakfast. What might be in any food served here? he asked himself.

Hunger is more than an empty stomach, Dasein thought. *I can go without a meal.*

"What I wish," Dasein said, "is to know why you're here."

"The doctor thought I might be the safest one," Burdeaux said. "I, myself, was an outsider once. I can recall how it was."

"They tried to kill you, too?"

"Sir!"

"Well . . . did you have accidents?" Dasein asked.

"I do not share the doctor's opinion about . . . acci-

185

dents," Burdeaux said. "Once . . . I thought— But I can see now how wrong I was. The people of this valley wish to harm no man."

"Yet, you're here because the doctor decided you'd be the *safest*," Dasein said. "And you haven't answered my question: Did you have accidents?"

"You must understand," Burdeaux said, "that when you don't know the ways of the valley, you can get into . . . situations which . . ."

"So you *did* have accidents. Is that why you asked for secret packages from Louisiana?"

"Secret packages?"

"Why else did you have them sent to Porterville?"

"Oh, you know about that." Burdeaux shook his head, chuckled. "Haven't you ever hungered for the foods of your childhood? I didn't think my new friends would understand."

"Is that what it was?" Dasein asked. "Or did you wake up one morning shaking with fear at what the Jaspers in the local food was doing to you?"

Burdeaux scowled, then: "Sir, when I first came here, I was an ignorant *nigger*. Now, I'm an educated Negro . . . *and* a Santarogan. I no longer have the delusions which I . . ."

"So you *did* try to fight it!"

"Yes . . . I fought it. But I soon learned how foolish that was."

"A delusion."

"Indeed; a delusion."

To remove a man's delusions, Dasein thought, *is to create a vacuum. What rushes into that vacuum?*

"Let us say," Burdeaux said, "that I shared your delusions once."

"It's normal to share the delusions of one's society," Dasein murmured, half to himself. "It's abnormal to develop private delusions."

"Well put," Burdeaux said.

Again, he wondered: *What rushed into the vacuum? What delusions do Santarogans share?*

For one thing, he knew they couldn't see the un-

186

conscious violence which created *accidents* for outsiders. Most of them couldn't see this, he corrected himself. There was a possibility Piaget was beginning to understand. After all, he'd put Burdeaux in here. And Jenny—*"Stay away from me! I love you!"*

Dasein began to see Santarogans in a new light. There was something decorously Roman about them . . . and Spartan. They were turned in upon themselves, unfriendly, insular, proud, cut off from exchange of ideas that might . . . He hesitated on this thought, wondering about the TV room at the Inn.

"The room you tried to hide from me," Dasein said. "At the Inn—the room with the television receivers . . ."

"We didn't really want to hide that from *you*," Burdeaux said. "In a way, we hide it from ourselves . . . and from chance outsiders. There's something very alluring about the sickness that's poured over TV. That's why we rotate the watchers. But we cannot ignore it. TV is the key to the outside and it's gods."

"It's gods?" Dasein suddenly remembered his dream.

"They have very practical gods outside," Burdeaux said.

"What's a practical god?" Dasein asked.

"A practical god? That'a a god who agrees with his worshipers. This is a way to keep from being conquered, you see."

Dasein turned away from Burdeaux to stare up at the green ceiling. *Conquer the gods?* Was that the dream's chronic frustration?

"I don't understand," he murmured.

"You still carry some of the outside's delusions," Burdeaux said. "Outside, they don't really try to understand the universe. Oh, they say they do, but that's not really what they're up to. You can tell by what they do. They're trying to conquer the universe. Gods are part of the universe . . . even man-made gods."

"If you can't beat 'em, join 'em," Dasein said. "To keep from being conquered, a practical god agrees with his attackers. Is that it?"

"You're just as perceptive as Jenny said you'd be," Burdeaux said.

187

"So outsiders attack their gods," Dasein said.

"Anything less than abject submission has to have some attack in it," Burdeaux said. "You try to change a god? What's that except accusing the god of not agreeing with you?"

"And you get all this from the TV?"

"All this from . . . " Burdeaux broke into a chuckle. "Oh, no, Doctor Gil . . . You don't mind if I call you Doctor Gil?"

Dasein turned to stare at the questioning look on Burdeaux's face. *Doctor Gil.* To object would be to appear the stiffnecked fool. But Dasein felt that agreement would be a step backward, the loss of an important battle. He could see no way to object, though.

"Whatever you wish," Dasein said. "Just explain this about the TV."

"That's . . . our *window* on the outside," Burdeaux said. "That whole world of the permanent expediency out there, that whole world is TV. And we watch it through . . ."

"Permanent expediency?" Dasein tried to raise himself on his elbows, but the effect set his burned arms to throbbing. He sank back, kept his gaze on Burdeaux.

"Why, of course, sir. The outside works on the temporary expedient, Doctor Gil. You must know that. And the temporary always turns into the permanent, somehow. The temporary tax, the necessary *little* war, the temporary brutality that will cease as soon as certain conditions end . . . the government agency created for the permanent *interim* . . ."

"So you watch the news broadcasts and get all this from . . ."

"More than the news, Doctor Gil. All of it, and our watchers write condensed reports that . . . You see, it's all TV out there—life, everything. Outsiders are spectators. They expect everything to happen *to* them and they don't want to do more than turn a switch. They want to sit back and let life happen to them. They watch the late-late show and turn off their TVs. Then they go to bed to sleep—which is a form of turning themselves off just like the TV. The trouble is, their late-late show is often later

188

than they think. There's a desperation in not being able to recognize this, Doctor Gil. Desperation leads to violence. There comes a morning for almost every one of those poor people outside when they realize that life hasn't happened to them no matter how much TV they've watched. Life hasn't happened because they didn't take part in it. They've never been onstage, never had anything real. It was all illusion . . . delusion."

Dasein absorbed the intensity of the words, their meaning and what lay under them. There was a terrifying sense of truth in Burdeaux's words.

"So they get turned off," Dasein murmured.

"It's all TV," Burdeaux said.

Dasein turned his head, looked out the window.

"You really ought to eat something, Doctor Gil," Burdeaux said.

"No."

"Doctor Gil, you're a wise man in some things, but in others . . . "

"Don't call me wise," Dasein said. "Call me experienced."

"The food here is the very best," Burdeaux said. "I'll get it and serve you myself. You don't have to fear a . . ."

"I've been burned enough times," Dasein said.

"Fire won't crack a full pot, Doctor Gil."

"Win, I admire you and trust you. You saved my life. I don't think you were supposed to, but you did. That's why Doctor Piaget sent you in here. But an *accident* could happen—even with you."

"You hurt me to say that, Doctor Gil. I'm not the kind feeds you with the corn and chokes you with the cob."

Dasein sighed. He'd offended Burdeaux, but the alternative . . . It occurred to Dasein abruptly that he was sitting on a special kind of bomb. Santaroga had abated its attack on him, probably in part because of his present helplessness. But the community was capable of returning to the manufacture of *accidents* if and when he should ever want something not permitted here.

At the moment, Dasein wanted nothing more than to be far away from here. He wanted this desperately despite the

189

certain knowledge this desire must be on the proscribed list.

The door beside Burdeaux opened. A nurse backed into the room pulling a cart. She turned. Jenny!

Dasein ignored his burns, lifted himself on his elbows.

Jenny stared at him with an oddly pained expression. Her full lips were thrust out almost in a pout. The long black hair had been tied back in a neat bun. She wore a white uniform, white stockings, white shoes—no cap.

Dasein swallowed.

"Miss Jenny," Burdeaux said. "What do you have on that cart?"

She spoke without taking her gaze from Dasein. "Some food for this madman. I prepared it myself."

"I've been trying to get him to eat," Burdeaux said, "but he says no."

"Would you leave us for a while, Win?" she asked. "I want . . ."

"The doctor said I wasn't to let . . ."

"Win, please?" She turned toward him, pleading.

Burdeaux swallowed. "Well . . . since it's you . . ."

"Thank you, Win."

"Twenty minutes," Burdeaux said. "I'll be right out in the hall where you can call me if you need."

"Thank you, Win." She turned her attention back to Dasein.

Burdeaux left the room, closed the door softly.

Dasein said: "Jen, I . . ."

"Be quiet," she said. "You're not to waste your strength. Uncle Larry said . . ."

"I'm not eating here," Dasein said.

She stamped a foot. "Gil, you're being . . ."

"I'm being a fool," he said. "But the important thing is I'm alive."

"But look at you! Look at . . ."

"How's Harry Scheler?"

She hesitated, then: "He'll live. He'll have some scars, and for that matter so will you, but you . . ."

"Have they figured out what happened?"

"It was an accident."

190

"That's all? Just an accident?"

"They said something about the line from the fuel pump being broken . . . a bad electrical connection to one of the lights and . . . "

"An accident," Dasein said. "I see." He sank back into his pillow.

"I've prepared you some coddled eggs and toast and honey," Jenny said. "You've got to eat something to keep up . . ."

"No."

"Gil!"

"I said no."

"What're you afraid of?"

"Another accident."

"But I prepared this myself!"

He turned his head, stared at her, spoke in a low voice: "Stay away from me. I love you."

"Gilbert!"

"You said it," he reminded her.

Her face paled. She leaned against the cart, trembling. "I know," she whispered. "Sometimes I can feel the . . . " She looked up, tears streaming down her face. "But I *do* love you. And you're hurt now. I want to take care of you. I *need* to take care of you. Look." She lifted the cover from one of the dishes on the cart, spooned a bite of food into her mouth.

"Jenny," Dasein whispered. The look of hurt on her face, the intensity of his love for her—he wanted to take her in his arms and . . .

A wide-eyed look came over Jenny's face. She reached both hands to her throat. Her mouth worked, but no sound came forth.

"Jenny!"

She shook her head, eyes staring wildly.

Dasein threw back the covers of his bed, winced as movement increased the pain along his arms. He ignored the pain, slid his feet out to a cold tile floor, straightened. A wave of dizziness gripped him.

Jenny, hands still at her throat, backed toward the door.

Dasein started toward her, hospital nightshirt flopping

191

around his knees. He found movement difficult, his knees rubbery.

Abruptly, Jenny slumped to the floor.

Dasein remembered Burdeaux, shouted: "Help! Win! Help!" He staggered, clutched the edge of the cart. It started to roll.

Dasein found himself sitting helplessly on the floor as the door burst open. Burdeaux stood there glaring at him, looked down at Jenny who lay with her eyes closed, knees drawn up, gasping.

"Call the doctor," Dasein husked. "Something in the food. She ate some . . . "

Burdeaux took one quick breath of awareness, whirled away down the hall, leaving the door open.

Dasein started to crawl toward Jenny. The room wavered and twisted around him. His arms throbbed. There was a whistle in Jenny's gasping breaths that made him want to dash to her, but he couldn't find the strength. He had covered only a few feet when Piaget rushed in with Burdeaux right behind.

Piaget, his round face a pale blank mask, knelt beside Jenny, motioned toward Dasein, said: "Get him back in bed."

"The food on the cart," Dasein rasped. "She ate something."

A blonde nurse in a stiff white cap wheeled an emergency cart in the door, bent over Piaget's shoulder. They were cut from Dasein's view as Burdeaux scooped him up, deposited him on the bed.

"You stay there, Doctor Gil," Burdeaux said. He turned, stared at the action by the door.

"Allergenic reaction," Piaget said. "Throat's closing. Give me a double tube; we'll have to pump her."

The nurse handed something to Piaget, who worked over Jenny, his back obscuring his actions.

"Atropine," Piaget said.

Again, he took something from the nurse.

Dasein found it difficult to focus on the scene. Fear tightened his throat. *Why am I so weak?* he wondered.

192

Then: *Dear God, she can't die. Please save her.*

Faces of more hospital personnel appeared at the door, wide-eyed, silent.

Piaget glanced up, said: "Get a gurney."

Some of the faces went away. Presently, there was a sound of wheels in the corridor.

Piaget stood up, said: "That's as much as I can do here. Get her on the gurney—head lower than her feet." He turned to Dasein. "What'd she eat?"

"She took . . . " Dasein pointed to the food cart. "Whatever it is, she took the cover off. Eggs?"

Piaget took one stride to the cart, grabbed up a dish, sniffed at it. His movement opened the view to the door for Dasein. Two orderlies and a nurse were lifting Jenny there, carrying her out the door. There was one glimpse of her pale face with a tube dangling from the corner of her mouth.

"Was it a poison?" Burdeaux asked, his voice hushed.

"Of course it was a poison!" Piaget snapped. "Acts like aconite." He turned with the dish, rushed out.

Dasein listened to the sound of the wheels and swift footsteps receding down the hall until Burdeaux closed the door, shutting out the sound.

His body bathed in perspiration, Dasein lay unresisting while Burdeaux eased him under the blankets.

"For one moment there," Burdeaux said, "I . . . I thought you'd hurt Jenny."

She can't die, Dasein thought.

"I'm sorry," Burdeaux said. "I know you wouldn't hurt her."

"She can't die," Dasein whispered.

He looked up to see tears draw glistening tracks down Burdeaux's dark cheeks. The tears ignited an odd anger reaction in Dasein. He was aware of the anger swelling in him, but unable to stop it. Rage! It was directed not at Burdeaux, but at the disembodied essence of Santaroga, at the collective *thing* which had tried to use the woman he loved to kill him. He glared at Burdeaux.

"Doctor Larry won't let anything happen to Jenny," Burdeaux said. "He'll . . . "

Burdeaux saw the expression in Dasein's eyes, instinctively backed away.

"Get out of here!" Dasein rasped.

"But the doctor said I was to . . . "

"Doctor *Gil* says you get the hell out of here!"

Burdeaux's face took on a stubborn set. "I'm not to leave you alone."

Dasein sank back. What could he do?

"You had a very bad shock reaction last night," Burdeaux said. "They had to give you blood. You're not to be left alone."

They gave me a transfusion? Dasein wondered. *Why didn't they kill me then? They were saving me for Jenny!*

"You all care so much for Jenny," Dasein said. "You'd let her kill me. It'd destroy her, but that doesn't make any difference, does it? Sacrifice Jenny, that's your verdict, you pack of . . . "

"You're talking crazy, Doctor Gil."

As quickly as it had come, the anger left Dasein. Why attack poor Win? Why attack any of them? They couldn't see the monkey on their back. He felt deflated. Of course this was crazy to Burdeaux. One society's reason was another's unreason.

Dasein cursed the weakness that had seized his body.

Bad shock reaction.

He wondered then what he would do if Jenny died. It was a curiously fragmented feeling—part of him wailing in grief at the thought, another part raging at the fate which had shunted him into this corner . . . and part of him forever analyzing, analyzing . . .

How much of the shock had been a Jaspers reaction? Had he become sensitized the way Santarogans were?

They'll kill me out of hand if Jenny dies, he thought.

Burdeaux said: "I'll just sit here by the door. You be sure to tell me if you need anything."

He sat down facing Dasein, folded his arms—for all the world like a guard.

Dasein closed his eyes, thought: *Jenny, please don't die.* He recalled Piaget telling how Harry Scheler had known of the brother's death.

194

An empty place.

Where do I sense Jenny? Dasein asked himself.

It bothered him that he couldn't probe within himself somewhere and be reassured by Jenny's presence. That kind of reassurance was worth any price. She had to be there. It was a thing any Santarogan could do.

But I'm not a Santarogan.

Dasein felt that he teetered on the razor's edge. One side held the vast unconscious sea of the human world into which he had been born. On the other side—there, it was like the green waters of a lake—serene, contained, every droplet knowing its neighbors.

He heard a door open, felt a storm begin in the unconscious sea, sensed a breeze stirring the surface of the lake. The sensation of balancing receded. Dasein opened his eyes.

Piaget stood in the middle of the room. He wore a stethoscope around his neck. There was a feeling of fatigue around his eyes. He studied Dasein with a puzzled frown.

"Jenny?" Dasein whispered.

"She'll live," Piaget said. "But it was close."

Dasein closed his eyes, took a deep breath. "How many more *accidents* like that can we take?" he asked. He opened his eyes, met Piaget's gaze.

Burdeaux came up beside Piaget, said: "He's been talking crazy, Doctor Larry."

"Win, would you leave us for a bit?" Piaget asked.

"You sure?" Burdeaux scowled at Dasein.

"Please," Piaget said. He pulled up a chair, sat down beside the bed, facing Dasein.

"I'll be right outside," Burdeaux said. He went out, closed the door.

"You've upset Win and that's rather difficult to do," Piaget said.

"Upset . . . " Dasein stared at him, speechless. Then: "Is that your summation of what's happened?"

Piaget looked down at his own right hand, made a fist, opened it. He shook his head. "I didn't mean to sound flippant, Gilbert. I . . . " He looked up at Dasein. "There must be some reasonable, rational explanation."

"You don't think the word *accident* explains all this?"

"An accident prone . . . "

"We both know there's no such thing as an accident prone in the popular sense of that label," Dasein said.

Piaget steepled his hands in front of him, leaned back. He pursed his lips, then: "Well, in the psychiatric view . . . "

"Come off that!" Dasein barked. "You're going to fall back on the old cliché about 'a neurotic tendency to inflict self-injury,' a defect in ego-control. Where did I have any control over the work on that bridge? Or the boy with the bow and arrow or . . . "

"Boy with a bow and arrow?"

Dasein thought to hell with his promise, told about the incident at the park, added: "And what about the garage hoist or the fire? For that matter, what about the poison in the food Jenny . . . Jenny, of all people! the food that she . . . "

"All right! You have grounds to . . . "

"Grounds? I've an entire syndrome laid out in front of me. Santaroga is trying to kill me. You've already killed an apparently inoffensive young man. You've almost killed Jenny. What next?"

"In heaven's name, why would we . . . "

"To eliminate a threat. Isn't that obvious? I'm a threat."

"Oh, now really . . . "

"Now, really! Or is it perfectly all right if I take Jenny out of this crazy valley and blow the whistle on you?"

"Jenny won't leave her . . . " He paused. "Blow the whistle? What do you mean?"

"Now, who's making the angels weep?" Dasein asked. "You protest that you love Jenny and won't have her hurt. What more terrible thing is there than to have her be the instrument of my death?"

Piaget paled, drew two ragged breaths. "She . . . There must be . . . What do you mean blow the whistle?"

"Has a Labor Department inspector ever looked into the child labor situation out at your *school*?" Dasein asked. "What about the State Department of Mental Hygiene? Your records say no mental illness from Santaroga."

"Gilbert, you don't know what you're talking about."

"Don't I? What about the antigovernment propaganda in your newspaper?"

"We're not antigovernment, Gilbert, we're . . ."

"What? Why, I've never seen such a . . . "

"Allow me to finish, please. We're not antigovernment; we're anti-*outside*. That's a cat of quite different calico."

"You think they're all . . . insane?"

"We think they're all going to eat themselves up."

Madness, madness, Dasein thought. He stared at the ceiling. Perspiration bathed his body. The intensity of emotion he'd put into the argument with Piaget . . .

"Why did you send Burdeaux to watch over me?" Dasein asked.

Piaget shrugged. "I . . . to guard against the possibility you might be right in your . . . "

"And you picked Burdeaux." Dasein turned his eyes toward Piaget, studied the man. Piaget appeared to be warring with himself, nervously clenching and unclenching his fists.

"The reasons should be obvious," he said.

"You can't let me leave the valley, can you?" Dasein asked.

"You're in no physical condition to . . . "

"Will I ever be?"

Piaget met Dasein's gaze. "How can I prove to you what we really . . . "

"Is there any place here where I can protect myself from accidents?" Dasein asked.

"Protect yourself from . . . " Piaget shook his head.

"You want to prove your honorable intentions," Dasein said.

Piaget pursed his lips, then: "There's an isolation suite, a penthouse on the roof—its own kitchen, facilities, everything. If you . . . "

"Could Burdeaux get me up there without killing me?"

Piaget sighed. "I'll take you up there myself as soon as I can get a . . . "

"Burdeaux."

"As you wish. You can be moved in a wheelchair."

"I'll walk."

"You're not strong enough to . . . "

"I'll find the strength. Burdeaux can help me."

"Very well. As to food, we can . . . "

"I'll eat out of cans picked at random from a market's shelves. Burdeaux can shop for me until I'm . . . "

"Now, see here . . ."

"That's the way it's going to be, doctor. He'll get me a broad selection, and I'll choose at random from that selection."

"You're taking unnecessary . . . "

"Let's give it a try and see how many accidents develop."

Piaget stared at him a moment, then: "As you wish."

"What about Jenny? When can I see her?"

"She's had a severe shock to her system and some intestinal trauma. I'd say she shouldn't have visitors for several days unless they . . . "

"I'm not leaving that isolation suite until I've convinced you," Dasein said. "When can she come to see me?"

"It'll be several days." He pointed a finger at Dasein. "Now, see here, Gilbert—you're not going to take Jenny out of the valley. She'll never consent to . . ."

"Let's let Jenny decide that."

"Very well." Piaget nodded. "You'll see." He went to the door, opened it. "Win?"

Burdeaux stepped past Piaget into the room. "Is he still talking crazy, Doctor Larry?"

"We're going to conduct an experiment, Win," Piaget said. "For reasons of Dr. Dasein's health and Jenny's happiness, we're going to move him to the isolation suite." Piaget jerked a thumb toward the ceiling. "He wants you to move him."

"I'll get a wheelchair," Burdeaux said.

"Dr. Dasein wants to try walking," Piaget said.

"Can he do that?" Burdeaux turned a puzzled frown on Dasein. "He was too weak to stand just a little . . ."

"Dr. Dasein appears to be relying on your strength," Piaget said. "Think you can manage?"

198

"I could carry him," Burdeaux said, "but that seems like a . . ."

"Treat him with the same care you'd treat a helpless infant," Piaget said.

"If you say so, Doctor Larry."

Burdeaux crossed to the bed, helped Dasein to sit on the edge of the bed. The effort set Dasein's head to whirling. In the fuzzy tipping and turning of the room, he saw Piaget go to the door, open it and stand there looking at Burdeaux.

"I'll take my evil influence elsewhere for the time being," Piaget said. "You don't mind, do you, Gilbert, if I look in on you shortly—purely in a medical capacity?"

"As long as I have the final say on what you do to me," Dasein said.

"It's only fair to warn you your bandages have to be changed," Piaget said.

"Can Win do it?"

"Your trust in Win is very touching," Piaget said. "I'm sure he's impressed."

"Can he . . ."

"Yes, I'm certain he can—with my instruction."

"All right then," Dasein said.

With Burdeaux's help, Dasein struggled to his feet. He stood there panting, leaning on Burdeaux. Piaget went out, leaving the door open.

"You sure you can manage, sir?" Burdeaux asked.

Dasein tried to take a step. His knees were two sections of flexing rubber. He would have fallen had it not been for Burdeaux's support.

"Do we go by elevator?" Dasein asked.

"Yes, sir. It's right across the hall."

"Let's get on with it."

"Yes, sir. Excuse me, sir." Burdeaux bent, lifted Dasein in his arms, turned to slip through the door.

Dasein glimpsed the startled face of a nurse walking down the hall. He felt foolish, helpless—stubborn. The nurse frowned, glanced at Burdeaux, who ignored her, punched the elevator button with an elbow. The nurse strode off down the hall, heels clicking.

Elevator doors slid open with a hiss.

Burdeaux carried him inside, elbowed a button marked "P."

Dasein felt his mouth go dry as the elevator doors closed. He stared up at a cream ceiling, a milky oblong of light, thinking: *They didn't hesitate to sacrifice Jenny. Why would they have a second thought about Burdeaux? What if the elevator's rigged to crash?*

A faint humming sounded. Dasein felt the elevator lift. Presently, the doors opened and Burdeaux carried him out. There was a glimpse of a cream-walled entrance foyer, a mahogany door labeled "Isolation" and they were inside.

It was a long room with three beds, windows opening onto a black tar roof. Burdeaux deposited Dasein on the nearest bed, stepped back. "Kitchen's in there," he said, pointing to a swinging door at the end of the room. "Bathroom's through that door there." This was a door opposite the foot of Dasein's bed. There were two more doors to the right of this one. "Other doors are a closet and a lab. Is this what you wanted, Doctor?"

Dasein met a measuring stare in Burdeaux's eyes, said: "It'll have to do." He managed a rueful smile, explained the eating arrangements.

"Canned food, sir?" Burdeaux asked.

"I'm imposing on you, I know," Dasein said. "But you were . . . like me . . . once. I think you sympathise with me . . . unconsciously. I'm counting on that to . . ." Dasein managed a weak shrug.

"Is this what Doctor Larry wants me to do?"

"Yes."

"I just pick cans from the shelves . . . at random?"

"That's right."

"Well, it sounds crazy, sir . . . but I'll do it." He left the room, muttering.

Dasein managed to crawl under the blankets, lay for a moment regaining his strength. He could see a line of treetops beyond the roof—tall evergreens—a cloudless blue sky. There was a sense of quiet about the room. Dasein took a deep breath. Was this place really safe? A Santarogan had picked it. But the Santarogan had been off balance with personal doubts.

For the first time in days, Dasein felt he might relax. A profound lassitude filled him.

What is this unnatural weakness? he wondered.

It was far more than shock reaction or a result of his burns. This was like an injury to the soul, something that involved the entire being. It was a central command to all his muscles, a compulsion of inactivity.

Dasein closed his eyes.

In the red darkness behind his eyelids Dasein felt himself to be shattered, his ego huddled in a fetal crouch, terrified. One must not move, he thought. To move was to invite a disaster more terrible than death.

An uncontrollable shuddering shook his legs and hips, set his teeth chattering. He fought himself to stillness, opened his eyes to stare at the ceiling.

It's a Jaspers reaction, he thought.

There was a smell of it in the room. The aroma gnawed at his senses. He sniffed, turned toward a metal stand beside the bed, a partly-opened drawer. Dasein slid the drawer all the way out to a stop, rolled onto his side to peer at the space he'd exposed.

Empty.

But there'd been a Jaspers *something* in the drawer— and that recently.

What?

Dasein swept his gaze around the room. Isolation suite, Piaget had said. Isolation of what? From what? For what?

He swallowed, sank back on the pillow.

The deliciously terrifying lassitude gripped him. Dasein sensed the green waters of unconsciousness ready to enfold him. By a desperate effort of will, he forced his eyes to remain open.

Somewhere, a cowering, fetal *something* moaned.

Faceless god chuckled.

The entrance door opened.

Dasein held himself rigidly unmoving, afraid if he moved his head to one side his face might sink beneath the upsurging unconsciousness, that he might drown in . . .

201

Piaget came into his field of vision, peering down at him. The doctor thumbed Dasein's left eyelid up, studied the eye.

"Damned if you aren't still fighting it," he said.

"Fighting what?" Dasein whispered.

"I was pretty sure it'd knock you out if you used that much energy at this stage," Piaget said. "You're going to have to eat before long, you know."

Dasein was aware then of the pain—a demanding hollow within him. He held onto the pain. It helped fight off the enfolding green waves.

"Tell you what," Piaget said. He moved from Dasein's range of vision. There came a scraping, a grunt. "I'll just sit here and keep watch on you until Win gets back with something you'll stuff into that crazy face of yours. I won't lay a hand on you and I won't let anyone else touch you. Your bandages can wait. More important for you to rest—sleep if you can. Stop fighting it."

Sleep! Gods, how the lassitude beckoned.

Fighting what?

He tried to frame the question once more, couldn't find the energy. It took all of his effort merely to cling to a tiny glowing core of awareness that stared up at a cream-colored ceiling.

"What you're fighting," Piaget said in a conversational tone, "is the climb out of the morass. Mud clings to one. This is what leads me to suspect your theory may have a germ of truth in it—that some stain of violence still clings to us, reaching us on the blind side, as it were."

Piaget's voice was a hypnotic drone. Phrases threaded their way in and out of Dasein's awareness.

" . . . experiment in domestication . . . " " . . . removed from ex-stasis, from a fixed condition . . . " " . . . must reimprint the sense of identity . . ." " . . . nothing new: mankind's always in some sort of trouble . . ." " . . . religious experience of a sort—creating a new order of theobotanists . . . " " . . . don't shrink from life or from awareness of life . . ." " . . . seek a society that changes smoothly, flowingly as the collective need requires . . ."

One of the faceless gods produced a thundering whisper

in Dasein's skull: *"This is my commandment given unto you: A poor man cannot afford principles and a rich man doesn't need them."*

Dasein lay suspended in a hammock of silence.

Fear of movement dominated him.

He sensed a world-presence somewhere beneath him. But he lay stranded here above. Something beckoned. Familiar. He felt the familiar world and was repelled. The place seethed with disguises that tried to conceal a rubble of pretensions, devices, broken masks. Still, it beckoned. It was a place in which he could fit, shaped to him. He sensed himself reaching toward it with a feeling of exuberant self-gratification, drew back. The rubble. It was everywhere, a blanket over life, a creamy ennui—soothing, cajoling, saccharine.

Still, it beckoned.

The lure was inexhaustible, a brilliant bag of pyrotechnics, a palette flooded with gross colors.

It was all a trick.

He sensed this—all a trick, a mass of signal clichés and canned reflexes.

It was a hateful world.

Which world? he asked himself. *Was it Santaroga . . .* or *the outside?*

Something grabbed Dasein's shoulder.

He screamed.

Dasein awoke to find himself moaning, mumbling. It took a moment to place himself. Where were the faceless gods?

Piaget leaned over him, a hand on Dasein's shoulder.

"You were having a nightmare," Piaget said. He took his hand away. "Win's back with the food—such as it is."

Dasein's stomach knotted in pain.

Burdeaux stood at his right next to the adjoining bed. A box piled with canned food rested on the next bed.

"Bring me a can opener and a spoon," Dasein said.

"Just tell me what you want and I'll open it," Burdeaux said.

"I'll do it," Dasein said. He raised himself on his elbows, Movement set his arms to throbbing, but he felt

203

stronger—as though he had tapped a strength of desperation.

"Humor him," Piaget said as Burdeaux̄ hesitated.

Burdeaux shrugged, went out the door across from the bed.

Dasein threw back the blankets, swung his feet out. He motioned Piaget back, sat up. His feet touched a cold floor. He took a deep breath, lurched across to the adjoining bed. His knees felt stronger, but Dasein sensed the shallowness of his reserves.

Burdeaux reappeared, handed Dasein a twist-handle can opener.

Dasein sat down beside the box, grabbed a fat green can out of it, not even looking at the label. He worked the opener around the can, took a proffered spoon from Burdeaux, lifted back the lid.

Beans.

An odor of Jaspers clamored at Dasein from the open can. He looked at the label: "Packed by the Jaspers Cooperative." There was a permit number, a date of a year ago and the admonition: "Not for sale in interstate commerce. Exposed Dec. '64."

Dasein stared at the can. *Jaspers?* It couldn't be. The stuff didn't ship. It couldn't be preserved out of . . .

"Something wrong?" Piaget asked.

Dasein studied the can: shiny, a glistening label.

"Beans with meat sauce and beef," read the yellow letters.

Dasein ignored the lure of the aroma from the can, looked in the box. He tried to remember whether the can had given off the characteristic hiss of a vacuum seal breaking as it had been opened—couldn't remember.

"What's wrong?" Piaget insisted.

"Can't be anything wrong," Burdeaux said. "That's all private stock."

Dasein looked up from the box. All the cans he could see bore the Co-op's label. *Private stock?*

"Here," Piaget said. He took can and spoon from Dasein's hands, tasted a bite of beans, smiled. He returned the can and spoon to Dasein, who took them automatically.

"Nothing wrong there," Piaget said.

"Better not be," Burdeaux said. "It came from Pete Maja's store, right off the private stock shelf."

"It's Jaspers," Dasein rasped.

"Of course it is," Piaget said. "Canned right here for local consumption. Stored here to preserve its strength. Won't keep long after it's opened, though, so you'd better start eating. Got maybe five, ten minutes." He chuckled. "Be thankful you're here. If you were *outside* and opened that can, wouldn't last more'n a few seconds."

"Why?"

"Hostile environment," Piaget said. "Go ahead and eat. You saw me take some. Didn't hurt me."

Dasein tested a bit of the sauce on his tongue. A soothing sensation spread across his tongue, down his throat. They were delicious. He spooned a full bite into his mouth, gulped it down.

The Jaspers went thump in his stomach.

Dasein turned, wide-eyed toward Burdeaux, met a look of wonder, dark brown eyes like African charms with butter-yellow flecks in them. The can drew Dasein's attention. He peered into it.

Empty.

Dasein experienced a sensation of strange recall—like the fast rewind on a tape recorder, a screech of memory: his hand in a piston movement spooning the contents of the can into his mouth. Blurred gulpings.

He recognized the *thump* now. It had been a thump of awareness. He no longer was hungry.

My body did it, Dasein thought. A sense of wonder enfolded him. *My body did it.*

Piaget took the can and spoon from Dasein's unresisting fingers. Burdeaux helped Dasein back into bed, pulled the blankets up, straightened them.

My body did it, Dasein thought.

There'd been a trigger to action—knowledge that the Jaspers effect was fading . . . and conscioussness had blanked out.

"There," Piaget said.

"What about his bandages?" Burdeaux asked.

Piaget examined the bandage on Dasein's cheek, bent close to sniff, drew back. "Perhaps this evening," he said.

"You've trapped me, haven't you?" Dasein asked. He stared up at Piaget.

"There he goes again," Burdeaux said.

"Win," Piaget said, "I know you have personal matters to take care of. Why don't you tend to them now and leave me with Gilbert? You can come back around six if you would."

Burdeaux said: "I could call Willa and have her . . . "

"No need to bother your daughter," Piaget said. "Run along and . . . "

"But what if . . . "

"There's no danger," Piaget said.

"If you say so," Burdeaux said. He moved toward the foyer door, paused there a moment to study Dasein, then went out.

"What didn't you want Win to hear?" Dasein asked.

"There he goes again," Piaget said, echoing Burdeaux.

"Something must've . . . "

"There's nothing Win couldn't hear!"

"Yet you sent him to watch over me . . . because he was special," Dasein said. He took a deep breath, feeling his senses clear, his mind come alert. "Win was . . . *safe* for me."

"Win has his own life to live and you're interfering," Piaget said. "He . . . "

"Why was Win *safe?*"

"It's your feeling, not mine," Piaget said. "Win saved you from falling. You've shown a definite empathy . . . "

"He came from *outside,*" Dasein said. "He was like me . . . once."

"Many of us came from outside," Piaget said.

"You, too?"

"No, but . . . "

"How does the trap really work?" Dasein asked.

"There is *no* trap!"

"What does the Jaspers do to one?" Dasein asked.

"Ask yourself that question."

"Technically . . . doctor?"

206

"Technically?"

"What does the Jaspers do?"

"Oh. Among other things, it speeds up catalysis of the chemical transmitters in the nervous system—5 hydroxytryptamine and serotonin."

"Changes in the Golgi cells?"

"Absolutely not. Its effect is to break down blockage systems, to open the mind's image function and consciousness formulation processes. You *feel* as though you had a better . . . an *improved* memory. Not true, of course, except in effect. Merely a side effect of the speed with which . . . "

"Image function," Dasein said. "What if the person isn't capable of dealing with all his memories? There are extremely disagreeable, shameful . . . dangerously traumatic memories in some . . ."

"We have our failures."

"Dangerous failures?"

"Sometimes."

Dasein closed his mouth, an instinctive reaction. He drew in a deep breath through his nostrils. The odor of Jaspers assailed his senses. He looked toward the box of cans on the adjacent bed.

Jaspers. Consciousness fuel. Dangerous substance. Drug of ill omen. Speculative fantasies flitted through Dasein's mind. He turned, surprised a mooning look on Piaget's face.

"You can't get away from it here in the valley, can you?" Dasein asked.

"Who'd want to?"

"You're hoping I'll stay, perhaps help you with your failures."

"There's certainly work to be done."

Anger seized Dasein. "How can I think?" he demanded. "I can't get away from the smell of . . . "

"Easy," Piaget murmured. "Take it easy, now. You'll get so you don't even notice it."

Every society has its own essential chemistry, Dasein thought. *Its own aroma, a thing of profound importance, but least apparent to its own members.*

207

Santaroga had tried to kill him, Dasein knew. He wondered now if it could have been because he had a different smell. He stared at the box on the bed. Impossible! It couldn't be anything that close to the surface.

Piaget moved around to the box, tore a small, curling strip of paper from it, touched the paper to his tongue. "This box has been down in storage," he said. "It's paper, organic matter. Anything organic becomes impregnated with Jaspers after a certain exposure." He tossed the paper into the box.

"Will I be like that box?" Dasein asked. He felt he had a ghost at his heels, an essence he couldn't elude. The lurking presence stirred in his mind. "Will I . . ."

"Put such thoughts out of your mind," Piaget said.

"Will I be one of the failures?" Dasein asked.

"I said stop that!"

"Why should I?"

Dasein sat up, the strength of fear and anger in him, his mind crowded by suppositions, each one worse than its predecessor. He felt more exposed and vulnerable than a child running from a whipping.

With an abrupt shock of memory, Dasein fell back to the pillow. *Why did I choose this moment to remember that?* he asked himself. A painful incident from his childhood lay there, exposed to awareness. He remembered the pain of the switch on his back.

"You're not the failure type," Piaget said.

Dasein stared accusingly at the odorous box.

Jaspers!

"You're the kind who can go very high," Piaget said. "Why do you really think you're here? Just because of that silly market report? Or because of Jenny? Ah, no. Nothing that isolated or simple. Santaroga calls out to some people. They come."

Dasein looked sidelong at him.

"I came so you people could get the chance to kill me," Dasein said.

"We don't want to kill you!"

"One moment you suspect I may be right, the next you're denying it."

208

Piaget sighed.

"I have a suggestion," Dasein said.

"Anything."

"You won't like it," Dasein said.

Piaget glared at him. "What's on your mind?"

"You'll be afraid to do it."

"I'm not . . . "

"It's something like a clinical test," Dasein said. "My guess is you'll try not to do it. You'll look for excuses, anything to get out of it or to discontinue it. You'll try to misunderstand me. You'll try to break away from . . ."

"For the love of heaven! What's on your mind?"

"You may succeed."

"Succeed in what?"

"Not doing what I suggest."

"Don't try to crowd me into a corner, Gilbert."

"Thus it starts," Dasein said. He held up a hand as Piaget made as though to speak. "I want you to let me hypnotize you."

"What?"

"You heard me."

"Why?"

"You're a native," Dasein said, "thoroughly conditioned to this . . . consciousness fuel. I want to see what's under there, what kind of fears you . . ."

"Of all the crazy . . . "

"I'm not some amateur meddler asking to do this," Dasein said. "I'm a clinical psychologist well versed in hypnotherapy."

"But what could you possibly hope to . . ."

"What a man fears," Dasein said. "His fears are like a 'homing beacon.' Home in on a man's fears and you find his underlying motivations. Under every fear, there's a violence of no mean . . . "

"Nonsense! I have no . . . "

"You're a medical man. You know better than that."

Piaget stared at him, silently measuring. Presently, he said: "Well, every man has a death fear, of course. And . . ."

"More than that."

209

"You think you're some kind of god, Gilbert? You just go around . . . "

"Doth the eagle mount up at thy command, and make her nest on high?" Dasein asked. He shook his head. "What do you worship?"

"Oh . . . religion." Piaget took a deep breath of relief. "Thou shalt not be afraid for the terror by night; nor for the arrow that flieth by day; nor for the pestilence that walketh in darkness; nor for the destruction that wasteth at noonday. Is that it? What do . . ."

"That is *not* it."

"Gilbert, I'm not ignorant of these matters, as you must realize. To stir up the areas you're suggesting . . . "

"What would I stir up?"

"We both know that cannot be predicted with any accuracy."

"You're doing things as a community . . . a group, a society that you don't want me digging into," Dasein said. "What does that society really worship? With one hand, you say: 'Look anywhere you like.' With the other hand, you slam doors. In every action of . . . "

"You really believe some of us tried to . . . kill you . . . for the community?"

"Don't you?"

"Couldn't there be some other explanation?"

"What?"

Dasein held a steady gaze on Piaget. The doctor was disturbed, no doubt of that. He refused to meet Dasein's eyes. He moved his hands about aimlessly. His breathing had quickened.

"Societies don't believe they can die," Piaget said. "It must follow that a society, as such, does not worship at all. If it cannot die, it'll never face a final judgment."

"And if it'll never face judgment," Dasein said, "it can do things as a society that'd be too much for an individual to stomach."

"Perhaps," Piaget muttered. "Perhaps." Then: "All right, then. Why examine me? I've never tried to harm you."

Dasein looked away, taken aback by the question. Out

210

the window he could see through a frame of trees a stretch of the hills which enclosed Santaroga. He felt himself enclosed by that line of hills, entangled here in a web of meanings.

"What about the people who have tried to kill me?" Dasein asked shortly. "Would they be fit subjects?"

"The boy, perhaps," Piaget said. "I'll have to examine him anyway."

"Petey, the Jorick boy," Dasein said. "A failure, eh?"

"I think not."

"Another *opening person* . . . like me?"

"You remember that?"

"Then, you said societies die, that you'd cut yourselves off here . . . with Jaspers."

"We had a speaking then, too, as I recall it," Piaget said. "Have you really opened now? Are you seeing? Have you become?"

Dasein abruptly remembered Jenny's voice on the telephone: "Be careful." And the fear when she'd said: "They want you to leave."

In this instant, Piaget became for him once more the gray cat in the garden, silencing the birds, and Dasein knew himself to be alone yet, without a group. He remembered the lake, the perception of perception—knowing his own body, that communal knowledge of mood, that sharing.

Every conversation he'd had with Piaget came back to Dasein then to be weighed and balanced. He felt his Santaroga experiences had been building—one moment upon another—to this instant.

"I'll get you some more Jaspers," Piaget said. "Perhaps then . . . "

"You suspect I'm fluttery behind the eyes?" Dasein asked.

Piaget smiled. "Sarah clings to the phrases of the past," he said, "before we systematized our dealings with Jaspers . . . and with the outside. But don't laugh at her or her phrases. She has the innocent eye."

"Which I haven't."

"You still have some of the assumptions and prejudices of the not-men," Piaget said.

211

"And I've heard too much, learned too much about you, ever to be allowed to leave," Dasein said.

"Won't you even try to become?" Piaget asked.

"Become what?" Piaget's crazy, almost-schizophrenic talk enraged him. *A speaking! A seeing!*

"Only you know that," Piiaget said.

"Know what?"

Piaget merely stared at him.

"I'll tell you what I know," Dasein said. "I know you're terrified by my suggestion. You don't want to find out how Vina's roach powder got into the coffee. You don't want to know how Clara Scheler poisoned her stew. You don't want to know what prompted someone to push me off a float. You don't want to know why a fifteen-year-old boy would try to put an arrow through me. You don't want to know how Jenny poisoned the eggs. You don't want to know how a car was set up to crush me, or how my truck was rigged as a fire bomb. You don't want to . . ."

"All right!"

Piaget rubbed his chin, turned away.

"I told you you might succeed," Dasein said.

" '*Iti vuccati*' " Piaget murmured. " 'Thus it is said: Every system and every interpretation becomes false in the light of a more complete system.' I wonder if that's why you're here—to remind us no positive statement may be made that's free from contradictions."

He turned, stared at Dasein.

"What're you talking about?" Dasein asked. Piaget's tone and manner carried a suddenly disturbing calmness.

"The inner enlightenment of all beings dwells in the self," Piaget said. "The self which cannot be isolated abides in the memory as a perception of symbols. We are conscious as a projection of self upon the receptive content of the senses. But it happens the self can be led astray— the self of a person or the self of a community. I wonder . . ."

"Stop trying to distract me with gobbledygook," Dasein said. "You're trying to change the subject, avoid . . ."

"A . . . void," Piaget said. "Ah, yes. The void is very pertinent to this. Einstein cannot be confined to mathematics. All phenomenal existence is transitory, relative. No particular thing is real. It is passing into something else at every moment."

Dasein pushed himself upright in the bed. Had the old doctor gone crazy?

"Performance alone doesn't produce the result," Piaget said. "You're grasping at absolutes. To seek any fixed thing, however, is to deal in false imagination. You're trying to strain soap from the water with your fingers. Duality is a delusion."

Dasein shook his head from side to side. The man was making no sense at all.

"I see you are confused," Piaget said. "You don't really understand your own intellectual energy. You walk on narrow paths. I offer you new orbits of . . . "

"You can stop that," Dasein said. He remembered the lake then, the husky feminine voice saying: *"There's only one thing to do."* And Jenny: *"We're doing it."*

"You must adapt to conditional thought," Piaget said. "In that way, you'll be able to understand relative self-existence and express the relative truth of whatever you perceive. You have the ability to do it. I can see that. Your insight into the violent actions which surround . . . "

"Whatever you're doing to me, you won't stop it, will you?" Dasein asked. "You keep pushing and pushing and . . ."

"Who pushes?" Piaget asked. "Are you not the one exerting the greatest . . . "

"Damn you! Stop it!"

Piaget looked at him silently.

"Einstein," Dasein muttered. "Relativity . . . absolutes . . . intellectual energy . . . phenomenal . . ." He broke off as his mind lurched momentarily into a speed of computation very like what he had experienced when deciding to hurdle the gap in the bridge.

It's sweep-rate, Dasein thought. *It's like hunting submarines—in the mind. It's how many search units you can put to the job and how fast they can travel.*

As quickly as it had come, the sensation was gone. But Dasein had never felt as shaken in his life. No immediate

213

danger had triggered this ability . . . not this time.

Narrow paths, he thought. He looked up at Piaget in wonder. There was more here than fell upon the ears. Could that be the way Santarogans thought? Dasein shook his head. It didn't seem possible . . . or likely.

"May I elaborate?" Piaget asked.

Dasein nodded.

"You will have remarked the blunt way we state our relative truths for sales purposes," Piaget said. "Conditional thought rejects any other approach. Mutual respect is implicit, then, in conditional thought. Contrast the market approach of those who sent you to spy upon us. They have . . ."

"How fast can you think?" Dasein asked.

"Fast?" Piaget shrugged. "As fast as necessary."

As fast as necessary, Dasein thought.

"May I continue?" Piaget asked.

Again, Dasein nodded.

"It has been noted," Piaget said, "that sewer-peak-load times tend to match station breaks on TV—an elementary fact you can recognize with only the briefest reflection. But it's only a short step from this elementary fact to the placement of flow meters in the sewers as a quite accurate check on the available listening units at any given moment. I've no doubt this already is being done; it's so obvious. Now, reflect a moment on the basic attitudes toward their fellowmen of people who would do this sort of thing, as opposed to those who could not find it in themselves to do it."

Dasein cleared his throat. Here was the core of Santaroga's indictment against the *outside*. How did you use people? With dignity? Or did you tap their most basic functions for your own purposes? The *outside* began to appear more and more as a place of irritating emptiness and contrived blandishments.

I'm really beginning to see things as a Santarogan, Dasein thought. There was a sense of victory in the thought. It was what he had set out to do as part of his job.

"It isn't surprising," Piaget said, "to find the 'N-square' law from warfare being applied to advertising and politics—other kinds of warfare, you see—with no real

214

conversion problem from one field to the other. Each has its concepts of concentration and exposure. The mathematics of differentials and predictions apply equally well, no matter the field of battle."

Armies, Dasein thought. He focused on Piaget's moving lips, wondering suddenly how the subject had been changed to such a different field. Had Piaget done it deliberately? They'd been talking about Santaroga's blind side, its fears . . .

"You've given me food for speculation," Piaget said. "I'm going to leave you alone for a while and see if I can come up with something constructive. There's a call bell at the head of your bed. The nurses are not on this floor, but one can be here quite rapidly in an emergency. They'll look in on you from time to time. Would you like something to read? May I send you anything?"

Something constructive? Dasein wondered. *What does he mean?*

"How about some copies of our valley newspaper?" Piaget asked.

"Some writing paper and a pen," Dasein said. He hesitated, then: "And the papers—yes."

"Very well. Try to rest. You appear to be regaining some of your strength, but don't overdo it."

Piaget turned, strode out of the room.

Presently, a red-haired nurse bustled in with a stack of newspapers, a ruled tablet and a dark-green ballpoint pen. She deposited them on his nightstand, said: "Do you want your bed straightened?"

"No, thanks."

Dasein found his attention caught by her striking resemblance to Al Marden.

"You're a Marden," he said.

"So what else is new?" she asked and left him.

Well, get her! Dasein thought.

He glanced at the stack of newspapers, remembering his search through Santaroga for the paper's office. They had come to him so easily they'd lost some of their allure. He slipped out of bed, found his knees had lost some of their weakness.

215

The canned food caught his eye.

Dasein rummaged in the box, found an applesauce, ate it swiftly while the food still was redolent with Jaspers. Even as he ate, he hoped this would return him to that level of clarity and speed of thought he'd experienced at the bridge and, briefly, with Piaget.

The applesauce eased his hunger, left him vaguely restless—nothing else.

Was it losing its kick? he wondered. Did it require more and more of the stuff each time? Or was he merely becoming acclimated?

Hooked?

He thought of Jenny pleading with him, cajoling. *A consciousness fuel. What in the name of God had Santaroga discovered?*

Dasein stared out the window at the path of boundary hills visible through the trees. A fire somewhere beneath his field of view sent smoke spiraling above the ridge. Dasein stared at the smoke, feeling an oddly compulsive mysticism, a deeply primitive sensation about that unseen fire. There was a spirit signature written in the smoke, something out of his own genetic past. No fear accompanied the sensation. It was, instead, as though he had been reunited with some part of himself cut off since childhood.

Pushing back at the surface of childhood, he thought.

He realized then that a Santarogan did not cut off his primitive past; he contained it within a membranous understanding.

How far do I go in becoming a Santarogan before I turn back? he wondered. *I have a duty to Selador and the ones who hired me. When do I make my break?*

The thought filled him with a deep revulsion against returning to the *outside*. But he had to do it. There was a thick feeling of nausea in his throat, a pounding ache at his temples. He thought of the irritant emptiness of the *outside*—piecemeal debris of lives, egos with sham patches, a world almost devoid of anything to make the soul rise and soar.

There was no substructure to life *outside*, he thought, no

underlying sequence to tie it all together. There was only a shallow, glittering roadway signposted with flashy, hypnotic diversions. And behind the glitter—only the bare board structure of props . . . arfd desolation.

I can't go back, he thought. He turned to his bed, threw himself across it. *My duty—I must go back. What's happening to me? Have I waited too long?*

Had Piaget lied about the Jaspers effect?

Dasein turned onto his back, threw an arm across his eyes. What was the chemical essence of Jaspers? Selador could be no help there; the stuff didn't travel.

I knew that, Dasein thought. *I knew it all along.*

He took his arm away from his eyes. No doubt of what he'd been doing: avoiding his own responsibility. Dasein looked at the doors in the wall facing him—kitchen, lab . . .

A sigh lifted his chest.

Cheese would be the best carrier, he knew. It held the Jaspers essence longest. The lab . . . and some cheese.

Dasein rang the bell at the head of his bed.

A voice startled him, coming from directly behind his head: "Do you wish a nurse immediately?"

Dasein turned, saw a speaker grill in the wall. "I'd . . . like some Jaspers cheese," he said.

"Oh . . . Right away, sir." There was delight in that feminine voice no electronic reproduction could conceal.

Presently, the red-haired nurse with the stamp of the Marden genes on her face shouldered her way into the room carrying a tray. She placed the tray atop the papers on Dasein's nightstand.

"There you are, doctor," she said. "I brought you some crackers, too."

"Thanks," Dasein said.

She turned at the doorway before leaving: "Jenny will be delighted to hear this."

"Jenny's awake?"

"Oh, yes. Most of her problem was an allergenic reaction to the aconite. We've purged the poison from her system and she's making a very rapid recovery. She wants to get up. That's always a good sign."

217

"How'd the poison get in the food?" Dasein asked.

"One of the student nurses mistook it for a container of MSG. She . . . "

"But how'd it get in the kitchen?"

"We haven't determined yet. No doubt it was some silly accident."

"No doubt," Dasein muttered.

"Well, you eat your cheese and get some rest," she said. "Ring if you need anything."

The door closed briskly behind her.

Dasein looked at the golden block of cheese. Its Jaspers odor clamored at his nostrils. He broke off a small corner of the cheese in his fingers, touched it to his tongue. Dasein's senses jumped to attention. Without conscious volition, he took the cheese into his mouth, swallowed it: smooth, soothing flavor. A clear-headed alertness surged through him.

Whatever else happens, Dasein thought, *the world has to find out about this stuff.*

He swung his feet out of bed, stood up. A pulsing ache throbbed through his forehead. He closed his eyes, felt the world spin, steadied himself against the bed.

The vertigo passed.

Dasein found a cheese knife on the tray, cut a slice off the golden brick, stopped his hand from conveying the food to his mouth.

The body does it, he thought. He felt the strength of the physical demand, promised himself more of the cheese . . . later. First—the lab.

It was pretty much as he'd expected: sparse, but sufficient. There was a good centrifuge, a microtome, a binocular microscope with controlled illumination, gas burner, ranks of clean test tubes—all the instruments and esoteria of the trade.

Dasein found a container of sterile water, another of alcohol, put bits of the cheese into solution. He started a culture flask, made a control slide and examined it under the microscope.

A threadlike binding structure within the cheese leaped into vision. As he raised magnification, the threads

218

resolved into spirals of elongated structure that resembled cells which had been blocked from normal division.

Dasein sat back, puzzled. The thread pattern bore a resemblance to fungoid mycelium spawn. This agreed with his early surmise; he was dealing with a type of fungus growth.

What was the active agent, though?

He closed his eyes to think, realized he was trembling with fatigue.

Easy does it, he thought. *You're not a well man.*

Some of the experiments required time to mature, he told himself. They could wait. He made his way back to bed, stretched out on the blankets. His left hand reached out to the cheese, broke off a chunk.

Dasein became aware of his own action as he swallowed the cheese. He looked at the crumbled specks on his fingers, rubbed them, felt the oily smoothness. A delicious sense of well-being spread through his body.

The body does it, Dasein thought. *Of itself, the body does it. Could the body go out and kill a man? Very likely.*

He felt sleep winding about his consciousness. The body needed sleep. The body would have sleep.

The mind, though, built a dream—of trees growing to gigantic size as he watched them. They leaped up with swift vitality. Their branches swept out, leafed, fruited. All basked under a sun the color of golden cheese.

12

Sunset was burning orange in the west when Dasein awoke. He lay, his head turned toward the windows, looking out at the blazing sky, his attention caught in a spell akin to ancient sun worship. The ship of life was headed down to its daily rest. Soon, steel darkness would claim the land.

A click sounded behind Dasein. Artificial light flooded the room. He turned, the spell broken.

Jenny stood just inside the door. She wore a long green robe that reached almost to her ankles. Green slippers covered her feet.

"It's about time you woke up," she said.

Dasein stared at her as at a stranger. He could see it was the same Jenny he loved—her long black hair caught in a red ribbon, full lips slightly parted, dimple showing in her cheek—but furtive smoke drifted in her blue eyes. There was the calm of a goddess about her.

Something eternally of the past moved her body as Jenny stepped farther into the room.

A thrill of fear shot through Dasein. It was the fear an Attic peasant might have experienced before a priestess at Delphi. She was beautiful . . . and deadly.

"Aren't you going to ask how I am?" she asked.

"I can see you're all right," he said.

She took another step toward him, said: "Clara brought Jersey Hofstedder's car over and left it for you. It's down in the garage."

Dasein thought of that beautifully machined automobile—another bauble to attract him.

"And what have you brought—this time?" he asked.

"Gil!"

"There's no food in your hands," he said. "Is it a poisoned hatpin, perhaps?"

Tears flooded her eyes.

"Stay away from me," he said. "I love you."

She nodded. "I do love you. And . . . I've felt how dangerous I could be . . . to you. There've been . . . " She shook her head. "I knew I had to stay away from you. But not any more. Not now."

"So it's all over," he said. "Let bygones be bygones. Wouldn't a gun be quicker?"

She stamped a foot. "Gil, you're impossible!"

"*I'm* impossible?"

"Have you changed?" she whispered. "Don't you feel any . . . "

"I still love you," he said. "Stay away from me. I love you."

She bit her lip.

"Wouldn't it be kindest to do it while I'm asleep?" he asked. "Never let me know who . . . "

"Stop it!"

Abruptly, she ripped off the green robe, revealing a white, lace-edged nightgown beneath. She dropped the robe, pulled the gown over her head, threw it on the floor, stood there naked, glaring at him.

"See?" she said. "Nothing here but a woman! Nothing here but the woman who loves you." Tears ran down her cheeks. "No poison in my hands . . . Oh, Gil . . . " His name came out as a wail.

Dasein forced his gaze away from her. He knew he couldn't look at her—lovely, lithe, desirable—and retain any coolness of judgment. She was beautiful and deadly—the ultimate bait Santaroga offered.

There was a rustling of cloth near the door.

He whirled.

She stood once more clothed in the green robe. Her cheeks were scarlet, lips trembling, eyes downcast. Slowly, she raised her eyes, met his stare.

"I have no shame with you, Gil," she said. "I love you. I

want no secrets between us at all—no secrets of the flesh
... no secrets of any kind."

Dasein tried to swallow past a lump in his throat. The
goddess was vulnerable. It was a discovery that caused an
ache in his chest.

"I feel the same way," he said. "Jen . . . you'd better
leave now. If you don't . . . I might just grab you and rape
you."

She tried to smile, failed, whirled away and ran out of
the room.

The door slammed. There was a moment's silence. The
door opened. Piaget stood in the opening looking back into
the foyer. The sound of the elevator doors closing came
clearly to Dasein. Piaget came in, closed the door.

"What happened with you two?" he asked.

"I think we just had a fight and made up," Dasein said.
"I'm not sure."

Piaget cleared his throat. There was a look of confidence
in his round face, Dasein thought. It was not a judgment
he could be sure of, however, in the unmapped land of
concentration. At any rate, the look was gone now,
replaced by a wide-eyed stare of interest in Dasein.

"You're looking vastly improved," Piaget said. "You've
a better color in your face. Feeling stronger?"

"As a matter of fact I am."

Piaget glanced at the remains of the cheese on the
nightstand, crossed and sniffed at it. "Bit stale," he said.
"I'll have a fresh block sent up."

"You do that," Dasein said.

"Care to let me look at your bandages?" Piaget asked.

"I thought we were going to let Burdeaux work on my
bandages."

"Win had a small emergency at home. His daughter's
getting married tomorrow, you know. He'll be along later."

"I didn't know."

"Just getting the new couple's house built in time,"
Piaget said. "Bit of a delay because we decided to build
four at once in the same area. Good location—you and
Jenny might like one of them."

"That's nice," Dasein said. "You all get together and

build a house for the newlyweds."

"We take care of our own," Piaget said. "Let's look at those bandages, shall we?"

"Let's."

"Glad to see you're being more reasonable," Piaget said. "Be right back." He went out the lab door, returned in a moment with a supply cart, stationed the cart beside Dasein's bed, began cutting away the head bandages.

"See you've been puttering around the lab," Piaget said.

Dasein winced as air hit the burn on his cheek. "Is that what I've been doing, puttering?"

"What have you been doing?" Piaget asked. He bent, examined Dasein's cheek. "This is coming along fine. Won't even leave a scar, I do believe."

"I'm looking for the active agent in Jaspers," Dasein said.

"Been several attempts along that line," Piaget said. "Trouble is we all get too busy with more immediate problems."

"You've had a try at it?" Dasein asked.

"When I was younger."

Dasein waited for the head bandage to be tied off before asking: "Do you have notes, any summary of . . . "

"No notes. Never had time."

Piaget began working on Dasein's right arm.

"But what did you find out?"

"Got a broth rich in amino acids," Piaget said. "Yeastlike. You're going to have a scar on this arm, nothing alarming, and you're healing rapidly. You can thank Jaspers for that."

"What?" Dasein looked up at him, puzzled.

"Nature gives; nature takes away. The Jaspers change in body chemistry makes you more susceptible to allergenic reactions, but your body will heal five to ten times faster than it would *outside*."

Dasein looked down at his exposed arm. Pink new flesh already covered the burned area. He could see the scar puckering Piaget had noted.

"What change in body chemistry?" Dasein asked.

"Well, mostly a better hormone balance," Piaget said.

223

"Closer to what you find in an embryo."

"That doesn't square with the allergy reactions," Dasein protested.

"I'm not saying it's a simple thing," Piaget said. "Hold your arm out here. Steady now."

Dasein waited for the bandage to be completed, then: "What about structure and . . . "

"Something between a virus and a bacteria," Piaget said. "Fungusoid in some respects, but . . . "

"I saw cell structure in a sample under the microscope."

"Yes, but no nucleus. Some nuclear material, certainly, but it can be induced to form virusoid crystals."

"Do the crystals have the Jaspers effect?"

"No. They can. however, be introduced into the proper environment and after suitable development they will produce the desired effect."

"What environment?"

"You know what environment, Gilbert."

"The Co-op's cave?"

"Yes." Piaget finished exposing Dasein's left arm. "Don't think you'll have as much scar tissue on this side."

"What's unique about the cave environment?" Dasein asked.

"We're not certain."

"Hasn't anybody ever tried to . . . "

"We do have a great many *immediate* problems j st to maintain ourselves, Gilbert," Piaget said.

Dasein looked down, watched Piaget finish the bandage on the left arm. *Maintain themselves?* he wondered.

"Is there any objection to my looking into it?" Dasein asked.

"When you find time—certainly not." Piaget restored instruments and material to the cart, pushed it aside. "There. I think we'll be able to take the bandages off tomorrow. You're progressing beautifully."

"Am I really?"

Piaget smiled at him. "Insurance from the garage will take care of paying for your new car," he said. "I presume Jenny told you about the car."

"She told me."

224

"We're also replacing your clothing. Is there anything else?"

"How about replacing my freedom of choice?"

"You have freedom of choice, Gilbert, and a broader area from which to choose. Now, I have some . . . "

"Keep your advice," Dasein said.

"Advice? I was about to say I have some rather interesting information for you. Your suggestion that I look into the people you accuse of trying to kill you has borne some . . . "

"My suggestion that *you* look?"

"I took the liberty of going ahead with your suggestion."

"So you hypnotized some of them," Dasein said. "Did you prepare a Davis chart on their suscept . . . "

"I did *not* hypnotize them," Piaget snapped. "Will you be silent and listen?"

Dasein sighed, looked at the ceiling.

"I've interviewed several of these people," Piaget said. "The boy, Petey Jorick, first because he's a primary concern of mine, having just been released from . . . school. An extremely interesting fact emerges."

"Oh?"

"Each of these persons has a strong unconscious reason to fear and hate the *outside*."

"What?" Dasein turned a puzzled frown on Piaget.

"They weren't attacking you as Gilbert Dasein," Piaget said. "You were the *outsider*. There's a strong unresolved . . . "

"You mean you consider this good and sufficient . . . "

"The reasons are unconscious, as you suspected," Piaget said. "The structure of motivation, however . . . "

"So Jenny both loves me and hates me . . . as an *outsider*?"

"Get one thing straight, Gilbert. Jenny did not try to harm you. It was a student nurse who . . . "

"Jenny told me herself she prepared . . . "

"Only in the broadest sense is that true," Piaget said. "She did go to the diet kitchen and order your food and watch while it was prepared. However, she couldn't keep an eye on every . . . "

225

"And this . . . this hate of *outsiders*," Dasein said, "you think this is why some of your people tried to get me?"

"It's clearly indicated, Gilbert."

Dasein stared at him. Piaget believed this—no doubt of it.

"So all I have to watch out for as long as I live in Santaroga is people who hate outsiders?" Dasein asked.

"You have nothing to fear now at all," Piaget said. "You're no longer an outsider. You're one of us. And when you and Jenny marry . . . "

"Of all the nonsense I've ever heard," Dasein said. "This takes all the honors! This . . . this kid, Petey, he just wanted to put an arrow through me because . . . "

"He has a pathological fear of leaving the valley for college outside," Piaget said. "He'll overcome this, of course, but the emotions of childhood have more . . . "

"The roach powder in the coffee," Dasein said. "That was just . . . "

"That's a very unhappy case," Piaget said. "She fell in love with an outsider at college—much as Jenny did, I might add. The difference is that her friend seduced her and left her. She has a daughter who . . . "

"My god! You really believe this crap," Dasein said. He pushed himself against the head of the bed, sat glaring at Piaget.

"Gilbert, I find this far easier to believe than I do your wild theory that Santaroga has mounted a concerted attack against you. After all, you yourself must see . . . "

"Sure," Dasein said. "I want you to explain the accident at the bridge. I want to see how that . . . "

"Easiest of all," Piaget said. "The young man in question was enamored of Jenny before you came on the scene."

"So he just waited for the moment when . . . "

"It was entirely on the unconscious level, that I assure you, Gilbert."

Dasein merely stared at him. The structure of rationalization Piaget had built up assumed for Dasein the shape of a tree. It was like the tree of his dream. There was the strong trunk protruding into daylight—consciousness.

226

The roots were down there growing in darkness. The limbs came out and dangled prettily distracting leaves and fruit. It was a consistent structure despite its falsity.

There'd be no cutting it down, Dasein saw. The thing was too substantial. There were too many like it in the forest that was Santaroga. *"This is a tree, see? Doesn't it look like all the others?"*

"I think when you've had time to reflect," Piaget said, "you'll come to realize the truth of what . . . "

"Oh, no doubt," Dasein said.

"I'll, uh . . . I'll send you up some more fresh cheese," Piaget said. "Special stock."

"You do that," Dasein said.

"I quite understand," Piaget said. "You think you're being very cynical and wise right now. But you'll come around." He strode from the room.

Dasein continued to stare at the closed door long after Piaget had gone. The man couldn't see it, would never be capable of seeing it. No Santarogan could. Not even Jenny despite her love-sharpened awareness. Piaget's explanation was too easy to take. It'd be the official line.

I've got to get out of this crazy valley, Dasein thought.

He slipped out of bed just as the door opened and a hatless, chubby young student nurse entered with a tray.

"Oh, you're out of bed," she said. "Good."

She took the old tray off the nightstand, put the new one in its place, set the old one on a chair.

"I'll just straighten up your bed while you're out of it," she said.

Dasein stood to one side while she bustled about the bed. Presently, she left, taking the old tray with her.

He looked at what she had brought—a golden wedge of cheese, crackers, a glass and a bottle of Jaspers beer.

In a surge of anger, Dasein hurled the cheese against the wall. He was standing there staring at the mess when a soothing sensation on his tongue made him realize he was licking the crumbs off his fingers.

Dasein stared at his own hand as though it belonged to another person. He consciously forced himself not to bend and recover the cheese from the floor, turned to the beer.

There was an opener behind the bottle. He poured it into the glass, drank in swift gulps. Only when the glass was drained did he grow aware of the rich bouquet of Jaspers in the remaining drops of beer.

Fighting down a fit of trembling, Dasein put the glass on the nightstand, crawled into the bed as though seeking sanctuary.

His body refused to be denied. People didn't take Jaspers, he thought. Jaspers took people. He felt the expanding effect within his consciousness, sensed the thunder of a host jarring across the inner landscape of his psyche. Time lost its normal flow, became compressed and explosive.

Somewhere in a hospital room there were purposeful footsteps. The toggles of a switch slammed away from their connections to create darkness. A door closed.

Dasein opened his eyes to a window and starshine. In its illumination he saw a fresh wedge of cheese on his nightstand. The mess had been cleaned from wall and floor. He remembered Jenny's voice—soft, musical, rippling like dark water over rocks, a plaintive tremor in it.

Had Jenny been here in the dark?

He sensed no answer.

Dasein groped for the call buzzer at the head of his bed, pressed it.

A voice sounded from the speaker: "Do you wish a nurse?"

"What time is it?" Dasein asked.

"Three twenty-four a.m. Do you want a sleeping pill?"

"No . . . thanks."

He sat up, slid his feet to the floor, stared at the cheese.

"Did you just want the time?" the speaker asked.

"What does a full round of Jaspers cheese weigh?" he asked.

"The weight?" There was a pause, then: "They vary. The smaller ones weigh about thirty pounds. Why?"

"Send me a full round," he said.

"A full . . . Don't you have some now?"

"I want it for lab tests," he said, and he thought: *There! Let's see if Piaget was being honest with me.*

228

"You want it when you get up in the morning?"

"I'm up now. And get me a robe and some slippers if you can."

"Hadn't you better wait, doctor. If . . . "

"Check with Piaget if you must," Dasein said. "I want that round now."

"Very well." She sounded disapproving.

Dasein waited sitting on the edge of the bed. He stared out the window at the night. Absently, he broke off a chunk of the cheese on his nightstand, chewed it and swallowed.

Presently, the foyer door produced a wedge of light. A tall, gray-haired nurse entered, turned on the room's lights. She carried a large wheel of golden cheese still glistening in its wax sealer.

"This is thirty-six pounds of prime Jaspers cheese," she said. "Where shall I put it?" There were overtones of outrage and protest in her voice.

"Find a place for it on one of the lab benches," he said. "Where are the robe and slippers?"

"If you'll be patient, I'll get them for you," she said. She shouldered her way through the lab door, returned in a moment and crossed to a narrow door at the far end of the room, opened it to reveal a closet. From the closet she removed a green robe and a pair of black slippers which she dumped on the foot of Dasein's bed.

"Will that be all—sir?"

"That'll be all, for now."

"Hmmmph." She strode from the room, shut the foyer door with a final-comment thump.

Dasein took another bite of the cheese from his nightstand, put on the robe and slippers, went into the lab. The nurse had left the lights on. The round of cheese lay on an open metal bench at his right.

Alcohol won't kill it, he thought. *Otherwise, it couldn't be incorporated in the local beer. What does destroy it? Sunlight?*

He recalled the dim red light of the Co-op's cave.

Well, there were ways of finding out. He rolled back the sleeves of his gown, set to work.

229

Within an hour he had three-fourths of the round reduced to a milky solution in a carboy, set about feeding it through the centrifuge.

The first test tubes came out with their contents layered in a manner reminiscent of a chromatograph. Near the top lay a thin silver-gray band of material.

Dasein poured off the liquid, burned a hole in the bottom of a test tube and removed the solids intact by blowing into the hole he'd created. A bit of the gray material went on a slide and he examined it under the microscope.

There was the mycelium structure, distorted but recognizable. He smelled the slide. It was redolent of Jaspers. He put a hand to the microscope's variable light control, watched the specimen while rotating the control. Abruptly, the specimen began to shrivel and crystallize before his eyes.

Dasein looked at the light control. It was the spectrum-window type and, at this moment, was passing light in the Angstrom range 4000-5800. It was cutting off the red end, Dasein noted.

Another look through the microscope showed the specimen reduced to a white crystalline mass.

Sunlight, then.

What would do the job? he wondered. A bomb to open the cave? A portable sunlamp?

As he thought this, Dasein felt that the darkness outside the hospital parted to reveal a shape, a monster rising out of a black lake.

He shuddered, turned to the carboy of milky solution. Working mechanically, he put the rest of the solution through the centrifuge, separated the silver-gray band, collected the material in a dark brown bottle. The solution produced almost a pint of the Jaspers essence.

Dasein smelled the bottle—sharp and definite odor of Jaspers. He emptied the bottle into a shallow dish, caught a bit of the substance on a spatula, touched it to his tongue.

An electrifying sensation of distant fireworks exploded from his tastebuds through his spine. He felt he could see with the tip of his tongue or the tip of a finger. Dasein sensed his core of awareness becoming a steely kernel surrounded by desolation. He concentrated his energy, forced himself to look at the dish of Jaspers essence.

Empty!

What had destroyed it? How could it be empty.

He looked at the palm of his right hand. How close it was to his face! There were specks of silver-gray against the pink flesh.

Tingling pulses of awareness began surging out from his throat and stomach, along his arms and legs. He felt that his entire skin came alight. There was a remote feeling of a body slipping to the floor, but he felt that the floor glowed wherever the body touched it.

I ate the entire dish of essence, he thought.

What would it do—the active agent from more than thirty pounds of Jaspers cheese? What would it do? What was it doing? Dasein felt this to be an even more interesting question.

What was it doing?

As he asked the question of himself, he experienced anguish. It wasn't fear, but pure anguish, a sense of losing his grip on reality.

The steely kernel of selfdom! Where was it?

Upon what fundament of reality did his selfdom sit? Frantically, Dasein tried to extend his awareness, experienced the direct sensation that he was projecting his own reality upon the universe. But there was a projection *of* the universe simultaneously. He followed the lines of this projection, felt them sweep through him as though through a shadow.

In this instant, he was lost, tumbling.

I was just a shadow, he thought.

The thought fascinated him. He remembered the shadow game of his childhood, wondered what forms of shadows he could project by distorting the core of self. The wondering produced the effect of shapes. Dasein sensed a screen of awareness, a shapeless outline upon it. He willed the shape to change.

A muscled, breast-beating hero took form there.

Dasein shifted his emphasis.

The shadow became a bent-shouldered, myopic scientist

231

in a long gown. Another shift: It was naked Apollo racing over a landscape of feminine figures.

And again—a plodder bent beneath a shapeless load.

With a gulping sensation of *deitgrasp* Dasein realized he was projecting the only limits his finite being could know. It was an act of self-discovery that gave birth to a feeling of hope. It was an odd sort of hope, unfixed, disoriented, but definite in its existence—not a hope of discernment, but pure hope without boundaries, direction or attachments.

Hope itself.

It was a profound instant permitting him to grasp for a fleeting instant the structure of his own existence, his possibilities as a being.

A twisted, dented and distorted *something* crossed the field of Dasein's awareness. He recognized the kernel of selfdom. The thing had lost all useful shape. He discarded it, chuckling.

Who discarded it? Dasein wondered.

Who chuckles?

There was a pounding sound—feet upon a floor.

Voices.

He recognized the tones of the gray-haired nurse, but there was a tingling of panic in the sounds she made.

Piaget.

"Let's get him on the bed," Piaget said. The words were clear and distinct.

What was not distinct was the shape of a universe become blurred rainbows, nor the pressures of hands which blotted out the glowing sensation of his skin.

"It's difficult to become conscious about consciousness," Dasein muttered.

"Did he say something?" That was the nurse.

"I couldn't make it out." Piaget.

"Did you smell the Jaspers in there?" The nurse.

"I think he separated the essence out and took it."

"Oh, my god! What can we do?"

"Wait and pray. Bring me a straight-jacket and the emergency cart."

A straight-jacket? Dasein wondered. *What an odd request.*

232

He heard running footsteps. How loud they were! A door slammed. More voices. Such a rushing around!

His skin felt as though it were growing dark. Everything was being blotted out.

With an abrupt, jerking sensation, Dasein felt himself shrivel downward into an infant shape kicking, squalling, reaching outward, outward, fingers grasping.

"Give me a hand with him!" That was Piaget.

"What a mess!" Another male voice.

But Dasein already felt himself becoming a mouth, just a mouth. It blew out, out, out—such a wind. Surely, the entire world must collapse before this hurricane.

He was a board, rocking. A teeter-totter. Down and up—up and down.

A good run is better than a bad stand, he thought.

And he was running, running—breathless, gasping.

A bench loomed out of swirling clouds. He threw himself down on it, became the bench—another board. This one dipped down and down into a boiling green sea.

Life in a sea of unconsciousness, Dasein thought.

It grew darker and darker.

Death, he thought. *Here's the background against which I can know myself.*

The darkness dissolved. He was shooting upward, rebounding into a blinding glare.

Dark shapes moved in the glare.

"His eyes are open." That was the nurse.

A shadow reduced the glare. "Gilbert?" That was Piaget. "Gilbert, can you hear me? How much Jaspers did you take?"

Dasein tried to speak. His lips refused to obey.

The glare came back.

"We'll just have to guess." Piaget. "How much did that cheese weigh?"

"Thirty-six pounds." The nurse.

"The physical breakdown is massive." Piaget. "Have a respirator standing by."

"Doctor, what if he . . ." The nurse apparently couldn't complete the statement of her fear.

"I'm . . . ready." Piaget.

Ready for what? Dasein wondered.

By concentrating, he found he could make the glare recede. It resolved momentarily into a tunnel of clarity with Piaget at the far end of it. Dasein lay helplessly staring, unable to move as Piaget advanced on him carrying a carboy that fumed and smoked.

Acid, Dasein thought, interpreting the nurse's words. *If I die, they'll dissolve me and wash me away down a drain. No body, no evidence.*

The tunnel collapsed.

The sensation of glare expanded, contracted.

Perhaps, I can no longer be, Dasein thought.

It grew darker.

Perhaps, I cannot do, he thought.

Darker yet.

Perhaps, I cannot have, he thought.

Nothing.

13

"It was kill or cure," the yellow god said.

"I wash my hands of you," said the white god.

"What I offered, you did not want," the red god accused.

"You make me laugh," said the black god.

"There is no tree that's you," the green god said.

"We are going now and only one of us will return," the gods chorused.

There was a sound of a clearing throat.

"Why don't you have faces?" Dasein asked. "You have color but no faces."

"What?" It was a rumbling, vibrant voice.

"You're a funny sounding god," Dasein said. He opened his eyes, looked up into Burdeaux's features, caught a puzzled scowl on the dark face.

"I'm no sort of god at all," Burdeaux said. "What're you saying, Doctor Gil? You having another nightmare?"

Dasein blinked, tried to move his arms. Nothing happened. He lifted his head, looked down at his body. He was bound tightly in a restraining jacket. There was a stink of disinfectants, of Jaspers and of something repellent and sour in the room. He looked around. It was still the isolation suite. His head fell back to the pillow.

"Why'm I tied down like this?" Dasein whispered.

"What did you say, sir?"

Dasein repeated his question.

"Well, Doctor Gil, we didn't want you to hurt yourself."

"When . . . when can I be released?"

"Doctor Larry said to free you as soon as you woke up."

"I'm . . . awake."

"I know that, sir. I was just . . ." He shrugged, began unfastening the bindings on the sleeves of the jacket.

"How long?" Dasein whispered.

"How long you been here like this?"

Dasein nodded.

"Three whole days now, and a little more. It's almost noon."

The bindings were untied. Burdeaux helped Dasein to a sitting position, unlaced the back, slipped the jacket off.

Dasein's back felt raw and sensitive. His muscles reponded as though they belonged to a stranger. This was an entirely new body, Dasein thought.

Burdeaux came up with a white hospital gown, slipped it onto Dasein, tied the back.

"You want the nurse to come rub your back?" he asked. "You've a couple of red places there don't look too good."

"No . . . no thanks."

Dasein moved one of the stranger's arms. A familiar hand came up in front of his face. It was his own hand. How could it be his own hand, he wondered, when the muscles of the arm belonged to a stranger?

"Doctor Larry said no one ever took that much Jaspers ever before all at once," Burdeaux said. "Jaspers is a good thing, sir, but everybody knows you can get too much."

"Does . . . is Jenny . . . "

"She's fine, Doctor Gil. She's been worried sick about you. We all have."

Dasein moved one of the stranger's legs, then the other until they hung over the edge of the bed. He looked down at his own knees. It was very odd.

"Here, now," Burdeaux said. "Best you stay in bed."

"I've . . . I . . . "

"You want to go to the bathroom? Best I bring you the bedpan."

"No . . . I . . . " Dasein shook his head. Abruptly, he realized what was wrong. The body was hungry.

"Hungry," he said.

"Well, why didn't you say so? Got food right here waiting."

236

Burdeaux lifted a bowl, held it in front of Dasein. The rich aroma of Jaspers enveloped him. Dasein reached toward the bowl, but Burdeaux said, "Best let me feed you, Doctor Gil. You don't look too steady."

Dasein sat patiently, allowed himself to be fed. He could feel strength gathering in the body. It was a bad fit, this body, he decided. It had been draped loosely on his psyche.

It occurred to him to wonder what the body was eating—in addition to the Jaspers, which surrounded him and pervaded him with its presence. Oatmeal, the tongue said. Jaspers honey and Jaspers cream.

"There's a visitor waiting to see you," Burdeaux said when the bowl was empty.

"Jenny?"

"No . . . a Doctor Selador."

Selador! The name exploded on Dasein's conscience. Selador had trusted him, depended on him.

Selador had sent a gun through the mails.

"You feel up to seeing him?" Burdeaux asked.

"You . . . don't mind if I see him?" Dasein asked.

"Mind? Why should I mind, sir?"

Burdeaux's not the you *I meant,* Dasein thought.

There arose in Dasein then an urge to send Selador away. Such an easy thing to do. Santaroga would insulate him from the Seladors of the world. A simple request to Burdeaux was all it would take.

"I'll . . . uh, see him," Dasein said. He looked around the room. "Could you help me into a robe and . . . is there a chair I could . . . "

"Why don't I put you in a wheelchair, sir? Doctor Larry had one sent up for when you awakened. He didn't want you exerting yourself. You're not to get tired, understand?"

"Yes . . . yes, I understand. A wheelchair."

Presently, Dasein's bad-fit body was in the wheelchair. Burdeaux had gone to bring Selador, leaving the chair at the far end of the room from the foyer door. Dasein found himself facing a pair of French doors that opened onto a sundeck.

He felt he had been left alone in a brutally exposed position, his soul naked, wretched with fear. There was a heavy load on him, he thought. He felt embarrassment at the prospect of meeting Selador, and a special order of fright. Selador saw through pretense and sham. You could wear no mask before Selador. He was the psychoanalysts' psychoanalyst.

Selador will humiliate me, Dasein thought. *Why did I agree to see him? He will prod me and I will react. My reaction will tell him everything he wants to know about me . . . about my failure.*

Dasein felt then his sanity had been corroded into a pitted shell, a thing of tinsel and fantasy. Selador would stamp upon it with the harsh, jolting dynamics of his aliveness.

The foyer door opened.

Slowly, forcing himself to it, Dasein turned his head toward the door.

Selador stood in the opening, tall, hawk-featured, the dark skin and wildness of India encased in a silver-gray tweed suit, a touch of the same silver at the temples. Dasein had the sudden blurred sensation of having seen this face in another life, the lancet eyes peering from beneath a turban. It had been a turban with a red jewel in it.

Dasein shook his head. Madness.

"Gilbert," Selador said, striding across the room. "In the name of heaven, what have you done to yourself now?" The precise accents of Oxford hammered each word into Dasein's ears. "They said you were badly burned."

And thus it starts, Dasein thought.

"I . . . my arms and hands," Dasein said. "And a bit about the face."

"I arrived only this morning," Selador said. "We were quite worried about you, you know. No word from you for days."

He stopped in front of Dasein, blocking off part of the view of the sundeck.

"I must say you look a fright, Gilbert. There don't appear to be any scars on your face, though."

Dasein put a hand to his cheek. It was his cheek suddenly, not a stranger's. The skin felt smooth, new.

"There's the damnedest musky smell about this place,"

238

Selador said. "Mind if I open these doors?"

"No . . . no, go right ahead."

Dasein found himself wrestling with the feeling that Selador was not Selador. There was a shallowness to the man's speech and mannerisms all out of character with the Selador of Dasein's memory. Had Selador changed in some way?

"Lovely sunny day," Selador said. "Why don't I wheel you out on this deck for a bit of air. Do you good."

Panic seized Dasein's throat. That deck—it was a place of menace. He tried to speak, to object. They couldn't go out there. No words came.

Selador took the silence for agreement, wheeled Dasein's chair out the door. There was a slight jolt at the sill and they were on the deck.

Sunlight warmed Dasein's head. A breeze almost devoid of Jaspers washed his skin, cleared his head. He said: "Don't you . . . "

"Doesn't this air feel invigorating?" Selador asked. He stopped at a shallow parapet, the edge of the roof. "There. You can admire the view and I can sit on this ledge."

Selador sat down, put a hand on the back of Dasein's chair. "I would imagine that ward is wired for sound," Selador said. "I do not believe they can have listening devices out here, however."

Dasein gripped the wheels of his chair, afraid it might lurch forward, propel him off the roof. He stared down at a paved parking area, parked cars, lawn, strips of flowers, trees. The sense of Selador's words came to him slowly.

"Wired . . . for . . . " He turned, met amused inquiry in the dark eyes.

"Obviously, you're not quite yourself yet," Selador said. "Understandable. You've been through a terrible ordeal. That's obvious. I'll have you out of this place, though, as soon as you're able to travel. Set your mind at rest. You'll be safe in a *normal* hospital at Berkeley before the week's out."

Dasein's emotions boiled, an arena of dispute. *Safe!* What a reassuring word. *Leave?* He couldn't leave! But he had to leave. *Outside? Go to that hideous place?*

239

"Have you been drugged, Gilbert?" Selador asked. "You appear . . . so . . . so . . ."

"I've . . . I'm all right."

"Really, you're behaving rather oddly. You haven't asked me once what we found on the leads you provided."

"What . . . "

"The source of their petrol proved to be a dud. All quite normal . . . provided you appreciate their economic motives. Cash deal with an independent producer. The State Department of Agriculture gives their cheese and the other products of their Cooperative a clean bill of health. The real estate board, however, is interested that no one but Santarogans can buy property in the valley. It may be they've violated antidiscriminatory legislation with . . . "

"No," Dasein said. "They . . . nothing that obvious."

"Ah, ha! You speak in the fashion of a man who has discovered the closeted skeleton. Well, Gilbert, what is it?"

Dasein felt he'd been seized by a vampire of duty. It would drain the blood from him. Selador would feed on it. He shook his head from side to side.

"Are you ill, Gilbert? Am I wearying you?"

"No. As long as I take it slowly . . . Doctor, you must understand, I've . . ."

"Do you have notes, Gilbert? Perhaps I could read your report and . . . "

"No . . . fire."

"Oh, yes. The doctor, this Piaget, said something about your truck burning. Everything up in smoke, I suppose?"

"Yes."

"Well, then, Gilbert, we'll have to get it from your lips. Is there an opening we can use to break these people?"

Dasein thought of the greenhouses—child labor. He thought of the statistical few Santarogans Jaspers had destroyed. He thought of the narcotic implications in the Jaspers products. It was all there—destruction for Santaroga.

"There must be something," Selador said. "You've lasted much longer than the others. Apparently, you've been given the freedom of the region. I'm sure you must have discovered something."

240

Lasted much longer than the others, Dasein thought. There was naked revelation in the phrase. As though he had participated in them, Dasein saw the discussions which had gone into choosing him for this project. *"Dasein has connections in the valley—a girl. That may be the edge we need. Certainly, it gives us reason to hope he'll last longer than the others."*

It had been something like that, Dasein knew. There was a callousness in it that repelled him.

"Were there more than two?" he asked.

"Two? Two what, Gilbert?"

"Two other investigators . . . before me?"

"I don't see where that . . . "

"Were there?"

"Well . . . that's very discerning of you, Gilbert. Yes, there were more than two. Eight or nine, I suspect."

"Why . . . "

"Why weren't you told? We wanted to imbue you with caution, but we saw no need to terrify you."

"But you thought they were murdered here . . . by Santarogans?"

"It was all exceedingly mysterious, Gilbert. We were not at all sure." He studied Dasein, eyes open wide and probing. "That's it, eh? Murder. Are we in peril right now? Do you have the weapon I . . . "

"If it were only that simple," Dasein said.

"In heaven's name, Gilbert, what is it? You must have found something. I had such high hopes for you."

High hopes for me, Dasein thought. Again, it was a phrase that opened a door on secret conversations. How could Selador be that transparent? Dasein found himself shocked by the shallowness of the man. Where was the omnipotent psychoanalyst? How could he have changed so profoundly?

"You . . . you people were just using me," Dasein said. As he spoke, he recalled Al Marden's accusation. Marden had seen this . . . yes.

"Now, Gilbert, that's no attitude to take. Why, just before I left to come here, Meyer Davidson was inquiring after you. You recall Davidson, the agent for the investment corporation behind the chain stores? He was very much taken with you, Gilbert. He told me he was thinking of making a place for you on his staff."

Dasein stared at Selador. The man couldn't be serious.

"That would be quite a step up in the world for you, Gilbert."

Dasein suppressed an urge to laugh. He had the odd sensation of being detached from his past and able to study a pseudoperson, a might-have-been creature who was himself. The other Dasein would have leaped at this offer. The new Dasein saw through the offer to the true opinion Selador and his cronies held for "*that useful, but not very bright person, Gilbert Dasein.*"

"Have you had a look at Santaroga?" Dasein asked. He wondered if Selador had seen Clara Scheler's used car lot or the advertisements in the store windows.

"This morning, while I was waiting for visiting hours with you, I drove around a bit," Selador said.

"What did you think of the place?"

"My candid opinion? An odd sort of village. When I inquired directions of a native—their language is so brusque and . . . odd. Not at all like . . . well, it's not English, of course, full of Americanisms, but . . ."

"They have a language like their cheese," Dasein said. "Sharp and full of tang."

"Sharp! A very good choice of word."

"A community of individuals, wouldn't you say?" Dasein asked.

"Perhaps . . . but with a certain sameness to them. Tell me, Gilbert, does this have something to do with why you were sent here?"

"This?"

"These questions. I must say, you're talking like . . . well, damned if you don't sound like a native." A forced laugh escaped his dark lips. "Have you gone native?"

The question, coming from that darkly eastern face, couched in that Oxford accent, struck Dasein as supremely amusing. Selador, of all people! To ask such a question.

Laughter bubbled from Dasein.
242

Selador misinterpreted the response. "Well," he said, "I should hope you hadn't."

"Humanity ought to be the first order of interest for humans," Dasein said.

Again, Selador misinterpreted. "Ah, and you studied the Santarogans like the excellent psychologist you are. Good. Well, then—tell it in your own way."

"I'll put it another way," Dasein said. "To have freedom, you must know how to use it. There's a distinct possibility some people hunt freedom in such a way they become the slaves of freedom."

"That's all very philosophical, I'm sure," Selador said. "How does it apply to finding justice for our sponsors?"

"Justice?"

"Certainly, justice. They were lured into this valley and cheated. They spent large sums of money here and got no return on it whatsoever. They're not people to take such treatment lightly."

"Lured?" Dasein said. "No one would sell to them, that I'm sure. How were they lured? For that matter, how did they acquire a lease on . . ."

"This isn't pertinent, Gilbert."

"Yes, it is. How'd they get a lease on Santaroga land?"

Selador sighed. "Very well. If you insist. They forced a competetive bid on some excess State property and put in a bid . . ."

"One they were sure no one else would match," Dasein said. He chuckled. "Did they have a market survey?"

"They had a good idea how many people live here."

"But what kind of people?"

"What're you trying to say, Gilbert?"

"Santaroga's very like a Greek *polis*," Dasein said. "This is a community of individuals, not a collectivity. Santarogans are not anthill slaves to grubs and grubbing. This is a *polis*, small enough to meet human needs. Their first interest is in human beings. Now, as to justice for . . ."

"Gilbert, you're talking very strangely."

"Hear me, please, doctor."

"Very well, but I hope you'll make some sense out of this . . . this . . ."

"Justice," Dasein said. "These sponsors you mention, and the government they control, are less interested in justice than they are in public order. They have stunted imaginations from too-long and too-intimate association with an ingrown system of self-perpetuating precedents. Do you want to know how they and their machinations appear to a Santarogan?"

"Let me remind you, Gilbert, this is one of the reasons you were sent here."

Dasein smiled. Selador's accusatory tone brought not a twinge of guilt.

"Raw power," Dasein said. "That's how the *outside* appears to a Santarogan. "A place of raw power. Money and raw power have taken over there."

"Outside," Selador said. "What an interesting emphasis you give to that interesting word."

"Raw power is movement without a governor," Dasein said. "It'll run wild and destroy itself with all about it. That's a civilization of battlefields out there. They have special names: market area, trade area, court, election, senate, auction, strike—but they're still battlefields. There's no denying it because every one can invoke the full gamut of weaponry from words to guns."

"I do believe you're defending these Santaroga rascals," Selador said.

"Of course I'm defending them! I've had my eyes opened here, I tell you. I lasted much longer, did I? You had such high hopes for me! How can you be so damn' transparent?"

"Now you see here, Gilbert!" Selador stood up, glared down at Dasein.

"You know what gets to me, really gets to me?" Dasein asked. "Justice! You're all so damned interested in putting a cloak of justice and legality on your frauds! You give me a . . ."

"Doctor Gil?"

It was Burdeaux's voice calling from the doorway behind him. Dasein yanked back on his chair's left wheel, pushed on the right wheel. The chair whirled. All in the same instant, Dasein saw Burdeaux standing in the French doors,

244

felt his chair hit something. He turned his head toward Selador in time to see a pair of feet disappear over the edge of the roof. There was a long, despairing cry terminated by the most sickening, wet thud Dasein had ever heard.

Burdeaux was suddenly beside him, leaning on the parapet to peer down at the parking area.

"Oh my goodness," Burdeaux said. "Oh, my goodness, what a terrible accident."

Dasein lifted his hands, looked at them—*his* hands. *I'm not strong enough to've done that*, he thought. *I've been ill. I'm not strong enough.*

14

"A major contributing factor to the accident," Piaget said, "was the victim's own foolishness in standing that close to the edge of the roof."

The inquest had been convened in Dasein's hospital room—"Because it is at the scene of the accident and as a convenience to Doctor Dasein, who is not fully recovered from injuries and shock."

A special investigator had been sent from the State Attorney General's office, arriving just before the inquest convened at ten a.m. The investigator, a William Garrity, obviously was known to Piaget. They had greeted each other "Bill" and "Larry" at the foot of Dasein's bed. Garrity was a small man with an appearance of fragility about him, sandy hair, a narrow face immersed in a mask of diffidence.

Presiding was Santaroga's Coroner, a Negro Dasein had not seen before this morning—Leroy Cos: kinky gray hair and a square, blocky face of remote dignity. He wore a black suit, had held himself apart from the preinquest bustle until the tick of ten o'clock when he had seated himself at a table provided for him, rapped once with a pencil and said: "We will now come to order."

Spectators and witnesses had seated themselves in folding chairs brought in for the occasion. Garrity shared a table with an Assistant District Attorney who, it developed, was a Nis, Swarthout Nis, a man with the family's heavy eyelids, wide mouth and sandy hair, but without the deeply cleft chin.

In the two days since the tragedy, Dasein had found his emotions embroiled with a growing anger against Selador—*the fool, the damned fool, getting himself killed that way.*

Piaget, seated in the witness chair, summed it up for Dasein.

"In the first place," Piaget said, a look of stern indignation on his round face, "he had no business taking Doctor Dasein outside. I had explained Doctor Dasein's physical condition quite clearly."

Garrity, the State's investigator, was permitted a question: "You saw the accident, Doctor Piaget?"

"Yes. Mr. Burdeaux, having noted Doctor Selador wheel my patient onto the sundeck and knowing I considered this a physical strain on my patient, had summoned me. I arrived just in time to see Doctor Selador stumble and fall."

"You saw him stumble?" Swarthout Nis asked.

"Definitely. He appeared to be reaching for the back of Doctor Dasein's wheelchair. I consider it fortunate he did not manage to grab the chair. He could have taken both of them over the edge."

Selador stumbled? Dasein thought. A sense of opening relief pervaded him. *Selador stumbled! I didn't bump him. I knew I wasn't strong enough. But what did I bump? A loose board on the deck, perhaps?* For an instant, Dasein recalled his hands on the wheels of the chair, the firm, sure grip, the soft bump. *A board could feel soft,* he told himself.

Burdeaux was in the witness chair now corroborating Piaget's testimony.

It must be true then.

Dasein felt strength flow through his body. He began to see his Santaroga experience as a series of plunges down precipitous rapids. Each plunge had left him weaker until the final plunge had, through a mystic fusion, put him in contact with a source of infinite strength. It was that strength he felt now.

His life before Santaroga took on the aspects of a delicate myth held fleetingly in the mind. It was a tree in a Chinese landscape seen dimly through pastel mists. He sensed he had fallen somehow into a sequel, which by its existence had changed the past. But the present, here-and-

247

now, surrounded him like the trunk of a sturdy redwood, firmly rooted, supporting strong branches of sanity and reason.

Garrity with his sleepy questions was a futile incompetent. "You ran immediately to Dr. Dasein's side?"

"Yes, sir. He was quite ill and weak. I was afraid he might try to get out of the wheelchair and fall himself."

"And Dr. Piaget?"

"He ran downstairs, sir, to see what he could do for the man who fell."

Only the Santarogans in this room were fully conscious, Dasein thought. It occurred to him then that the more consciousness he acquired, the greater must be his unconscious content—a natural matter of balance. That would be the source of Santaroga's mutual strength, of course—a shared foundation into which each part must fit.

"Doctor Dasein," the Coroner said.

They swore Dasein in then. The eyes in the room turned toward him. Only Garrity's eyes bothered Dasein —hooded, remote, concealing, *outsider eyes.*

"Did you see Dr. Selador fall?"

"I . . . Mr. Burdeaux called me. I turned toward him and I heard a cry. When I turned back . . . Doctor Selador's feet were going over the edge."

"His feet?"

"That's all I saw."

Dasein closed his eyes, remembering that moment of electric terror. He felt he was using a tunnel-vision effect in his memory, focusing just on those feet. An accident—a terrible accident. He opened his eyes, shut off the vision before memory reproduced that descending wail, the final punctuating thud.

"Had you known Dr. Selador for a long time?"

"He was . . . yes." What was Garrity driving at from behind those hooded eyes?

Garrity produced a sheet of paper from a briefcase on his table, glanced at it, said: "I have here a page from Dr. Selador's journal. It was forwarded to me by his wife. One passage interests me. I'll read it to . . . "

248

"Is this pertinent?" Coroner Cos asked.

"Perhaps not, sir," Garrity said. "Again, perhaps it is. I would like Dr. Dasein's views. We are, after all, merely trying to arrive at the truth in a terrible tragedy."

"May I see the passage?" That was Swarthout Nis, the Assistant District Attorney, his voice suavely questioning.

"Certainly."

Nis took the paper, read it.

What is it? Dasein asked himself. *What did Selador write that his wife would send to a State investigator? Is this why Garrity came?*

Nis returned the paper to Garrity. "Keeping in mind that Dr. Selador was a psychiatrist, this passage could have many interpretations. I see no reason why Dr. Dasein shouldn't have the opportunity to throw light upon it, however—if he can."

"May I see this?" the Coroner asked.

Garrity stood, took the paper to Cos, waited while the Coroner read it.

"Very well," Cos said, returning the paper to Garrity. "The passage you've marked in red pencil presumably is what concerns you. You may question the witness about that passage if you wish."

Garrity turned, the paper held stiffly before him, faced Dasein. With occasional glances at the page, he read: "Dasein—a dangerous instrument for this project. They should be warned."

He lowered the paper. "What project, Dr. Dasein?"

There was a hush in the room as thick as fog.

"I . . . when did he write this?"

"According to his wife, it's dated approximately a month ago. I repeat: what project?"

Dasein groped in his memory. *Project . . . dangerous?*

"The . . . only project . . . " He shook his head. The passage made no sense.

"Why did you come to Santaroga, Dr. Dasein?"

"Why? My fiancée lives here."

"Your fiancée . . ."

"My niece, Jenny Sorge," Piaget interposed.

249

Garrity glanced at Piaget, who sat now in the front row of chairs, looked back to Dasein. "Didn't you come here to make a market survey?"

"Oh, that—yes. But I don't see how I could be dangerous to that . . ." Dasein hesitated, weighing the time nicely. ". . . unless he was afraid I'd have my mind too much on other things."

A soft rustle of laughter whispered through the room. The Coroner rapped his pencil, said: "I remind you this is a serious occasion. A man has died."

Silence.

Garrity looked once more to the page in his hand. The paper seemed to have gained weight, pulling down.

"What else is on that page from his journal?" Dasein asked. "Doesn't it explain what . . . "

"Who are the *they* who should be warned?" Garrity asked.

Dasein shook his head. "I don't know—unless it could be the people who hired us for the market study."

"You have prepared such a study?"

"I'll complete it as soon as I'm well enough to be released from the hospital."

"Your injuries," Garrity said, a note of anger in his voice. "Something was said about burns. I'm not at all clear about . . . "

"Just a moment, please," the Coroner said. "Dr. Dasein's injuries are not at issue here in any way other than how they bear on his being in a particular place at a particular time. We have had testimony that he was very weak and that Dr. Selador had wheeled Dr. Dasein's wheelchair out onto the sundeck."

"How weak?" Garrity asked. "And how dangerous?"

The Coroner sighed, glanced at Piaget, at Dasein, back to Garrity. "The facts surrounding Dr. Dasein's injuries are common knowledge in Santaroga, Mr. Garrity. There were more than a dozen witnesses. He was severely burned while saving a man's life. Dr. Dasein is somewhat of a hero in Santaroga."

"Oh." Garrity returned to his seat at the table, put the

page from Selador's journal on the briefcase. He obviously was angry, confused.

"I permit a considerable degree of informality in an inquiry such as this," Cos said. "Dr. Dasein has asked a question about the surrounding contents of that page. I confess the entries make no sense to me, but perhaps . . . " The Coroner left his question hanging there, his attention on Garrity.

"My office can add little," Garrity said. "There's an entry which obviously is a population figure; it's so labeled. There's a line . . . " He lifted the page. " 'Oil company checked out. Negative.' There's a rather cryptic: 'No mental illness.' Except for the one entry referring to Dr. Dasein . . . "

"What about the rest of the journal?" the Coroner asked. "Has your office investigated it?"

"Unfortunately, Mrs. Selador says she obeyed her husband's testamentary wishes and burned his journal. It contained, she said, confidential data on medical cases. This one entry she preserved and sent to us . . ." Garrity shrugged.

"I'm afraid the only man who could explain it is no longer living," the Coroner said. "If this was, however, a journal of medical data with reference to Dr. Selador's psychiatric practice, then it would seem the entry in question might be explained easily in rather harmless terms. The word *dangerous* can have many interpretations in a psychiatric context. It may even be that Dr. Dasein's interpretation is the correct one."

Garrity nodded.

"Do you have any more questions?" the Coroner asked.

"Yes. One more." Garrity looked at Dasein, a veiled, uncertain look. "Were you and Dr. Selador on friendly terms?"

Dasein swallowed. "He was . . . my teacher . . . my friend. Ask anyone at Berkeley."

A blank look of frustration came over Garrity's face.

He knows, Dasein thought. And immediately he wondered what it was Garrity *could* know. There was nothing

251

to know. An accident. Perhaps he knew Selador's suspicions about Santaroga. But that was foolishness . . . unless Garrity were another of the investigators looking into things that were none of his business.

Dasein felt his vision blur and, staring at Garrity, saw the man's face become a death's-head skull. The illusion vanished as Garrity shook his head, jammed Selador's journal page into the briefcase. A rueful smile appeared on his face. He glanced at the Coroner, shrugged.

"Something amuses you, Mr. Garrity?" the Coroner asked.

The smile vanished.

"No, sir. Well . . . my own thought processes sometimes. I've obviously allowed an unhappy woman, Mrs. Selador, to send me on a wild goose chase."

The investigator sat down, said: "I've no more questions, sir."

Abruptly, Dasein experienced a moment of insight; Garrity's thoughts had frightened the man! He'd suspected a vast conspiracy here in Santaroga. But that was too fantastic; thus, the smile.

The Coroner was closing his inquiry now—a brief summation: all the facts were in . . . an allusion to the pathologist's gory details—"massive head injuries, death instantaneous"—a notation that a formal inquest would be held at a date to be announced. Would Mr. Garrity wish to return for it? Mr. Garrity thought not.

It dawned on Dasein then that this had been a show for Garrity, something to set his mind at ease. Tiny bits of Piaget's preinquest conversation with Garrity returned to Dasein, fitted into a larger pattern. They'd been in school together—*outside!* Of course: old friends, Larry and Bill. One didn't suspect old friends of conspiracy. Reasonable.

It was over then—death by misadventure, an accident.

Garrity was shaking hands with Coroner Cos, with Piaget. Would Piaget be coming out to their class reunion? If his practice permitted . . . but Garrity certainly must know how it was with country doctors. Garrity understood.

"This was a terrible thing," Garrity said.

Piaget sighed. "Yes, a terrible tragedy."

Garrity was pausing at the foyer door now. There were knots of people behind him waiting for the elevator, a buzz of conversation. He turned, and Dasein thought he saw a look of angry speculation on the man's face.

Piaget bent over Dasein then, shutting off the view of the door. "This has been a strain on you and I want you to get some rest now," Piaget said. "Jenny's coming in for a minute, but I don't want her staying too long."

He moved aside.

The foyer doorway stood open and empty.

"Understand?" Piaget asked.

"Yes . . . Jenny's coming."

What was that look in Garrity's eyes? Dasein asked himself. A black savage in Africa might have peered that way into a white man's shiny city. Strange . . . angry . . . frustrated man. If Meyer Davidson and his crew chose Garrity for an investigator—there'd be a dangerous one. That'd be a bridge to cross in its own time, though . . . if at all. Many things could happen to a man out there in the wide-wide world. Dasein could feel it—Santaroga was preparing itself to reach out there.

That's why I was chosen, he thought. *And Burdeaux . . . and the others . . . whoever they are. The only good defense is a good offense.*

This was a disturbing thought that sent trembling agitation through Dasein's stomach and legs.

Why am I trembling? he wondered.

He tried to recapture the thought that had disturbed him, failed. It was brief unimportant disturbance, a momentary ripple on a lake that otherwise was growing calmer and calmer. Dasein allowed the sensation of calm green waters to flow over and around him. He grew aware he was alone in the room with Jenny.

There was calmness personified: blue eyes with laugh wrinkes at their edges, full lips smiling at him. She wore an orange dress, an orange ribbon in her dark hair.

Jenny put a package on his nightstand, bent over and kissed him—warm lips, a deep sense of peace and sharing. She pulled away, sat down beside him, held his hand.

Dasein thought she had never looked more beautiful.

"Uncle Larry says you're to rest this afternoon, but you can be released from the hospital by Saturday," she said.

Dasein reached out, ran his fingers through her hair—silky-smooth, sensuous hair. "Why don't we get married Sunday?" he asked.

"Oh, darling . . . "

Again, she kissed him, pulled back, looked prim. "I better not do that anymore today. We don't want to weaken you." The dimple flickered in her cheek. "You want to be fully recovered and strong by Sunday."

Dasein pulled her head down against his neck, stroked her hair.

"We can have one of the houses in the new section," she whispered. "We'll be near Cal and Willa. Darling, darling, I'm so happy."

"So am I."

She began describing the house to him, the garden space, the view . . .

"You've chosen one of them already?"

"I was out there—dreaming, hoping . . . "

The house was everything she'd ever longed for—it was important for a woman to have the right house in which to begin life with the man she loved. There was even a big garage with room for a shop . . . and a lab.

Dasein thought of Jersey Hofstedder's car sitting in the garage she described. There was a sense of continuity in the thought, a peasant complacency involving "good things" and "vintage crops."

His attention focused on the package Jenny had put on his nightstand.

"What's in the package?"

"Package?"

She lifted her head, turned to follow the direction of his gaze. "Oh, that. The gang at the Co-op—they put together a 'get-well' package for you."

"Jaspers?"

"Of course." She sat back, straightened her hair.

Dasein had a sudden vision of himself working in the wrapping line at the Co-op.

"Where will I work?" he asked.

254

"Uncle Larry wants you in the clinic, but we'll both get a month of honeymoon leave. Darling—it's going to be so long until Sunday."

In the clinic, Dasein thought. *Not as a patient, thank God.* He wondered then which god he was thanking. It was a odd thought, without beginning and without end, a bit of string hanging in the green lake of his mind.

Jenny began unwrapping the package on the night-stand—a wedge of golden cheese, two bottles of beer, dark wheat crackers, a white container that sloshed when she moved it. He wondered when they had been exposed.

Dasein had the sudden feeling that he was a moth in a glass cage, a frantic thing fluttering against his barriers, lost, confused.

"Darling, I'm tiring you." Jenny put her hand on his forehead. It soothed him, calmed him. The moth of his emotions settled on a strong green limb. The limb was attached to a tree. He felt the trunk of the tree as though it were himself—strong, an infinite source of strength.

"When will I see you?" he asked.

"I'll come by in the morning."

She blew him a kiss, hesitated, bent over him—the sweet fragrance of Jaspers about her breath, a touch of lips.

Dasein stared after her until the foyer door closed.

A momentary anguish touched him, a fleeting sense that he'd lost his grip on reality, that this room was unreal without Jenny in it. Dasein grabbed a chunk of the golden cheese, stuffed it in his mouth, felt the soothing Jaspers presence, his awareness expanding, becoming firm and manageable.

What's reality, anyway? he asked himself. *It's as finite as a bit of cheese, as tainted by error as anything else with limits.*

He settled his mind firmly then onto thoughts of the home Jenny had described, pictured himself carrying her across the threshold—his wife. There'd be presents: Jaspers from 'the gang,' furniture . . . Santaroga took care of its own.

It'll be a beautiful life, he thought. *Beautiful . . . beautiful . . . beautiful . . .*